Their Secret He

By Michael J. Rowbottom

© Michael J.Rowbottom
All rights reserved.

Author's note:

The idea for this story first came to me in 1993 but it has taken until now to emerge properly into the world. At that time I was a TV reporter for Central ITV based around Oxford and while I don't name the location in the text it is loosely based on that admirable city. My life brought me into contact with a great many people from different walks of life including the medical profession and the heroine of this story is based on one of those, although so heavily disguised that I hope even she wouldn't recognise herself. None of these characters existed and certainly not with the names I have used, but their type have had manifestations elsewhere in the country; in fact shortly after I finished this draft an investigation in London revealed widescale abuse of care children in local authorities by the very people who should have been protecting them. I use the geography of Oxford and my knowledge of many of its institutions because so much of the story originated from people there. I had to set it in an area I knew and as Spike Milligan noted, unforgettably: "Everybody's got to be somewhere!"

There was a smell of fried bacon in the kitchen, the comforting warmth of the cooker pervaded the lower half of the house, taking the edge off the early April chill.

"I don't see why we have to have the central heating off so early in the year," said the middle-aged woman with a kindly face preparing the meal,

"Don't be so irritable, Pauline. It's not that cold, anyway it's spring, we shouldn't need it." He smirked in the direction of a third member of the family. "Isn't that right, David?"

"Yes, Dad," said the boy.

"You don't have to agree with everything your dad says," said the woman. "He's not always right." She was finding it hard to keep a straight face. She concentrated on her cooking. Scrambled eggs and bacon with toast, she stirred them in the pan, the aroma filled the air. The other two stared at her. Her mouth cracked a little, it was the detonator which set off an explosion of mock indignation throughout the kitchen.

"I saw you, Pauline, you're laughing." Her husband convulsed with mirth.

She tried to regain herself. "No I'm not," she said before dissolving into a fit of giggles. "Yes you are, Mum, yes you are," shouted the boy hysterically.

There was a loud knock at the door.

"I'll get it," shouted the man, still laughing. He opened the door, took stock of what he saw and smiled in welcome.

"Good morning, officer, how can I help?"

There were two police officers at the door and someone in civilian clothes.

A woman officer, looking severe, spoke.

"Are you John Maclean?"

"Yes, that's correct," said the man.

"Mr Maclean I am here with my colleague to ensure that the social services are able to carry out their duties without interference."

"Who is it, John?" cried his wife from the kitchen.

"What duties are you talking about?" he said.

The one in civilian clothes stepped forward. "We're taking David back into our care Mr Maclean, we believe he's in severe moral danger while he lives with you."

"I said who is it, John?" his wife said this time standing in the hallway, "The police! What do they want?"

John Maclean looked at her, shock written across his face, "David!" he stuttered.

"What do you mean?"

"Mrs Maclean, I am Elaine Easterbrook from the social services Department. I have just explained to your husband that we have come to collect David."

"I don't understand."

"We have reason to believe that David is being abused."

There was a brief pause while the information sank in. Then John Maclean shouted, "That's bloody crazy."

David had appeared behind the two adults at the door. "Ah, David," said the social worker. "Will you come with me!" It was made to sound like a request, but it clearly was not.

Maclean was quicker this time. "Oh no he doesn't, he's staying here."

He made to push shut the door. Pauline stood dumbfounded, David looked confused. The other police officer, silent until this moment, jammed his foot into the door and with the help of the woman police officer forced it back again.

"Come along, Mr Maclean, or we'll be forced to restrain you."

The man's face, untrained in deception, betrayed his fury too easily. "What's happening here!" he shouted and tried to force back the door.

The two police officers grabbed him by the arms and held him, one put a hand over his mouth. Pauline Maclean looked on without a sound, The boy cast his eyes around in all directions, then a pair of hands picked him up and carried him away.

"Where are you taking me?" he cried.

"Somewhere safe, David."

The woman broke her silence and screamed. "Who told you these lies."

The social worker looked straight back at her, coldly.

"David did"

Her thoughts drifted back eighteen years to when she got the letter saying she'd been accepted at med school; the leaps of joy, the screeching about the house waving the note to her parents and her underwhelmed brother, the feeling that she'd won the lottery of life before she'd even started; where did all that go?

It was Monday morning – she assumed it was Monday, she'd been at the hospital for so many hours she couldn't be certain, no sleep and no let up. She sighed deeply at the pile of paperwork on her desk. She had the urge to swipe it all on to the floor and just walk out, but she kept it down. Instead she stretched, then yawned; there was no one else in the room but she cupped her mouth with her hand from habit.

She thought she loved her work. But did she really? The office was such a dull place, nothing happened there of importance, it was badly decorated and cramped. She belonged on the wards or in the clinics, not hemmed into a tiny cell like this.

Perhaps she could allow herself the luxury of a cup of coffee and half an hour away from the hospital, the staff, her interfering superiors, the peeling walls. Yes, and sod the paperwork for a few minutes. She picked up her coat, there was still a chill on the mid-spring day, then looked guiltily down at the pile on her desk. She grabbed a file, it said R.I.S.K. in the top right corner. She would take a glance at it while she was out. She closed the door and kept her head down in case anyone was passing. It was only for a few minutes, surely they could let her have that!

Desire's was quiet. It was just before nine on a Monday morning. She was virtually alone. She sat amid the mock Gallic atmosphere trying to get into it by thinking of the French word for a white coffee.

She glanced around the salon resting her gaze on the 1930s aviation posters, or affiches as the cafe insisted on calling them. Every now and then a poster print of one of the impressionists popped up.

Not that she knew a Degas from a Banksy; it was hard enough trying to be a paediatrician, culture had to take a side seat.

Une creme, she remembered, that's a white coffee in French. She'd stopped bothering after GCSE and now regretted it. The cafe doorbell rang, she looked automatically towards the entrance. She watched two men walk in, one was wearing jeans and a windcheater and carried what looked like a video camera with a professional-looking tripod, the other was better dressed with a collar and tie, slightly older and she looked at him for longer than she meant to.

He caught her eye before she could look away. He smiled and called out confidently, "Good morning." She mouthed a reply with a reserved smile then quickly lowered her head and buried herself in the file. She was tired. Working around the clock at 36 wasn't as easy as it had been ten years before – and it hadn't been easy then.

The two men sat on the other side of the salon at a petite table surrounded by cheap green Belle Epoque style chairs. There was an echo as they scraped the furniture against the tiles in the near empty café. The aroma of filtered coffee was cocooning and warm.

The well dressed one sat in a position giving him a view of his companion and the only other occupant of the cafe, herself. He raised his eyes to her just as she began to lower hers again.

Interesting, he thought, late thirties, attractive and slim. He dwelt awhile on the mid-length black hair. Not dirty but it needed a wash to liven it up again.

"How's Diane?" asked his companion.

"Well, I think." The voices echoed through the salon, there was nothing to absorb it, only the other customers' ears. He looked up again to see if she had reacted, she was smiling directly at him. A sense of humour as well. But his companion had just wrecked his chances, whatever they might have been. He looked at him again, seriously this time, and murmured under his breath, "Thanks Steve, I owe you!"

"No worries," said the other, while smurking. "Nice to know you're sticking to the straight and narrow."

"Unlike your leg which I am about to make bent and twisted."

"You'll thank me in the end."

"Bollocks...", he realised his voice was rising, he let it fall back. It still hurt, Diane, even though it was obviously over and gone. The coffee came, he made no comment about the slops which had overflowed on to his saucer, neither did the waitress who had the dawning of recognition in her eye. He raised his eyebrows in mock defeat and made a small show of pouring it back into the cup.

His phone buzzed, he checked it, a Whatsapp message. "It's Jonesy," he said to his companion, "He's spitting tacks because I got to the office first and got this plush little job."

"Serves him right, be on time, no excuses!" said his companion.

"I'll read it to you: "Jammy fucker. I'm on the motorway to Manchester to cover some poxy sub-literate pop princess up for speeding."

They both laughed, then he spoke out loud the words he tapped into his phone, "Don't forget to get her to sing a line from one of her songs. They won't be happy if you miss it!"

"That's not true is it," said his companion,

"Put it this way, he'd get brownie points if he managed it. Not news, though, is it?"

"Not for you maybe, it probably is for a few hundred thousand viewers and ...," he assumed a faux pomposity, "That's who we serve."

She was mesmerised by the conversation. She ought to take her eyes away but she felt like walking on the edge this morning. Flirting, why not! Grey eyes, tie neatly knotted, clean shaven, nice voice. She finally lowered her gaze, her smile stayed.

She heard them chuckle, she looked up again; they were smiling back at her. She looked directly into the smart one's eyes and, illogically, thought he was laughing at her. The waitress returned to the mens' table with a smile and a determined look.

"Scuse me for askin' but ain't you the bloke on the tele, David Prester."

He hid his irritation from the girl, but in looking away with an attempted smile the awkwardness caught the eye of the other woman in the café..

"Simon Preston, yes, thanks for recognising me." The waitress said nothing more, she pushed in alongside him, brandished her phone at arm's length and clicked. He knew what to do, he smiled briefly and asked her name.

"Sharon."

"Hello, Sharon, nice to meet you!"

"Coffee's coming up," she gave him a look and then perfunctory thanks and clacked away.

"I'm Steve Topping, by the way," said the other man.

"Whatever," said Sharon without looking back. Preston laughed out loud.

The doctor watched discreetly. Shame, he'd seemed nice. But a puffed up TV star she didn't care about.

Those were the last moments of ordinary life she would remember for a long time. A loud detonation, amplified by the tall buildings close together, changed their lives for ever. The doctor froze momentarily. The two men did the opposite and leaped for the door, one carrying the TV camera. Her temporary freeze was quickly replaced by shock like an electric current sweeping from the top of her chest through her whole body. She could see what was happening, but not hear.

Preston scrambled open the door, looked along the street and fell to the floor. The cameraman was a couple of seconds behind, switching on as he emerged. "Get down!" The last syllable was smothered by another explosion, amplified by the high buildings. He reeled back, rolled over and lay prone. He fought to bring himself back. He looked around the street, then raised himself on to his elbows and shook his head. The other was a couple of feet away. They saw a young man, not much more than a boy, brandishing a sawn-off shotgun and holding a middle aged woman with his other arm.

A few metres away a man lay bleeding on the pavement. Preston couldn't make out much about him, just that there was blood and he was wearing a grey raincoat. He wasn't moving.

He couldn't see if anyone else was hurt.

"He's let off two," Topping whispered behind him, "He's put another in the left barrel."

After the crash of the explosion, and its echo, there was a silence. Preston could hear the faint humming of the camera. It would normally be overwhelmed by the ambience but everything else had gone so quiet that it was faintly audible close up. It was pointing towards the gunman. Steve Topping never let his fear get in the way of a good picture. Fine, thought Preston, but not when he's right next to *me* with a manic gunman close by. Topping looked into the viewfinder.

"Have you got him close up?"

"Shut up!"

Preston nodded. and whispered "OK!"

The youth had his back to them now and Preston had a chance to look at him. He appeared to have nothing other than the shotgun. The hostage woman started to whimper by his side but thank God she wasn't screaming. He whispered, "We either crawl back into the cafe and hope he never saw us, or we get very brave and try to talk him round." Topping snapped at him. "He doesn't look much like wanting a conversation right now, does he."

"Maybe he'll calm down".

"Well I'm no betting man. All I've seen is him reloading that shotgun. He's used it twice and I think he'll do it again." Risks were part of the job, foolhardiness was not. Preston looked at the cafe door two metres from them and guessed how long it would take to crawl back without being noticed. Then all bets were off. The youth turned around again, still clutching the hostage with his left hand. His eyes scanned the street until they settled on them.

And on Topping's camera.

He brought the sawn off shotgun down until the deep black eyes of its twin barrels were staring at the two men on the pavement.

The doctor raised her head; there was only her and the waitress inside the café now. Her heart beat furiously. So this was what Medicins Sans Frontieres put up with daily. One look through the window had been enough. She'd dived straight under the flimsy table and waited there.

The waitress stood motionless and expressionless by the till, she could be seen easily through the window.

There was a boy with a gun of some sort. His attention was somewhere else, not on the café anyway. She got up unsteadily, still expecting another blast to come through the window and finish them both off. Nothing happened.

She moved towards the waitress and shook her. Probably not the best treatment for shock but she couldn't worry about that now. The girl's eyes responded dully. Come on, get a grip! She pushed her through an opening behind the counter, into a back room and threw her a tea towel. "Stay there and wipe yourself down!" she said, quietly. The girl looked at her emptily, still clutching her phone. "It's all right, stay there, don't move. He's not looking at us… at the moment." She left her there, ducked down and made her way to the door, steeling herself for what she might see. As she got within a foot of the cafe front her knees started to shake. There was the sound of sirens in the distance.

"Think you can talk your way out of this?" Topping whispered.

"If I start to speak he'll shoot, I'm certain," Preston replied.

He looked around the street hurriedly, there was no escape route! He always had an escape route. One of the ten commandments of street reporting: don't go in unless you've already sussed a way out. And he hadn't done it this time, he'd just charged in. Idiot!

The youth stared at them. The woman in his grip was petrified. He looked at her, to avoid the youth's eyes, but he couldn't keep it up. He kept going back to the gun. It was bigger than anything else in the street.

"STOP FILMING" shouted the youth in a strangely powerless, light voice which belied the authority of the weapon in his hand. Preston spoke over his shoulder, "Turn it off, Steve!"

Topping ignored him and spoke directly to the youth, "It's not running, honestly."

For God's sake, Steve, now is not the time for that, thought the reporter.

"Turn it off!" replied the boy behind the gun.

"Look, I'm turning the on/off switch, all right!"

Preston looked at the camerman as he fiddled with a switch which he knew full well would make no difference to whether it was working or not, it was the automatic white balance, only the tint would be affected.

"Don't antagonise him!" he whispered, urgently. Topping scowled and ignored him.

"Turn that FUCKING CAMERA the other way," yelled the youth in his high pitched squeal.

"Just do it, will you!" said the reporter.

"OK, I'll point it away from you," said the cameraman. Preston breathed a sigh of relief.

Topping moved the camera around a 30 degree angle. But he also pressed a button by the side of the lens which would widen the scope. He heard the whir of the lens motor in the silence of the street. Surely everyone else must have heard it, no matter how quiet the manufacturer's claimed it to be. He stared straight at Topping. His mouth was completely dry, he couldn't say it but he hoped his look would say to the camerman, "What The FUCK are you doing!" Topping stared back, expressionless. He was probably mentally mouthing something about lily-livered reporters. Well, Fuck you Steve, and thank you very much!

"Who told you I was here!" squealed the almost dispossessed voice. He hadn't heard the lens motor after all, one small miracle, anyway.

"You're the man with the words," muttered Topping.

His heart sank further. What could he say with a dry mouth and no words to fill it! Come on, you can talk for hours when you don't need to. Summon up a couple of seconds now.

"We had no idea you were here." His voice was shaky and higher than his normal baritone, the words sounded so stupid. "We were just having a coffee, just here." He pointed to the coffee shop behind him."

"Why!"

Why have a cup of coffee? Why not have a cup of coffee! Why would he care about having a coffee?
Then it struck him that the sirens had stopped.

The messages were ordinary in so far as they were what she expected, but they didn't lack brutality, that was a constant. Nothing to break up her weekend, though! She could have done with the distraction, shame! The duty DI obviously didn't think so.

Trying to work your way through a break-up only a day after it happened is one way of dealing with it. Some go into a shell, others go flat out to smother the feelings and that was Di Sanders' way this time. It had only been a few months and she thought she'd loved Simon Preston, but she was wrong and so was he. She wouldn't call him for at least a couple of days. There were still some clothes, a couple of books, that sort of thing. But right now she didn't want the angst of it.

Which was the more depressing, her problems or the weekend log? She sighed, at least it was only a broken romance, not a shattered limb, or wrecked family. She went through the list, one by one, and read them out loud.

"Mother and two-year old daughter to Refuge after attack by estranged husband. Mother, four-year old son, one year-old daughter to parents after father threatened all three with chip pan fat." Only the occasional one stood out. "Father to hospital after wife attack with knife." She leaned back in her chair.

"Tony, do you think there's a market for a card game called Unhappy Families. You could have Mr Axeman, Mr Bully, Mr Wimp."

Her new DC looked back with a wry smile. She could never tell with him. She didn't know if he resented her or fancied her. She could do without either today.

"Bad weekend?" Just the hint of a knowing smile from him.
"Could have been better.".
"Maybe Mr Drunk, Mr Inadequte, Mr Limpdick... Someone's probably come up with it already,"
Funny. She smiled. "How are your messages looking?"

"The usual: mutilation, victimisation, and hate. Uniform dealt."

"Unhappy families, snap! It's a score draw."

The office tannoy crackled with static, then stopped.

She continued through her list: elderly woman dumped in a car park, no identification, no money, drooling at mouth. Taken to Accident and Emergency. She marked it and sent it to the DC. "One for you, Tony."

He opened it. "What's it got to do with us? Social Services problem, sounds like."

"Check it, please!" she said, firmly, as she scrolled down. Ah, there it was, no weekend was complete without one. A six-year old child taken into care by Social Services. Evidence of severe and continuous abuse over a long period.

She sighed. She knew what had to happen next. She sent this one to him as well. "Here it is, no Monday complete without it."

He glanced at the details then looked back at her. "I'll do this if you want, Di, I have to get used to it."

Technically he shouldn't call her Di, she was a sergeant and pitching for inspector, but she didn't much care, she wasn't so pompous. She had to be honest, sne didn't want this case herself, not this morning. But her guilt won.

"Stay where you are, DC King, there's plenty for you to be getting on with. Have a go at tracking down the old dear, it'll do your sense of chivalry no end of good." He cast his eyes down. Not a popular order. But when are they ever popular! "This is a job for Detective Sergeant Sanders of the Star Corps. I'm going to see the boy first, I'll see the parents afterwards." The false jollity went as quickly as it came. King wasn't convinced by it, nor was she.

But as she trawled through her emails after the weekend list she brightened if only for a few seconds.

"This'll please you, Tony, Juliet... I mean Chief Superintendent Neilson, has sent a note telling me to keep at it and she asks to be remembered to you."

"That's nice," said King, "We did get on well. Fast riser, though, it was only three years ago that she was an inspector and telling me how to be a detective."

"Picked it up fast, didn't she! Strange kind of copper is Juliet. I mean the chief super…"

"It's OK, I got the first name treatment too. I reckon it was the side-entry attitude. She never was a PC and came in with all that management speak from commerce."

Sanders looked across at King suspiciously and said, "Did you and she…?"

King smiled and said, "Let's say her interpretation of hierarchy is maybe different from what we're used to."

"And there was me thinking she was gay."

King smiled and said as he looked down, "Not always."

"Be careful, Tony, don't get used!"

"It's been a while since that and I think we all know how close she is to the chief."

Sanders did not respond but she knew well enough that Juliet Neilson and Petra Fairbrother shared a lot. She smiled again, picked up her bag, put her phone in a jacket pocket and left the office.

She'd been gone five minutes when the crackling tannoy erupted into a fury of noise and urgency. King ditched everything and grabbed his body armour.

A cacophony of phones overwhelmed the office, music to a news editor's ears. Geoff Donald took a few moments to savour it. Then one next to him rang and he grabbed it.

"Newsdesk."

It was a local tipoff reporter.

"There's something big going off in the city centre. Sirens everywhere for a few minutes, then nothing. But we've been getting calls from all over saying the plod are out in force."

"Any more?"

"Nothing from the Plod. They're staying dead quiet. I know something's up."

"What about radio messages?"

"Not much help. They were just told to switch off their sirens but keep the blues on."

"Right, I'll get on to it."

Donald didn't wait for a response, he touched the End button and yelled out to the Newsroom, "Guns going off in Castleton City Centre, get on the phones and find out what it is – police, ambulance, fire, local shops, everything. Get on it!"

An assistant said, "Do you want to bring Jonesy back?"

"No, we need that story, but give him a call and tell him he MUST get her singing a song for us!"

"What?"

"I know, no chance but it'll piss him off and that's what I want. He was late this morning."

Now, didn't he have a reporter and crew in the city centre, Topping and Preston? They were out early on an easy feature; time to get real gentlemen.

The loudest thing the reporter could hear was his own breathing. He could barely make out the shaky voice behind his left shoulder.

"Is she alright?" It was a woman's voice, trying to sound controlled but how could it in this grimy café doorway with a sawn-off shotgun pointing at them? Preston's first reaction was to shout at her to shut up, but he checked it. He turned his head and saw it was the woman in the cafe. She was crouching out of the youth's eyeline.

"Stay quiet, he's got a gun trained on us!" If it was possible to scream in a soft whisper, that was it.

"Is she hurt?" she repeated, firmly, gesturing in the direction of the woman in the youth's grasp.

"I don't know! And the old man's certainly not looking good, but there's nothing you can do. Get back now!" Couldn't she see the danger?

"Look you ... ", she held back from saying stupid man but she thought it as forcefully as if she'd shouted it through a megaphone "I'm a doctor, there may be something I can do. What exactly can *you* do, anyway?"

The arrogant bastard!

"Not much and nothing at all if I – or you – get shot." Finally she pulled away from the doorway but did not go back inside. Perhaps he knew something that she didn't.

Detective Sergeant Sanders was almost out of the building into the police garage when she heard the tannoy. All available officers to the Market Square. Armed siege in progress. Firearms officers already present.

She was available. She got into her unmarked BMW, checked her body armour and drove out. She'd been on the road for sixty seconds when her radio told all cars to stop their sirens. She hadn't even turned hers on.

The youth waved the gun erratically, sometimes directly in line with Preston, sometimes with Topping. Occasionally it would be pointed at a random target elsewhere in the now empty street. The woman he held in his rough grasp was hanging from him lifelessly – although he didn't think she was actually dead, probably paralysed with fear, thought Preston. The grip had never softened on her. The youth had the determination of a madman.

If he couldn't crawl back into the café, he would have to somehow argue it out. There hadn't been any more shooting, that was a start, Preston's breathing began to ease, although his heart still thumped and fluttered. They might get away with this. If he could just find his calmest, deepest, least panicked voice and talk the youth down from his rage.

He took a deep breath and prepared to say something, projecting from the very base of his diaphragm in a way that only fear will make happen. Then his phone sounded, his heart started pounding uncontrollably. Next to another gunshot it was the last thing he wanted to hear, but there it was, as clear as the brilliant sunshine in the street.

"Turn it off for God's sake!" hissed Topping.

Preston fumbled inside his jacket trying to retrieve it. When he did the swipe wouldn't work. His nervous fumbling fingers danced over it uselessly. He pressed everything he could. The sound carried on. The youth stared straight at them; so did the gun with its two round, unblinking black holes.

Preston was sweating, he couldn't make the bloody thing stop! He gasped for air. "Where is it? Where the fuck is it?" he muttered, desperately.

The phone sounded twice more. The youth let the woman go, she fell to the ground in a heap and lay there, still. The gunman was oblivious to her. Preston saw the dead look in his eye and involuntarily spilled out in a high, blurty squeal, "Don't worry, it's nothing, it's just my phone," then gasped for more air. The youth shouted in his own surprisingly high-pitched voice, "What's going on. What's that noise." Preston made a supreme effort to calm himself and managed finally to swipe his phone towards the red. The phone stopped and he fell back in a heap, gasping, heart pumping blood so hard it felt like it would burst through his eyes. The youth walked slowly towards them.

He knew he had to do something now. He stood up shakily to say it was a mistake. The words started to force themselves out on their own as if he was just a conduit for them not their owner.

The crouching doctor heard every word as she crouched by the café door. She heard the TV manikin start to say something. "Look, It was just...", the rest was lost in the roar of another explosion. She let out an involuntary cry as she fell back through the door into the café. Then she heard two less loud, sharper explosions. She scrambled to her knees to look back into the street. She still had a clear view. The youth seemed to stand for a fraction of a second, really still. Then he started to crumple slowly to the ground clutching his thigh, dropping the gun as he fell. But clearly it had already done its damage. The cartridge pellets had been discharged straight at the TV people in front of the café. There was broken glass right next to her. The shotgun pellets had gone into the window. She looked back into the street, the youth was still lying in the road clutching his thigh with one arm, the other hung uselessly and was bleeding. She heard a slow moaning coming from him. He'd dropped the weapon and it lay a metre away from his left arm. There was no sound from the people in front of her.

She breathed in deeply. Was it still loaded? Could he still fire it? Later she would see this as the moment of her life she would look back on and acknowledge that it defined who she was. Would she cower back under the table, or do what she believed she was meant to do: ease suffering, save life? A shiver gripped her body. Come on Louise, she told herself, now's the time to prove you could survive in Syria. She pushed herself back out of the door, squashing down her fear as she moved. She emerged through the doorway then stopped short as the sight sank in.

She was used to people being ill, children had died on her before now and she hated that. But she was always in a position where she could do her best to control it. Not here. This was carnage. She'd had no part in this. There was a gathering pool of blood just in front of her. It wasn't big but it threatened her. A few yards away she saw more blood coming from the youth. He was one of two figures on the ground with a third lying a little way off. She turned her attention to the reddening bodies next to her.

"It's all right, I'm a doctor, where does it hurt," she asked the TV showpony. There was an urgency in her voice which she hoped sounded like authority instead of the fear it actually was. Preston writhed on the ground. His chest and shoulder were stinging with pain and blood had already seeped through his jacket.

"Bloody everywhere," he gasped. "What about Steve?"

She cast her eyes around quickly, taking in as much as she could, quickly assessing her priorities. There was the man who'd carried the camera, he was a metre away and had taken several pellets in the leg. She shifted towards Topping and asked the same question. He grimaced, his replies came through clenched teeth. But he wasn't bleeding so seriously that it needed her immediate attention. The paramedics could deal with it, probably better than her. She turned back to Preston. His chest was peppered with broadening bloodstains.

"Can you breathe?"

"More easily than a few minutes ago."

"I need to undo your shirt and see the damage in case it went deep."

"Deep?"

"Your heart's close by."

Preston said nothing more but let her do her work.

"I think you're lucky Mr Preston, none of it has got beyond the ribs. The Hospital can patch you up."

"Lucky!", he gasped, then, "You know who I am?"

It was the last thing to happen before the mayhem; it had stuck.

"I couldn't help but know with the pantomime the waitress put on for you."

"Who are you, then?"

"Louise Brown, senior registrar paediatrician."

"You're a children's doctor?"

She pulled his shirt back together. "Don't worry, you qualify."

"Good to know."

"Sure about that?"

Yes, he was sure about that. What did she mean? Then realisation: ouch, what had he done to deserve that? He opened his mouth to ask but she had already moved to the side of the old man.

A uniformed chief inspector barked an order to an armed team a few metres away. "Get in there now! The gun's on the floor".

Police and paramedics filled the street, high viz jackets bent over the wounded figures. Blue uniforms in body armour and carrying guns charged in and surrounded the youth on the ground. Two of them had shot him moments before, one in the thigh, the other in an arm. His weapon had fallen too far away for him to reach and he was now powerless. If Preston had been capable he would have seen how the stripping of the gun had reduced the youth's authority to nothing.

The chief inspector spoke into his radio, "It's safe, but it's a bloodbath." A crash team had pre-empted him, they raced into the street and went straight to the four injured bodies. The senior officer again spoke to his superior, "It's over sir...No he isn't dead as far as we can tell. He's badly hurt...The medics are looking at the others now."

The youth was bleeding heavily from his left femural artery, paramedics worked furiously to plug the wound. Dr Brown could see what they were doing and left them alone, that was their area, not hers, she would only get in the way. But he had already lost a lot of blood.

The mayhem can only have lasted for a couple of minutes, but in that short time no one saw the old woman who'd been held by the gunman, get up shakily from where she'd been dropped and quietly move away from the scene completely.

Di Sanders headed straight for the bleeding TV reporter, her mind churning with conflicting emotions. Was he hurt badly? Why was the idiot getting in the way? She should leave him to his silly games, she should run to care for him! They were over, no question about that, but more than a vestige of concern remained; he wasn't a bad man, not especially good either but who was?

Finally she said, "Is there nothing you will not do to get a story?" He tried to smile but his face contorted to a mask of pain, he was waiting for meds from the paramedics. Normally he'd be right back at her with a one-liner, but right now he was struggling. But Preston could never resist an audience, even an ex-lover hovering over his pellet-ridden body. So he dug deep.

"I won't eat snails, someone else can have that one." She smiled despite the situation but he was an annoying man. Dr Brown caught the eye of the detective sergeant as she left the old woman and the old man to the paramedics.

"Hello, I'm Louise Brown, I work at the hospital."

Sanders recognised her.

"I know, I've seen you in case conference meetings."

"Sorry, still in shock – and no sleep for 36 hours. Yes, you're Sergeant....Sergeant Sanders?

"Yes, I'm on the family Unit. And it's Di."

"I'm Louise." She looked down at Preston who was trying to conceal his discomfort, "Is he yours?"

"No, not any more. But he was up until a few hours ago."

"Oh, sorry…"

Preston chipped in, "You and me both!"

Sanders scowled at him and said, "All right, this isn't the time or the place."

Brown joined in, "I'm with her. Now be quiet! Wait for the paramedics to stretcher you into the ambulance."

She turned back to Sanders, "He's going to be all right. It's going to hurt but nothing's dangerously damaged that I could see. There's bleeding but no real blood loss."

"Thanks doc," said Preston, weakly, "Catch you later."

She allowed herself to smile, "You'll need a big hook, and I don't like worms."

As rejections go it was original but still Sanders watched the exchange irritatedly. She and Preston were finished but only since the weekend and it was too soon to be flirting with other women, especially in front of her.

Topping, hurting but smiling, jumped in and said: "Things were getting pretty dull. Do me a favour Doc." The doctor looked down at his pointing hand. "Turn that switch off on the camera." The doctor's eyes rolled heavenwards, but she did as she had been asked. Sanders looked on from another direction, she knew Topping but not very well. She gave him a reassuring smile. "Could be evidence, Steve."

"You'll have to speak to the big boys about that," he replied.

Sanders turned back to Preston. "Does that mean you, Simon?" she asked. The doctor allowed a chuckle despite herself and the situation. She was still a medical student at heart. Preston, regaining his composure and with it his enthusiasm for oneliners, saw an open goal.

"You need to ask, Di?"

"For God's sake, Simon!" said the detective.

The doctor, at this moment seeing the sisterhood being more important than a good joke, added, "Like I said, you qualify."

The two women exchanged glances and a quarter smile touched both sets of lips but disappeared as quickly as they arrived. They watched Topping and Preston being loaded into ambulances and then saw them driven away. Sanders was tempted to give a wave but thought better of it; they were finished after all, no matter what had happened here. The doctor tried to think of some useful words to say but they didn't come. She was better with parents and kids, not adults and their relationships, she had never really understood those. The moment passed.

Her phone sounded, the screen threw up a picture of her consultant and she knew she had some explaining to do. She excused herself, turned away from Sanders and walked the few metres back to the cafe. Her legs were shaky and she felt a weariness come over her which she knew could not just be from the long hours. There was no one in the cafe but she could still smell the aroma of roasted coffee.

She swiped her phone towards the green and said, "Louise Brown."

"Where the hell *are* you, Louise?"

The voice was demanding but not furious, more ironic with an edge.

"Paul, I'm sorry, I've been caught up in an incident in the town."

"You'll be caught up in something much worse if you don't get here bloody fast." He was only half joking.

"I'm serious Paul."

"So am I."

"Paul, stop, please! I've been helping at a shooting."

She gave him the full account. He softened, "What a nightmare, sorry for shouting. You were on duty last night weren't you?" He drew up the rostas he should know she was on call; still he scheduled this bloody meeting for first thing in the morning.

"I'm coming down off adrenaline at the moment."

"Have you had enough of a dose to get to this social services meeting."

Have a care for …. "I'll try Paul."

"Sorry Louise, you know how hard it is to get everyone here at the same time."

"OK I'll be late. I'm still shaky, give me half an hour."

"I wish I could but you're already late."

For god's sake! She looked down at her bag and saw the RISK file. The road to hell is paved with good intentions. "All right, yes I'm coming, *now*. All right!" She pressed the END button before her boss could get in any more jibes and she said something she would regret. She wasn't a consultant yet, she had to toe the line. Bastard, where was he when the bullets were flying. She paused, she liked him really. If only he wasn't married. She packed the file away in her bag, added the phone and walked towards the door, still unsteadily, but gathering strength. Just at the door she looked back and saw her coffee on the table, undisturbed by the previous 30 minutes. She went back and picked it up, then defiantly took a sip, it was cold and revolting. She banged the cup down and left.

Back at the hospital, she made her way to the second floor and went straight to the Ladies toilet. She rifled through her bag and brought out a makeup bag, then she looked in the mirror and saw what the last twenty four hours had done to her. This was stupid, she shouldn't be going to this meeting, she should go home to bed; or better still a town centre bar and a couple of double Southern Comforts.

She ran the eyeshadow brush over her lids, applied some powder and prayed it would camouflage the ravages of her last few hours. Time is really not on your side any more, she thought. It wasn't just the last few hours which were catching up on her, it was the entire thirty four years of her life.

It's getting to be hopeless, she again confided silently to the mirror.

She had wanted to be a doctor since she was 15. She did everything right, excelled at school, got top grades to get her into a London teaching hospital. She had dedicated herself to medicine, men came second which was to say last. If she ever got lonely she could find companionship, it wasn't hard for her. But as she had climbed the ladder she had less time even for that.

She was getting later and later for the meeting. She drew a deep breath, stood up erect and became Dr Louise Brown again. She slung her bag on her shoulder and put her makeup bag inside. The file she tucked under an arm. She walked out of the ladies lavatory and strode twenty yards down the corridor where she stopped, looked at her watch, took another deep breath, and opened the door.

She felt the eyes burning into her as she entered the room. Paul Bowes sat at the head of the table looking like a judge about to don a black cap. He looked down at his papers pointedly. She gritted her teeth, and squeezed an apology through them. Bowes grimaced.

"Nothing serious I hope", came an inquiry from the man on her right.

"All emergencies are serious", replied the Brown in her most doctor-like voice. Her mask stayed rigid. She cast her gaze down to her file but she wasn't looking at it, her eyes were in peripheral mode, that's how she noticed a new face.

Bowes broke in, "I'm sorry Dr Brown I haven't introduced you to Dr Martin Tench." She nodded and raised a half smile. He was too far away to shake his hand. "I introduced him to everyone else at the start of the meeting."

That was enough! He'd made his point.

"I'm sorry I missed it but I was tending to a shotgun victim in the ciry."

The room, already quiet, was reduced to silence, everyone looked at her.

Finally Tench spoke, "Are you sure you should be here?"

Thank you and no she damned well wasn't. But that was just too bad. "I'll take some time when we've finished. Now, shall we get on, I'm sorry to hold you up." The people gathered around the table exchanged glances and nods and some looked down at their papers again. The meeting restarted.

Child abuse was part of her job and it was the one part she hated – not the children, she cared deeply for them; no, it was the very thought of it. It made her feel weak to think of what some people did to their kids, and why. But she had a duty.

"There's another one for you, I'm afraid, Dr Brown", said Bowes, "David Maclean, six years old, brought in on Saturday. The details are in the file."

"Who examined him." enquired Brown, surprised but thankful that it had not been her.

"I did," said Martin Tench, grim-faced,looking directly at her.

"Is there any reason why I wasn't called to it?" she asked, she had been on duty after all.

"No it came from our friends here," said Bowes, looking at the social services representatives. You hadn't started duty yet.

She turned to Tench, "What's the evidence?"

"Apart from what the social services had gleaned from his teacher ..." he looked to the principle social worker, "...it's all in the file."
"Was any of it recent".
Tench opened his mouth to speak but Bowes cut him off. "We've already covered most of this Dr Brown. Perhaps you can pick it up later." That was the second put down from him in less than five minutes. Even the social workers picked up something. They were supposed to be friends for goodness sake. "Yes of course", she replied airily with a confidence she did not feel. The mask staying rigidly in place. She wrote a note in her file.

Robin Humphries was a decent enough lawyer; he believed everyone had a right to justice, he steered a straight path, he enjoyed his family and his life. He was not a man of great means but his comfortable house just outside the city on a new, well-to-do estate, and his well-established reputation, lent him substance.
Now he was on unfamiliar territory. He didn't want this case. Just because he'd done some conveyancing work for the Macleans a few years ago did not mean he was the family solicitor. They'd never called on him for anything else. The fact was he was at home with oaths, wills, contracts and the detail of everyday life, not this criminal stuff – still less child abuse allegations.
Now he stood in the family court with the bench in front, the Macleans behind, and his opposing lawyer from the social services at his side. He'd very occasionally been to court while training but had avoided it ever since. Now he was here and was hating every second of it.
His lack of experience was hindering his judgement and he knew it. He wasn't sure if he believed John and Pauline Maclean. If Social Services had taken away their son he assumed there had to be a reason. Humphries drew breath, looked behind to the Macleans who fretted anxiously in the rear benches, turned, and addressed the magistrates.
"Your worships the evidence before you is far from conclusive," he knew it would have no effect but he carried on,

"Mr and Mrs Maclean are determined that there has been no abuse in their household, neither by them nor anyone else".

He paused to study the bench. Three impassive faces stared back. The one on the left, a woman of about sixty, had a cold look which would have frozen the most ardent of advocates and Humphries was not that. He was not certain, even after an hour of face-to-face discussion, if the Macleans were properly defendable.

He'd only agreed to be there because he was a decent man and knew they had to be represented, that was everyone's right. The request – no, pleading – had come in only an hour before and he didn't have time to find them a specialist family lawyer. So green was he in this environment that he wasn't even sure if his light grey, double-breasted suit, was the proper way to dress there. No one had said anything.

He continued to the bench, "Clearly we must accept the evidence of abuse, that seems to be incontrovertible, but Mr and Mrs Maclean are adamant that they had nothing to do with it. Furthermore they point to ten years of unblemished fostering of children in care".

The chairman of the bench looked up.

"Are you able to help, Mr Johnson?" the chairman addressed the local authority solicitor.

"Your worships whether or not there is no evidence from the past ten years, there most certainly is evidence now. This remains a hearing for an extension of the place of safety order subject to a full care order. Such details may emerge later."

Johnson was a fair man in Humphries' eyes, but he had a job to do, and sometimes he overdid it. They had locked horns over more than one planning application in the past. That said Humphries had to admire the other lawyer's versatility – from architect's drawings to this: quite a leap and one which he wasn't managing at all well.

He looked behind to the Macleans. They stared on, miserable, without understanding. It had been just a broth of words signifying nothing to them. The magistrates panel huddled together for a few seconds then the chairman spoke.

"We will retire!".

The room stood as they left their seats and filed through a door at the front of the court. The court clerk followed them. Humphries turned to Johnson, "What do you think?"

"Seems cut and dried. The medical evidence is there, so is the teacher."

"Mr Humphries!" He had been neglecting his clients. He turned around to face John Maclean.

"What's happening, why have they gone out of the room."

Humphries himself rarely understood the secret rituals which were conducted in the rooms behind the magistrates bench. Sometimes it was simply to have a cup of coffee, other times it was probably serious deliberation. He doubted that on this occasion but he could not tell that to Maclean. He tried to sound convincing. "They're weighing up the evidence to see if David stays with the authority or goes back to you".

"Surely they believe us. I mean you told them we didn't do it. You told them nothing like this has ever happened at our place".

Humphries glanced across to Maclean's wife who sat motionless throughout. She had said very little in their brief talk beforehand. Short, neat, no perfume, ordinary. Was she a submissive bystander allowing it to happen; or was she genuinely in shock?

They waited for what seemed like an hour, but when Humphries looked at his watch he saw it had been only ten minutes. The magistrates filed back in, the court stood. Maclean rejoined his wife. Humphries and Johnson faced the bench. The chairman took his seat, cleared his throat and started to speak. The ice woman on the left remained frozen and forbidding. Humphries could see what was coming despite his inexperience. He braced himself internally.

"David Maclean will stay in care in the interim," said the chairman dispassionately. At the back of the court Maclean sighed loudly. His wife broke into a coughing fit and he comforted her with an arm.

Louise Brown walked out of the Conference Room and headed straight for the ladies staff toilet brushing off the newcomer, Dr Martin Tench, on the way. His "How about a coffee Dr Brown?" wafted in her slipstream. The lavatory door banged shut behind her. She sat in one of the cubicles and let the mask slip as she took out a tissue and dabbed her eyes. She sat there for ten minutes silently weeping amid intermittent waves of anger. Then she dabbed her eyes one last time, collected herself and left her sanctuary.

The staff restaurant was one of the few places in the hospital where doctors, nurses, porters and administrators could get away from the pressures of the public they served. The constant worries of people concerned about themselves, their relatives, or nothing at all could make for a bitter life if they weren't careful.

Brown entered believing that here at least she was among friends. She could mitigate her loneliness here. Another way was children; they asked few questions. She could give them affection and they would not query or complicate, just accept it.

She looked around the crowded tables trying to find Tench. She spotted him sitting with Paul Bowes. Her heart sank, she did not want to speak to Bowes right now; she *did* want to speak to Tench.

She surprised herself at her disappointment. And she was annoyed that Tench had made such an impression before she had a chance to examine it; she'd only met him a few minutes before, where was her judgement?

She approached the table smiling. "Dr Tench I'm sorry if I seemed rude earlier, I've been on call all night and a shotgun being fired in my direction doesn't make for a calm life."

"Hardly, it's the sort of thing which could end it. It's Martin, by the way and I think we can cut you some slack this morning of all mornings."

"Thank you, and it's Louise."

Tench took her hand and smiled warmly. She felt a slight shiver but didn't try so hard to beat it down this time.

"It was an experience I've never had before. I don't want anything like it again."

"I'm not surprised. I bet your hormones are all over the place…!"

What did he say?

He saw her face change and said, "Adrenaline overload...not..."

She relaxed and smiled. If they were all over the place now it might no longer have been because of the adrenaline.

She heard a grunt and looked down to see Bowes grinning.

They talked some more; he had been a registrar at a large Hampshire hospital and was now moving up to senior, the same as her. He was relatively young, attractive and with a voice which would melt the North Pole if global warming failed. She needed to be careful. But what eyes! She found herself imagining... best to stop before that even got started..

Bowes watched with a half smile on his face. He said nothing but he caught her eye, briefly and she coquettishly thought he was jealous.

She looked down and fiddled with her coffee cup.

THREE DAYS LATER

He enjoyed the round-the-clock TV to begin with - endless hours of box sets and constant news on CNN, BBC and Sky News; what wasn't to like? But three days in he was kicking against it; no one to butt heads with, just be there, sitting upright now at last, but still letting the TV do all the work, his brain straining against nothing. Boring, he wanted a scrap – not a physical one, he'd never wanted that in is life and now would certainly not have been a good time to start with his chest looking like a magnified pepper pot. No, he wanted an argument with someone – the nurses were fabulous, but it wasn't in their job description, he had to be careful in case they took it for aggression, which it was, but not against them. Anyway, they didn't have the time, nor did the doctors who should have been more fertile territory. So he'd spent the last hour arguing with himself just to keep in shape. The only disadvantage was that whilst he won every time, he also lost.

He hoped he would be allowed home today, his observations had been good for the last 12 hours: blood pressure back to normal – for him, anyway – no secondary infections from the pellet wounds, heart rate at a respectable level and his breathing deeper and regular again, There was the pain from the bruising around his ribs and the shallow entry wounds from the pellets, but painkillers would deal with that he was sure. If not that then a decent single malt.

Home! Great! Of course, although he didn't have anyone there to soothe his pained brow, he couldn't ask Di to suspend their break up to nurse him, but there was always that versatile single malt. He was on a general ward and would be glad to be away from it. There were sick people there and they didn't have much to say for themselves except that they knew him from the tele and then complain about their conditions. They hadn't been much bothered by his wounds either, a perfunctory nod, a "How awful for you," then a demand to know the gossip about the newscasters on the programme.

He wasn't about to let anything slip, even when they'd put him on a mild titration of Morphine, now reduced to paracetomol; some things you shared, others you didn't. Now he was about to leave he regretted his decision not to accept a private room. The TV company wanted to pay for it but he had some principles, he thought, and they included getting the same treatment as everyone else.

Noble! Also stupid! He should have taken it; the neighbouring patients and, worse, their relatives, had made it hell, but once he was there he couldn't opt out without a PR mess. It would only take one patient or a member of staff to get in touch with a tabloid with a line about him being too good for the likes of them. As it was everybody everywhere had a camera on their phone which they would use without thinking – like their lives hadn't been lived unless they had been put on YouTube. He hadn't dared even fart without carefully filtering it through his bedclothes, he could easily find himself unwillingly being mocked on a late night TV comedy show. As you live, so shall you die, he thought as the irony struck him.

The man in the bed to his left shifted and groaned with discomfort; he'd had a hernia operation with complications. It was as much as he could glean. He heard a rustling and the sound of voices from around the corner of his bay. He recognised one of them but couldn't hear the words clearly so the face eluded him. Then she appeared at the end of his bed. The doctor from the shooting. Why, he wondered, was she here?

"Mr Preston, how are you?"

"You'll have to forgive me I…"

"Doctor Louise Brown. I was there with you."

He replied, almost dismissively, she thought, "What brings you here?"

What had brought her there? An intense moment shared? The desire to bond through their mutual experience? Well, if it was that he wasn't biting and she began to feel foolish but she carried on.

"I'd meant to visit sooner… but I've been catching up on sleep – or at least trying to. I get jumpy."

"You get used to it." So matter of fact he might have been parking his car instead of being shot in the chest. He worked for a regional TV station, how many times did he face gunfire doing that? She wished she hadn't come, it was only courtesy and it didn't look like he wanted reassurance. Prick!

But she was there so she persevered, "I'm surprised to hear that. Have you faced a lot of danger out here in the British provinces?"

"Not much. Why?"

"So how do you get used to it?

"You do tours in Afghanistan, Iraq and Syria." Beyond dismissive now; offhand!

But it didn't sound like he was lying.

"I see. This must seem quite run of the mill, then?"

"Nope, never been shot before. It had to be in an English provincial town, didn't it? And a shotgun, not even a high velocity rifle."

What! He actually wanted it to be more serious?

"Are you sure you know what you're saying? "

Then his face changed and the ironic smirk was replaced by a smile.

"Just bragging rights. War wounds are a badge of pride in my game… well, they are in my old game." He looked her straight in the eye, "I don't play it any more – at least I didn't think I did." He looked down at his chest ruefully and rubbed it.

She kept quiet, he filled the gap, "I was a foreign correspondent for ITN. "

"Really?" she asked, half-heartedly.

"Takes a lot to impress you, doesn't it Miss Kiddies doctor!"

Yes, it did, but he was beginning to be more interesting. No less annoying, though, in fact, if anything, more so.

"Mr Maclean if you don't tell me everything I can't help you!"

John Maclean stared back, his wife by his side, both muted.

"The police say you did it, the social workers say you did it, even the boy's teacher has testified that she heard David say he had been abused. I need more than just your denial".

Humphries was still flapping around in a world he didn't understand. His attempts to get rid of this disagreeable case to someone more used to the ugliness of it were proving useless and he began to fear he was saddled with it. He'd always gone his own way as a lawyer, he did well enough without having resort to a partnership. Now it would be so useful to be in a gang where they shared the specialisms around. But here he was, still offering his next to useless advice. Nevertheless he was still a solicitor and he was obliged to persevere. Despite his loud protestations to Maclean he sensed that not everything added up. There had never been any issues before with this couple, they seemed perfectly good people and had taken such a shine to David that they'd adopted him permanently after fostering him for a year.

Maclean finally spoke, quietly, hurt, "Mr Humphries, I have told you, and I have told the social services I did not abuse David, or anyone else who has been fostered by us."

The trouble was nothing the Macleans had said was strong enough to convince Humphries of their innocence, only the way they said it. And he knew enough about the law to know bad people can deceive. The evidence was piling up and they had nothing to counter it with but their denials. Worse, the institutions were lining up – social services, teachers, police – big guns and hard to shift once set.

Maclean spoke again: "Not only are we being accused of something which has not happened, other people are getting to hear about it. Our reputation is being destroyed and for nothing!"

Humphries paused: it would be unusual to put a reputation before the welfare of a child, wouldn't it? On the other hand the Macleans were a simple couple, they had little ambition beyond their small house on the outskirts of the city. He worked as a jobbing carpenter, she stayed at home. If there was still a working class they represented it. And the only thing they would leave this earth with was their reputation.

"How do we make you believe we have never done anything like this. It's against my nature. All we wanted was to be able to help, to give some love. We've been doing this for ten years and we have never touched a kid beyond a pat on the head." For a moment his dignity left him and the power of his rage took over. "We're not fucking child molesters. Do you understand?" The last words were roared, there was rage in this mild-mannered man.

Humphries' heart beat hard, conveyancing didn't bring this kind of passion and he struggled to calm himself.

"All right Mr Maclean, please, shouting won't get us anywhere!" He waited while Maclean's fury slowly ebbed then he resumed, "We somehow have to convince the police, and the social services..." he emphasised the "And", "that you did not have anything to do with it. How are we going to do that?"

"We didn't do it Mr Humphries!"

Humphries opened his hands and raised them slightly. "Well if you didn't do it, who did?"

He was young, though not fit according to the medics. They also thought he should be in a lot better condition for someone in his late teens. They hadn't taken to him, why would they, he'd shot up the High Street and given them more work than they needed. Now he was silent in the bed. They gave him pain relief because that was their job, but anything else, like comfort and human contact, forget it! Let him stew. And not everyone was too bothered about his patient-confidentiality either, which is why King had so much detail, albeit sotto voce. The kid had taken two bullets and had been in a bad way for three days. His right thigh and right shoulder had been smashed up and would take time to repair. He was injured badly enough that the medics had stopped cuffs being put on him – not that he was going anywhere.

King had been deputed to interview him at the earliest possible moment. It fell to him because there seemed a departmental link at the time, and even if there wasn't they were short staffed and there had to be some doubling up.

This was that earliest possible moment – probably too early but the medics weren't fussed, so he found himself at the bed trying to get some sense out of the sullen figure in front of him. So far they hadn't even got his name. There had been nothing in his clothes, no one had come forward to claim him. All they had was the sawn-off shotgun, but the prints were useless and he'd dropped it far enough away that no blood could get on it, so no DNA. And while the medics were unusually flexible he knew better than to just take a hair from his head for DNA sampling. He'd have to answer for that in court at some time and he'd be back in uniform stuck on the ground floor. He hadn't joined the police to be PC Plod, he'd already passed his sergeant's and inspector's exams and was looking to move up as soon as he could. So he would play by the rules, but any information was useful and while the medics should have been more discreet there was no rule to say he couldn't hear it.

The kid was a mess. The hospital had cleaned him up so that his hair was washed but he still had the air of a scruffy, unfed urchin. The skeletal face was pale and defeated, and his eyes transmitted a ferocity which remained no matter what King said.

King was no deep thinker and not yet even a good judge of people so it was easy for his contempt to rise. The lad was immobilised in his plaster and bandages. His wounds had needed immediate surgery and he was on a constant drip of morphine based painkillers. He was dopey but conscious. King tried again, "You'll have to speak sometime, you can't stay silent forever!" The youth looked at him with his angry eyes as if to say, "Yes I can!" but his lips did not move.

"Tell us your name!"

Silence! King got out his notebook and busied himself making imaginary notes. The youth remained defiantly still, only his breathing betrayed that he was alive.

"There had to be a reason for it. You do know what you've done?" Nothing. "You've almost killed a man." He waited, but still nothing came. "You scared a woman half to death... and badly injured a TV Crew".

The boy's eyes widened.

"Ah, so you are alive".

Not for long, the youth retreated into his frozen mask. "Come on!" He spoke softly, "Where did you get the gun?" The youth closed his eyes and reopened them. It was movement but hardly encouraging. The detective thought about giving up, but that would not be acceptable to his boss, or in the end himself.

"You can't just ignore what you've done. It won't go away"

Still nothing but sod it, he was going to talk at the bastard just to annoy him. "You know the first man you shot is in intensive care? If he ever regains consciousness... and that's not likely...then he'll have nothing left to think with." He stopped again. "He lost so much blood it starved his brain of oxygen"

Now King was ranting and he didn't care, "He's in a bad way, he may never come round. What did he do to you to deserve that? Did you just decide to have a morning out at a shooting gallery!. Was it just a game for you?"

The youth shifted his body slightly, a reaction at last! He opened his mouth and spoke, "You're all the same," came the squeaky voice which had terrorised the city centre. Four more words than they had before.

"Why am I the same?" said King.

The youth kept a snarl on his lips and stayed silent for a few seconds then cast his eyes down and repeated less vehemently, more in supplication, "You're all the same!"

"All right, have it your way, but you'll have to talk sometime!"

He walked towards the door and called a uniformed officer back.

She fought to get her work head back where it should be. Her mission was to make inspector before 35 and superintendent by 40. Unlike her junior, DC King, she hadn't been fast-tracked but had impressed anyway. However, she wouldn't do it if she let her emotions get in the way, wasn't that why she'd ditched Preston in the first place?

She'd liked him, still liked him, and seeing him shot up in a café doorway had been harder than she thought. Yes, he was an arrogant bastard, full of himself, a know-it-all annoyance a lot of the time; but he was funny and sexy and he'd cared for her in his own way. But Preston was a security risk – or he would be if she went to Special Branch as she knew she had to if she was to continue her promotion plans.

He hadn't been slow to tap her up for information during their short time together and sometimes she'd been able to help him without compromising herself. But there would come a time when that conflict would arise and just how loyal would he be? She liked him, probably loved him, certainly cared for him, but she did not trust him and that, in the end, meant it was over for them, it had to. Without trust what do you have?

Now her work head was returning and that sliver of logic slipped in and helped her reset herself.

There had been so much going on at the incident she hadn't had time to sort it, but now Preston had been put in a box her mind roamed more. It had been niggling at the back of her mind for days: who was the kid with the shotgun? He was familiar in a vague way. She never got a full look at him, the face had been hidden and by the time she got close he was covered in an oxygen mask and being loaded into the ambulance.

"Tony, get the News View website up and look up the report from the shooting, I'm not signed on yet."

"What are you looking for?" asked King.

"The kid. There was something about him which has been bugging me. I might know him from somewhere."

"Now you tell me. I've looked at this stuff 50 times already."

"Yes, but I haven't," she said, adding steel to her voice.

King did as he was told and accessed the News View report. The camerawork was shaky and poorly focused so even if there was a full shot it was indistinct. Sanders had been around Preston for long enough to know that the immediacy and drama overrode any questions about picture-clarity. She stared hard at the boy then muttered quietly, "He's one of the orphans."

King looked round at her. "Sarge?""

"Just an idea. The kid looks like someone I came across a few years ago. She stared hard at the image.

"I don't suppose this will get any better, will it?"

"It's already in HD."

She sighed. "OK, Tony, history lesson: seven years ago when I was still in uniform there used to be an orphanage a few miles out of town at Bulmington."

History had never been King's strong point, but he listened.

"One day sometime in the middle of spring we got a call from one of the local tradesmen, it might have been a plumber, to say that the place was locked up."

"You mean everything, every door and window?"

"Yes, and all the kids had been locked inside, there was nobody from the management; no manager, no nurses, nobody".

King listened.

"We never got to the bottom of it and my involvement was pretty small, CID took it over. But I wanted to know what happened."

King's interest peaked, he was a copper and a detective at that. He smelled something and liked the scent.

"How could that be?"

"No idea, all the records had gone. For all we know there may never have been any".

"And you think this lad is one of them?"

"Could be. If he's nineteen now, and we don't even know that for sure, then he would have been eleven at the time. He should have changed beyond recognition. I only saw them for a short while. I was just brought in to do an emergency nursemaid job."

"So why this now?"

"It was a haunted look he had, it reminded me of it all again. They were under some kind of spell and wouldn't speak, but I spent time with him … at least I think I did. Never got a name, though!"

"So they never told you what happened?"

"We couldn't get a word out of them. I remember they were nervous, but we never knew what led to it."

King was hooked. "So where did they all go?"

"Sorry Tony I don't know, one of the council care homes I suppose. I never got the chance to look into it any deeper… and I haven't got the time now. I have to be at the social services department."

Sanders made to leave the room.

"Just one thing, Di." She stopped and tried not to look irritated. She may not have been a sergeant for very long but she'd earned the rank.

"What was this orphanage called?"

That was easy, it had never left her.

"The James Institute. Got to go. Check it out!"

She rushed out of the door, King was already typing into his laptop and didn't register her departure.

Preston moved gingerly, the soreness in his chest could take him by surprise as the weaker painkillers wore off. He was on his way home but had a mission before he called the office to let them know. He knew they'd be all over him with a car and help and that was all fine, but not before he'd got this out of the way.

He picked up his bag with it's light load of a tablet, electric toothbrush and a couple of paperbacks and stopped instantly, surprised by the sharp pains in his pecs and upper abs. He put down the bag and resolved to collect it later from the nurses' station when someone else could carry it. He moved slowly towards the door realising for the first time just how much every muscle in his body was engaged in the act of walking. He took a couple of painkillers from the supply the nurses had given him and decided to tough it out – the endorphins would kick in as he got moving.

He shuffled out to a long corridor with branches off indicating different wards. He continued his slow progress for 50 metres until he came to the ward he was looking for. He turned into its entrance, beginning to feel freer in his movement, and saw the uniformed policeman outside.

"Simon Preston. Are you feeling better?" Then, "You

shouldn't be here you know!"

Preston smiled fraternally and pointed at the door.

"I wanted to take a look. "

"Strictly off limits Simon, even to you, especially you!"

Nothing was off limits to Simon Preston, ever!

"Just forget you saw me."

"Simon he's the centre of an investigation, it might even be for murder. I can't just forget I saw you. Now stop it and we'll say no more about it!"

Young one with an eye on promotion and keeping his slate clean. They'd met before but only to exchange smiles and limited words.

"He did nearly kill me you know", said Preston with a sense of not entirely fake grievance.

The uniform had nothing against Preston, but he had strict orders, and this officer, at least, believed in the chain of command and doing the right thing.

" I know how you must feel. But I can't let you in".

Preston shrugged his shoulders: "OK I give in. I guess I'll just have to wait until the trial."

He turned on his heel, did his best to hold back the wince as the pain in his pecs reasserted itself, and headed back to the corridor.

The officer said to his retreating back, "I'm sorry, Simon".

"I know".

He went back to the corridor and shuffled along to the next ward before ducking into it. The officer thought he'd won, but nothing was off-limits to Preston. One of the nurses glanced at him, any other time he would have glanced back, she was worth it, but not now. He gave no acknowledgement but tried to look fascinated by the contents of the board. He prayed she wouldn't come up to ask him what he was doing there, especially if she recognised him.

No, too busy.

Ten minutes elapsed before he headed out to the corridor again and back to the youth's ward. The guard was sitting on a chair by the door looking at his phone. It was getting close to his changeover time because he was looking at his watch as well. Preston hung back in the corridor on the off chance that he might still be able to do it. He wasn't disappointed. A minute later another officer approached from the other direction. He could make out their conversation.

"I'll be with you in a sec. I just need to get something from the hospital shop, then I'll take over."

"Don't worry, it's all quiet, he's not going anywhere, he can't move. I'll come with you and get a cup of tea." Naughty boy, deserting his post. But Preston wasn't about to raise the alarm, the very opposite in fact. The two moved off with a glance down the ward entrance. They walked past Preston's still pained form as he pressed it hard against the corridor wall and prayed that he wasn't standing on the route to the teashop. He was lucky again. They walked past and Preston was partially concealed by the door, he waited for them to disappear. He had to be quick, the tea stand was only a few metres away but concealed behind a corner.

He opened the door and walked in. The youth looked up. Now he would get a chance to see what he had wanted to see for the last three days. He looked into the boy's eyes and stared hard. The youth stared back but there was no recognition. He didn't seem to have any idea that he had shot this man.

Preston had wanted the satisfaction of seeing fear in the eyes, and it was there all right, but not for him. The boy's face a showed a map of emotions with rage and fear prominent, and defeat everywhere. Just for a fleeting moment pity crept into his heart. But it was crushed by another spasm from his pecs. He stared hard into the youth's eyes, fuelled by his own outrage.

But nothing came back.

The social worker listened but said nothing until this moment. "If that is the case then we have a catastrophe on our hands. The Macleans have been fostering children for ten years. How many others will have been affected?"

The plummy voice surprised Sanders; this was no ordinary social worker, he was aiming for the director's job and who knew what after that. Well, not on her back he wouldn't.

"The Macleans deny everything." There were shrugs and frustrated hand gestures around the table as Martin Tench, Paul Bowes and Louis Brown, found ways to express dissatisfaction without saying so. The social services rottweiler did nothing, but his department should have weeded the Macleans out a long time ago, what could he say!

"For the moment, on the current evidence ..." she looked at Tench, "and my own interview with David, I think there's a case for prosecution. The question is..." she looked now at the social worker, "Do you think it's wise to pursue, or should there be an attempt at reconciliation?"

"Not from what I saw, Sergeant, you've seen what I found in my examination report?" intervened Tench. "It's just not safe. I think we should go for prosecution." No-one dissented:

They were alone in the room. Preston made sure the door was in exactly the same position as when he entered it. He could see if anyone was coming. He kept one eye on that and the other on the kid, or *man* as the law would now insist a 19 year-old was – assuming he was nineteen, and that had yet to be proven.

This cowering, beaten down specimen had shot him and Topping and virtually killed someone else. Preston of all people could afford not to understand. He could see the kid was going nowhere but he still wanted to see cuffs, or even chains, on his bed, just to make a vengeful point. Then, as Preston considered the many ways he would like to hurt the slimeball before him, he spoke. It was that same pitiful whining voice he remembered from the café doorway and Preston's limited energy drained as he fought back the memory. But he stayed standing and stared at the face.

Then it spoke, "Are you another one of them?"

What did that mean? No apology, not even a flicker of recognition by the looks of it. He added a bruised ego to his chest wounds.

"Another one of who?" He couldn't be bothered with the grammatically correct Whom, it would waste time.

"Another one of their *gang*!" The last said with a sneer.

What gang?

"No, I'm not. Don't you have any idea who I am?".

"You must be another copper, you're all the same"

"You shot me, that's why I'm here in the hospital,"

The high voice squeaked back in a mixture of alarm and relief, "You mean you're not a copper?"

"No. I repeat: you SHOT me!".

"I don't remember".

What! His chest sent a storm of pinpoint stings to his brain.

"I was with the camera by the coffee shop. Do you remember that!"

"I only remember getting that bastard".

The little shit had put him in a hospital bed for three days and he didn't remember!

"Which bastard?" he demanded, forcefully.

"He had it coming, and that cow with him".

"You mean the man you virtually killed?"

"He's not dead yet then?"

"Not as far as I know".

"Shame!"

"Why?"

"Why don't you ask him. Are you sure you're not a copper?"

"Yes quite *bloody* sure".

There was a noise outside the door. Preston looked round warily, but it passed without stopping.

"What's your name?" Silence. "All right where do you come from?" The snarl returned. There was no reply. "Look you owe me something."

"I don't owe anyone anything. I'm calling in what people owe me now".

"What do you mean by that".

"Why don't you ask that bastard. I doubt if he'd tell you even if he could."

"Why won't you tell me?"

The fear crept back into the youth's face. Preston moved slowly around the room until he came to the foot of the bed. The patient's notes were hanging off the end. There was a blank space where the name should go. The rest was filled in with drug prescriptions. None made any sense to him.

He repeated his question, slowly, with the hint of threat in his voice, "Why won't you tell me?"

"I've sworn never to say anything." He faltered, then he added with a returning sneer, "Why don't you ask that copper?"

Another voice broke the impasse.

"What are you doing here? You can't be here!"

The voice didn't come from the kid but from behind. Preston whirled round to see the changeover guard in the doorway, holding a cup of tea and about to speak into his lapel radio.

Bollocks!

Preston made his way back painfully to his ward bed and lay on it pondering. Gang?

A new voice burst into his reverie. "Lazy bastard, what won't you do to get out of doing a day's work. I draw the line at being shot, though, Presto."

The noise came from his friend and colleague, Mike Jones.

"Try it some time, Jonesy, then come back and say that!"

"No thanks, I'll keep working, it's safer. I bring stuff from the team." He was carrying a rucksack which he opened and emptied on the foot of the bed. "Grapes, of course, chocs, your ipad because you must be sick of hospital radio by now... and..," he handled the next item with discretion, looking around to make sure no one saw him, "a half bottle of Bushmills to keep you warm."

That caused Preston to laugh and almost simultaneously wince.

"You sly bastard, Jonesy. How's Janet?"

"As ever, she sends her love."

"Right back at her."

"And you're coming round for a meal after you get out, understood? She won't take no for an answer."

"I won't give it."

"Good man. So, any idea why this happened?"

Preston mentioned the kid and how he'd got in to see him, how he'd said nothing except about some 'Gang'.

"Gang," responded Jones, thoughtfully, "There's a mystery, you going to set DS Di on it?" said Jones.

Preston looked up from the grapes and said, "We broke up."

"Sorry, mate, you really liked her."

"Yeah, anyway, it's got me thinking," said Preston.

"Here we go," another RTS award on the way. You step on a turd and it turns to gold."

"I'm just lucky that way." He lifted the bottle of Bushmills. "Drink?"

"Rude not to," replied Jones.

They each took a nip from the opened bottle.

"So, did you get your speedy pop princess to sing for you?" said Preston mockingly.

"I didn't need to, we got there early…"

"What, that's not like you."

"Shut up! We set up the camera and she turned up before the rest of the pack got there, saw us and broke into song."

"Who would do that?"

"Attention-starved pop princesses would do that. Good job we got her going in, though, she wasn't smiling when she came out and her minders bundled her away. She was banned for six months. Great story. Geoff was going to lead with it because of the singing and drop yours down to second – only attempted murder after all with some of the best shots you could get. Run of the mill stuff, mate. Singing speeders, that's what the viewers want."

"Bastard, Jones!"

"I know, it's why you love me."

The Risk file was in front of her but Doctor Brown hadn't had time to give it her full attention. She was on call and looking forward to it with the enthusiasm of a sofa-bound salad-dodger forced to go for a run – not that the analogy applied to her beyond that, in truth she kept herself fit. She resolved to make it even worse by catching up on her paperwork, why punish yourself once when you can double the agony? That was the Catholic in her. She opened the Risk file at the David Maclean entry.

MACLEAN, DAVID.
Aged six.

Adopted by John and Pauline Maclean of...it gave the address.
Fostered by Macleans before adoption.
Born to Sally Collins aged fourteen at time of birth. Single parent.
Baby taken into care at six months.

There was nothing else, it was incomplete; not the first time a case file had been incomplete, but frustrating. Her colleagues still laughed at her when she produced her battered manila box files with their reams of paper. Why not use a tablet like everyone else, they would ask. But she'd kept to her way of doing things. Computers, clouds, tablets, phones? Security nightmare! With her trusty folder she knew where everything was. She left the IT stuff to her direct medical practice and her social life – even then at arm's length.

There was probably more to come from the social services, she would check at the next meeting, or tomorrow morning, if she had enough energy. Right now she had to get going. She closed the file and put it away, then headed for the paediatric ward for another night's work.

It was a high pitched voice with the fumbling pronunciation of a five-year-old and it screamed painfully, frighteningly. She was attending another young patient nearby and heard the noise.

"No, please don't do it...No."

The last word was louder and more pleading. "NO! NO! NO! Stop, Please stop!..."

Then he dissolved into frightened tears as a nurse gently shook him and said: "Come on Nicholas. It's all right now. You don't have to worry, no one's going to hurt you here. You're in the hospital now."

The boy awoke but the look of terror didn't go. The nurse stroked his head and tried to calm him, "It's all right, you're safe here. Don't be scared!"

He looked across at the doctor with unseeing eyes and said, pitifully, "Please don't let them do it to me! Not again, please!"

The two women looked at each other. A five-year-old's dreams are not evidence, they're not even a reliable guideline for paediatrician let alone the law courts. But she had been in this field too long not to know what it could mean was happening to the boy. She left him in the care of the nurse, telling her to give him a mild sleeping draught.

She went back to the pokey functional room and rolled back the bed only to find it remained unchanged from the previous occupant.

"Great", she sighed, and flopped onto it anyway.

He was known in the hospital but he was in casual clothes, no scrubs and certainly no stethoscope. An hour before he had finished a call on a burner-phone. Now he walked purposefully along a corridor, past ward entrances and echoing walls barely throwing back the muffled percussion of his soft-soled trainers. Away from the nonstop ED a hospital at night reflects the ghosts of its decades; it can be a solemn place threaded with concern and sometimes resentment.

His soft-shoes occasionally squeaked but no one else appeared in the corridor. He saw the opening to The Dependency Unit and followed the arrow off to the left. He fumbled for his photopass, held the barcode against the cardreader and walked through the yielding doors. He thanked the stars for the hospital's tardy IT service that they had yet to install a log of all card users and where they'd been. It would come eventually, but they were too busy shoring up their screw-ups elsewhere.

He looked to see if the duty staff nurse was at her desk but she was away somewhere. Good! There was a noise further down the ward in one of the far bays, he used its cover to duck in and out of the other bays.

There would be no name on the bed – miraculously - but he had a still on his phone sent 45 minutes before. It was an old shot but it would do.

He glanced around a corner: so far so good, if he could get away with not being seen it would be good; he wanted to avoid being trapped in a lie just in case.

He looked again for the staff nurse but she was nowhere to be seen. The noise from further down the ward continued and he assumed she must be attending to it. He ventured deeper into the ward looking in the bays and hoping the low light wouldn't defeat his sight. He reached into his jacket pocket and fingered a plastic syringe with the tip covered with a plastic guard; adrenalin taken from his own illicit store.

He glanced down at the chart on the bed next to him. He had a rush of excitement. There was no name, just some details of progress. By the looks of it he was pulling through, albeit slowly. This intervention was none too soon. He pulled out his phone and checked the picture against the patient. The years had not been kind but it was the same person.

Lucky! First stop and you find him. This should be quick. Mr Nowhere Man your time is up old chap, he thought as he again reached into his pocket and withdrew the syringe. He pulled the drip towards him and examined the top. He had never done this before but he was certain it would work, the alternative was a straight injection with the syringe but that would wake the old man up and alert the rest of the ward. No, a steady infusion of extra adrenalin would bring about what he wanted, a heart attack! He'd been badly shot and his recovery was fragile. They hadn't thought he'd make it through ICU, but he did and, anyway, it was easier to get to him here. He raised the syringe to the top of the plastic drip bag and tested its resistance, then hoped the hyperdermic, designed for yielding human skin, would be able to do the same on a plastic drip bag. He jammed the needle down, it took more pressure than he realised but it went in cleanly, then he pressed down the plunger. He could not make out the thin but powerful stream feeding into the intravenous mixture, but he knew it was going in. He emptied the syringe, pulled out the needle and replaced the plastic cap before returning it to his pocket. He waited for 60 seconds and saw the old man's heart rate quickly elevate. He could leave the hormone to do its work now. He walked back to the door, past the still empty nurses station, throwing the emptied syringe into a yellow sharps box on the side as he went.

He shuffled out with his muffled steps unheard, he didn't look back once. He never saw the old man's heart rev up, almost to a hundred and sixty beats a minute, nor did anyone else, because he was too weak to call, too distressed to raise any kind of alarm.

No-one but the old man would ever know what his last frantic seconds were like, no one ever saw him simply stop breathing as his overworked heart gave up the struggle.

His killer never saw the death mask, if he had he might have stopped to ponder, not for any sympathy or empathy, he had neither, but what fate might await him eventually. The old man's face did not relax into the eased contentment of a life well-lived.

Quite the opposite.

She applied blusher to her cheeks, trying to brush some life into them. Then she picked up her bag and walked into the office. Paul Bowes was already sitting at his desk with files open in front of him.

"Paul I must speak to you about a patient, Nicholas Carter."

"What about him?" said the consultant scrolling through his notes.

"I've got his notes here."

He looked up from his tablet to see paper files laid down in front of him.

"Old school, Lou?"

She smiled as she often did at her avuncular boss. Sometimes she found time to count her blessings as well as curses; one was that paediatricians wanted to look after children and bullying wasn't natural to them. She had never encountered one since specialising – although she'd been chastised many times herself, as she should have been.

"What's the problem?"

"I think he's being abused."

"Oh god! What's the evidence?"

She told him of the nightmare she had witnessed. His smile didn't disappear, but it reduced.

"Every kid has nightmares Lou, go carefully! Are you going to assume they're all being abused, because they're not!"

She was taken aback by the putdown. "Paul what's wrong.

You know it's a perfectly legitimate observation?"

The half smile maintained. "All right, it's not your fault. Sometimes it gets to you."

"What about this boy Carter, then?"

He picked up the notes and glanced through them quickly.

"I'll take a proper look later – In the meantime I have a mountain of paperwork to climb. So unless you want to help me with it…"

"Oh no you don't. I've been awake for two days, you're not pulling that on me."

"Right! So go home, get some sleep and see if the refreshed, vibrant you sees it the same way."

He raised his smile back to full and she responded the same way. She turned to leave, he said softly to her retreating back "We can't save the world, Lou, only tiny bits of it. It's dangerous to think we can!"

Maybe!

The voice was cold and hard: "You know what you have to do."

He knew. He led a lonely life in the bowels of the hospital, cutting up dead bodies and making reports. He had never been able to get on with living people, not in a true sense. He could talk to them, pretend to share their interests, but really there was no connection.

He had to carry out a post-mortem examination to establish the cause of death, discover it to be natural causes aggravated by shock from gunshot wounds, and then make sure all the blood and tissue samples were clean. An infusion of adrenaline had made his heart give out – he knew that before he'd even touched the corpse because he'd been told. His job was to clean up the blood samples in case they showed abnormal hormone presence.

He put the telephone down and went to the mortuary store where the old man's body had lain all night. Yes he knew what to do, and he would make a thorough job, after all he was well respected in his field.

The blood type was already known, all he had to do was take some samples and mix them with clean blood to dilute the solution. The DNA profile would be a nightmare but that wasn't his problem. Anyway, his caller was more than happy for the old bastard not to be ID'd. He took a fresh syringe and stuck it deep into the left radial artery.

Sharp scratch he muttered to himself in jest.

A studious man snapped shut the book he was reading on American Constitutional History and prepared to receive another dispatch of garbage for disposal.

He believed it best to work with a cheery smile, do the work, have a laugh and go back to his books. This book was a massive tome of 800 pages and cumbersome to drag around the hospital, but he preferred to read like that than from his phone, it seemed more real.

The box came in and his untutored but voraciously curious mind wanted to know more.

Here a box, there a box, what was in them he often wondered.

He opened it up and saw a couple of used dripbags, and a half full one. Those were always intriguing; there was a story behind every one, nearly always a sad one. The patient hadn't made it and the half-drained fluid had been taken from its hook, detached from its intravenous needle and thrown with the rest of the waste that had been keeping the late victim company in its final hours. He liked to imagine what had happened, it gave his days impetus. He took out the bag to weigh it in his hands, to try to feel the life force that was once depending on it. He held it close and squeezed it voluntarily in the hope that the physical action would somehow release its story to him; it did but he didn't know it. A fine jet of liquid hit him in the face. Well, he'd never known that to happen before. It spooked him, like the dead life was making one last protest at existence and he hastily replaced it in the box.

He was sure it wasn't supposed to do that, though; what was the point of a leaking drip? Bad quality control, a weakness in the manufacture? It wasn't his place to point it out, he was a lowly maintenance worker, bottom of the pile, below the porters, the care assistants, the nurses and light years from the doctors.

But he was a clever man for all his lack of life chances and that one stuck in his mind.

She went through three outfits before settling on a plain black piece. The accessories would make it live, but not garishly: a blue scarf and a silver broach. She toyed with the idea of wearing an NHS badge for a joke but thought it would be too obvious and she wanted him to be brighter than that. It had been a long time since she'd been asked out and she wasn't sure she liked it: the tension, the anticipation, the uncertainty. Work had let her get older without warning her what would happen.

Tonight, though, she would sparkle. The fatigue of the previous night's work was gone, blasted by the force of her expectation. She was aglow and blooming. She checked herself in the mirror. The black number helped, the makeup worked, the cautious smile finished it. Time to move up.

The world was different since she last went through these rituals. Fifteen years ago when she was active and single it was person-to-person, med-school colleagues, junior doctors, occasional senior doctors, one very senior doctor and a couple of nurses just to ring the changes. Then she met Peter and her dating days were over. She fell in love, fell into a relationship and stayed there. She'd still be there now if Peter hadn't died. But he did and the family she thought she'd have with him transferred itself to the Paeds Ward with a constant stream of surrogate sons and daughters.

She cared too much, more than most, but that was her way and she'd got this far and survived. To go the other way and shut herself down like so many of her colleagues would be to deny herself and her humanity; to betray herself. She'd take the pain, it had to be less draining than the alternative of emptiness never fully filled by sensation.

Tonight, though, she might go for a bit of that anyway. Tonight was not about families, or the past, it was about here and now and not before time. And, unless she screwed it up really stupidly, or he did, tonight would be about sex. She hadn't been starved for the last three years, but nor had she been sated. She'd had necessary sex, diet sex, enough for the nourishment of body and soul; but not from any date, she had not been courted or wooed, it was all from end-of-the-evening fatigue, or end-of-nightshift-delirium with the accelerant of wine.

Tonight was not that. This was slow and deliberate. His smile and that voice said gentleness and attention. Third date? Stupid rule, she'd get down to it tonight. She wasn't going to fall into the traps of her 20s, she would strike while the iron... well, let's get it hot first; she enjoyed the image for a moment.

A fleeting vision of Peter flashed through her mind and she moved quicky around the house putting his photos out of sight. Hers and Peter's house. She could talk about him another time.

The security phone hummed, but she'd seen him draw up. A black Mercedes, one year old registration. She surged – nerves, fear or excitement? The doctor in her knew it was a hormone release, the woman in her just went with it. She walked to the front door.

And there he was, cool as polar ice, dressed casually but with an attention to detail that shamed her. Smart and expensive pale blue jacket, tailored black slacks, a trendy and new black buttoned T-shirt with just the top left button undone; his black shoes were shined but not to perfection and – oh, shame, no socks! Still that guaranteed one thing for later and she was 99% certain that was how their evening would end.

"Well, Martin Tench, look at you when you're not being a doctor!"

"I'm always being a doctor. I hope I'm on time. Are you ready?"

Good start!

He moved through the dimmed corridors of the late-80s building. It had been conceived during a time of enlightenment and had deteriorated ever since. Now it was one of those shells which mar so many town centres. A testament to the power of concrete and bad taste. It was ugly but so was his work. And that's what he liked about it: socially deprived families, hardship, emotional dependency; all these things were his job, and his joy. He fed off them, and he fed them to the Network. Because out of this pool of misery housed within the decaying building there came a kind of fruit which he and his associates enjoyed tasting above all. No-one cared about them, they were unwanted, unloved, and ripe for the picking.

And he always harvested, he never stopped. All the undereducated, undernourished lost causes came to him and he feasted on them.

He came to a door which was not to his own office but for which he had a key. This had to be done now, it would arouse suspicion in the morning because the boy was nothing to do with his caseload. He opened the door and aimed straight for the laptop where he knew he would find it. It was locked, but he had a password He also had a way to hide the access if anyone wanted to dig later, he had the log-in details of several of the department's senior staff and he could get in under any of their names. That's what having a pliant IT serf did – just throw him a bone every now and then. He opened the application and sifted through the files until he came to the one he wanted. He opened it up and inspected the contents. Department policy was to put each part of case history on a separate page which made his job easier, as it had done with the other lad.

There was no resume, just his name and date of birth. That was followed by his mother's name and a short history. She was sixteen at the time of the birth, and from a family on the Links estate. There were a few paragraphs about her and that was all for that sheet. He would leave that. The next page was the one he needed. The child had gone straight into care, straight into the Network's garden of delight.

He highlighted the page and deleted it. Then he continued his scrutiny: he scrolled down through the pages taking in the reports and details until he came to one which made his face light up. The boy had been fostered directly afterwards, and guess who the foster parents were?

Then he strode out to his car. He had a phone call to make: things were taking a turn for the better.

His cold, unmoving face resembled those of the corpses he dissected. Pathologists often looked like death, it was the nature of their work, or perhaps that deadeyed personality was the kind who were attracted to it. The absence of life made every action echo in the darkened pathology laboratory at the hospital. He had been a member of the Network for nine years but it wasn't his only perversion, sometimes being alone with the cadavers ...

He turned off the corridor and into his room. He knew who the old man was but had kept quiet. He was in the Network in the early years when the cadaver he now sought had life coursing through it and was looking after their pleasure garden. It had been a long time but he could remember the name. He had a good memory. There was a woman involved somewhere along the line, but her name or involvement was misty. These days his memory was only good for the things that counted. He had done the post mortem that day. This was the last piece of the jigsaw.

The coroner would hear that the man had died from natural causes. He had a weak heart, it had overloaded, possibly because of the tension but that was not for him to say. He only needed to supply the facts, or in this case the false information. There was no doubt that heart tissue had been damaged. He had a massive heart attack brought on by unknown circumstances – of course he knew what it was, excess adrenaline driving blood through the coronary arteries at high pressure when they were already aeschemic. Result, overload, breaking off cholesterol plaque, blockage of artery, heart muscle starved, good night.

The only major concern was the blood analysis which he didn't do himself. But he had delayed sending it off that day. But enough, he had covered himself adequately, just in case of questions. He had timetabled the post mortems that day so that the old man was the final one. It had been too late to send the blood off so he had taken the sample and put it in the fridge.

Now came the second part of the plan. He took a small phial filled with dark red blood and with exactly the same markings as the one in the fridge, and he swapped them. No abnormal adrenalin was likely to show up in that. He closed the fridge door pocketing the real sample as he left. He would dispose of it at home. The echo of his footsteps died away quickly as the doors closed behind him.

The two women exchanged glances across the meeting room, but there was no sense of sisterhood, just ice. The doctor and the detective looked away simultaneously, Brown was at a loss to know why.

The senior social worker brought them to order, "Thanks for coming, everyone. I'll get straight to it: if the Macleans are as guilty as the reports suggest we have a catastrophe on our hands. They have been fostering for ten years and it raises the question…"

"How many others?" said Di Sanders.

"Yes, how many others? And why are we only finding out now?"

"But that means there could be an epidemic on our hands," said Brown.

"Yes, it does. I don't know if we can track them down – we might have to wait for them to come to us. All I ask is for you to maintain your vigilance in the hospital, in the police and we'll redouble our efforts to try and stamp it out."

"I don't envy you," said Paul Bowes, "We all know enough about them to know that they are expert at hiding what they do."

"Yes, we do, usually in plain sight," said the social worker, unnecessarily.

What a bloody mess, thought Sanders, and it had landed on her desk.

"So, sergeant, will you prosecute the boy's guardians?" Paul Bowes looked at Sanders directly but the social worker intervened before she could say anything.

Martin Tench weighed in, "Can we even countenance the idea of this boy returning to the Maclean home?" Not his decision to make but Louise Brown looked at him warmly. "In my opinion this boy has been systematically hurt over a long period. If he goes back it's certain to happen again".

There was a silence around the table.

Tench broke the spell.

"What do the Macleans have to say about it?"

"We haven't spoken directly to them since the night the boy was taken in" said Sanders. "They weren't interviewed by specialist officers so I don't want to say anything until I have spoken to them myself."

"Why has it taken so long?" inquired Bowes with an air of irritation in his voice.

Again, not his call. She became defiant.

"I'm sure I don't need to remind you of the events nine days ago Dr Bowes.

"Yes of course, but that's no reason to leave this case untouched. It's child abuse for goodness sake."

Steady Paul, thought Brown. Not like him to lose his rag, even over something like this. The social worker eased the tension. "The child is in a place of safety, we've seen to that." The Macleans were supposed to be a place of safety, thought Louise Brown, but she kept quiet. "You have to admit sergeant, that it has been a long period without any progress."

The words were precise. Diane Sanders was furious. It wasn't her fault, she had been seconded to work on the shooting incident like just about everyone else. She knew she had to speak to the Macleans. She knew she might have to arrest them, or at least John. But she also knew there were only so many hours in the day and if the superintendent says something must be done then so be it. She hid the frustration as she tried to retrieve some initiative.

"The Macleans are steadfastly denying everything".

The room stayed quiet, no one tried to cut her off. That was a relief.

"I am hoping to interview the family this week," She continued to hold the floor, "But for the moment, on the current evidence ..." she looked at Tench, "and my interview with David, I think there's a case for prosecution. Of course that will be down to the CPS. The question is..." she looked at the social worker, "do you think it's wise to pursue, or should there be an attempt at reconciliation?"

"Not with that level of abuse," said Tench, "It's not safe. We should go for prosecution." No-one dissented: Bowes appeared satisfied, Tench relieved, Brown agreed in principle but felt she ought to know more; she made a mental note to dig out David Maclean's complete history.

He delved into his secret phone to find the network list. He needed help and there were men who were in a position to do something. Senior people, junior people, but no nobodies. Each of them had a position which they had either reached or were on their way to reaching and which put them above suspicion. None of them could afford to be exposed, they knew how vital it was to keep their mouths shut and their eyes and ears open. The list extended into places and institutions which would terrify the normal population if they knew. They had to stay secret and sometimes there would be sacrifices to keep the rest of them safe. Usually it was someone who had been too careless. They knew what would happen. One man's needs were nothing against the needs of the many.

He scrolled down the list picking out names, like the senior politician with his ministerial office number. He kept that one to one side. It was something to be used only in the most serious emergency because it was so influential. The situation hadn't reached that stage.

But there were numbers lower down the pecking order which could be brought into play soon. Numbers in the police, the media, lawyers' chambers, and most of all in the places most likely to give the opportunity for their activities: the people who look after kids.

He scanned the list twice and narrowed it down to three names. One thing was certain.

The Maclean Family was not on that list.

The modest home looked exactly what it was. Tidy and unassuming. A lower middle class abode with all Di Sanders expected. A smart television, the obligatory sofa, a satellite dish outside which was probably no longer needed and a garden gnome on the small lawn. This was the home of Mr and Mrs Average. There were no plaster ducks on the wall but everyone's entitled to some variation thought the detective. She had been met at the door by Pauline Maclean who had expressed some surprise at her being there. Now she was sitting with both of them. Her phone video camera worked silently.

"Mr and Mrs Maclean I must tell you that I am here about your adopted son David".

John Maclean breathed in deeply, his wife stayed quiet, resigned it seemed to Sanders.

"You will already know of the medical examination and David's evidence".

"Are you here to arrest us!"

"No Mr Maclean, not at the moment but I can't rule that out".

"In that case I want our solicitor to be with us".

"It will make it a lot easier at the moment if I simply speak to you. It's up to you if you wish to remain silent but it isn't going to help".

"Everything has been done with Mr Humphries so far, so I don't see why that should change".

Sanders was looking for signs which she thought might give him away. There was nothing material in the room like suspicious videos, or pornographic books. But then if they had ever been there they would have been taken out the moment David went.

She tried to take Maclean in as she talked. She wanted to get a feeling about him, just something in his manner of speech which would betray what he really was. His words may deny but there may be something like being too angry, or too restrained, or a falseness which her police intuition might pick up.

"The fact is Mr Maclean we already have enough to prosecute you. It doesn't look remotely likely that David will ever be returned. If you keep quiet, then that's how it will stay and I shall have to arrest you at some stage."

The wife started at the words and spoke for the first time. "How is this happening to us." She started to sob. "All we wanted to do was help. We love David."

"Mrs Maclean this evidence could not be more clear! He has been abused systematically over a lengthy period. That's what the doctor says, and what David confirms".

John Maclean comforted his wife then turned to the detective sergeant.

"David has never said anything to us about being abused but I can promise you it wasn't here. No child we have looked after has ever been abused by me or anyone I know. The idea is disgusting. It's so completely against what we stand for".

"How long have you had him!"

"He was adopted six months ago, he'd been with us for six months before that".

"How did you receive him in the first place".

"He was a social services referral".

"Do you know where he came from before that?"

"Of course we know where he came from. We have his history in the desk." His fury erupted from nowhere.

"Why did you decide to adopt him".

It was a tricky question.

"Look, I'm not going to say any more without my solicitor being here." The anger remained. Cover-up thought Sanders... and yet...!

"I'm sorry you feel that way Mr Maclean. We'll just have to see what happens now."

The paper copy of the RISK file was in front of her but Louise Brown hadn't had time to give it her full attention. She knew it was old school and was often mocked for it but she felt more confident with things committed to paper, they took more than a keystroke to lose. She would get around to looking at it again once she'd got over the resentment of being there yet again.. Would she get any sleep tonight or would there be so much to do that she would be a walking zombie for the following seventy two hours.

Her phone sounded..

"Hello!" She didn't identify herself.

"Louise?"

She recognised the voice.

"Mr Preston... how did you get my number?"

"Surely you can call me Simon now," he said.

"I said how did you get my number?

"You gave it to me."

No she had not. She was careful to a fault about giving out her number.

"Anyway, never mind that, I wondered if you fancied... "

She sensed what he was about to say: no, she did not. She cut him off before he could complete his sentence, "If you're not prepared to tell me how you got my number, then there can be no trust between us - I know we shared something ... terrifying... but don't think you can take advantage of that, Mr Preston. Now please don't call again!"

She pressed the red end icon and breathed out deeply. then when she'd recovered herself, she opened the Risk file at the David Maclean entry.

MACLEAN,DAVID.

Aged six.

Adopted by John and Pauline Maclean of...it gave the address.

Fostered by Macleans before adoption.

Born to Sally Collins aged fourteen at time of birth. Single parent.

Baby taken into care at six months.

There was nothing else. Where was the rest of it? She closed the file and put it away, then headed for the paediatric ward for another night's work.

It was a comfortable, well-to-do detached home in suburbia. Preston was sitting in the well-furnished dining room enjoying the hospitality of Mike and Janet Jones. Janet was a fine cook and Preston had made room for this break because of it.

"So, what happened with Di then, Presto?" asked Jones.

"I was disappointed for you," added Janet.

Preston took a breath and said, "Me too. Two different worlds. She's a rule taker, she has to be, I'm not as you well know."

"I do," said Jones, laughing, "You've pulled a few stunts in your time."

"I'm not alone in that, Jonesy, I could learn something from you."

All three laughed. Janet cleared some plates as she said, "Shame, though, I thought you were a good couple."

"Well, we gave it a go," said Preston, sitting back, "It was fun, for the first few weeks, anyway, then it started to fall apart."

Jones proferred a bottle of New Zealand red and asked, "Sure you won't indulge?"

"Thanks but it gets in the way of the painkillers. I don't know how, but this is a rule I'll take."

Janet said, "Sensible, I wish Mike would be more abstemious."

"Nothing wrong with a little drink every now and again," said Jones.

"Hazard of the job," added Preston, "I look forward to when I can do it again."

Janet sat back down and said, "So, goodbye to Di. Anyone else in the pipeline, so to speak?"

"What about that doctor you got caught in the doorway with?" added Jones.

"We'll have colonised Andromeda before that happens," said Preston, ruefully.

"So you'd like to?" asked Janet.

"We'd have to be on better terms before I could think about that," said Preston and went on to explain why his encounters had so far been in arctic conditions.

"Playing hard to get," said Jones.

Janet smiled at him and said, "I have no idea how I can be married to a man who has such little understanding of women. Cool is how you play it to begin with, until the man makes you smile, then you warm up. It seems that our master charmer hasn't managed that yet so I'd have to accept that it's where she wants to be. You'd know otherwise, Simon, sorry!"

"Jones put a zip across his mouth and said, "Whatever you say, dear. Change the subject: any more on that supposed gang you were telling me about in the hospital?"

"Bits and pieces, it's a sparse jigsaw at the moment. I don't really know what it adds up to. I've been thinking about how I can get to the kid to see if he'll give me more. He owes me something, after all!"

"He certainly does," said Janet. "Now, have some fruit salad before you go!"

Preston didn't need to be asked twice.

They were short of uniform sergeants so she had been volunteered by her superintendent. Her nights had been lonely recently anyway, so it wasn't so bad. She was there because the rulebook said there had to be a sergeant, they only had to be on duty and available, they didn't have to be sitting at a desk all night. She called the inspector in the control room to let him know she'd be on a force radio if needed.

"How long do you think you'll be?"

"About two hours."

She put the phone in her bag, checked her radio and went out into the station yard to pick up the CID Astra. She drove out of the yard into the deserted street and pointed the car towards the hospital.

Coincidence makes the world an interesting place. Preston had gone home after his evening with the Joneses, but he couldn't settle to sleep. He had amused himself as best he could by watching the television. But he was preoccupied. At 1.45 he gave into his obsession, left his house, got into his car, and drove to the hospital. He'd spent the whole evening with his mind back at the shooting and what endured was the emptiness in the kid's eyes.

He parked in the hospital car park and made his way through a side entrance. There was a chance he would be recognised because of who he was, but he would minimise that. He knew his way well enough to be able to find the main corridor and get to the youth's room. He was gambling on the guard either being asleep or not there at all because of the time of night.

The time was now five past two in the morning, the only sound in the corridor was his echoing feet. His wounds were healing and he moved along more quickly than his last visit. He slowed as he approached the ward. The door was closed, there was no need for it to be open. That was useful. He sidled up and peered through the glass window at the top. He could see nothing. He grew bolder and put his head above the bottom ridge to be able to see more clearly. Still nothing! No guard, no nurse, no-one.

Had the youth been transferred to a prison?. He was pretty sure he hadn't, so why wasn't there anyone there? He pushed at the door gingerly, it opened without resistance. He entered the ward corridor and went up to the chair where the uniformed guard normally sat. It was still warm. He may not be far away. He resolved to get into the room before anyone came along and try to speak to the youth again. His hand closed on the door handle and he was just about to turn it when he was stopped in his tracks.

"What the Hell are you doing here!"

He spun round, it had been too good to be true. He looked in the direction of the familiar voice.

"Di!" He exclaimed.

She moved towards him, a uniformed officer by her side.

"You are not supposed to be here at any time of day, still less at two in the morning."

"Tell me something I don't know."

She turned to the uniform.

"All right John, I'll take care of this, go off and have a cup of tea!"

The uniform looked at her in surprise; she returned the look with ice, a look which said: I'm a sergeant, don't forget it!

"OK Sarge, I'll be in the nurses' canteen."

"And may God rest your soul," said Preston.

They watched him walk out of the door and listened to his footsteps fade down the corridor.

"How have you been, Di?"

"Fine. Why are you here?"

This was not the version he was used to, this was professional Di. No point in playing on their past. On the other hand they weren't strangers. Worth a go?

"Di, if I tell you what I know, will you do the same?"

Her face betrayed nothing.

"We don't do pillow talk any more, remember! I know too well what you'll do to get a story."

She did. But it cut both ways.

"Look, I might have something, that's why I'm here. Cards on the table?"

She nodded without expression.

"I hated the little sod to begin with. Why should he push me around just because he had a gun in his hand! I mean there's not much to him is there. He's a wimp without the gun. I just want to talk to him."

Her cold front stayed.

"I was shot you know?"

Her eyes flashed angrily.

"Stop that! I won't be manipulated by you – especially you!"

"Why are you here then? It's gone two in the morning."

"Police business and none of yours. You know as well as I do that I can't let you in there because you are a direct witness in an attempted murder charge."

"Yes, I know, but that's not the point. I'll accept I'm involved but you see..."

He paused for effect: "I've already spoken to him."

She was about to soften having made her point, but not now.

"You've done WHAT!"

He was treading none too lightly on their now brittle friendship.

"The day I came out of hospital."

"You know you could be charged for that."

"I know. What are you going to do, report me?"

What was she going to do? Dob him in when her own position was anything but certain? By rights she should not be there anyway. She was only helping Tony King.

And this slippery man had been her lover until only a short time ago.

"All right, maybe we're both in deeper than we should be."

"Not sure what that means."

"Too bad, that's all you're getting. Now, what can you tell me?"

"So you want to trade?"

"Tell me what you know and I'll see if it's worth the haggle!"

They were a few metres from the youth's door and speaking in low voices.

He knew from two months with her that detective sergeant wasn't her destination, just a station along the way and she was much tougher than him. He caved.

"He's linked to the old man who died the other night..."

"That's hardly surprising, he was the one who got shot first."

"...and the woman he was holding had something to do with it."

"I thought she was just an innocent hostage."

"So did everyone else."

Her face unfroze, her eyes registered interest, her voice softened.

"What exactly did he say?"

Preston told her about "asking the old bastard and the woman."

"And there was one thing which struck me about him. It changed my mind when I first got into his room. I said I hated him but when I saw him he was helpless."

"Without the gun you mean!"

"It was more than that. There was this look of fear in his face which had nothing to do with me."

"How do you know that?"

"I've seen fear before. I didn't expect it on the streets of a provincial English city, but it was the same as if it was Moscow, or Tehran."

She hated it when he flashed his passport at her like that and hated herself for the petulance it provoked in her. But she couldn't stop it.

"It's not much use then is it!"

He sighed and looked away.

"Your turn. Tell me what *you* know!"

"You think that's worth me risking a warning? I need better than that."

Preston's face sagged. She fought hard to disguise her triumph. She should be better than that. She gave him a bone.

"He hasn't said anything at all worth the name. I've played one idea through Tony King which I half remember from seven years ago."

Preston's face recovered.

"What happened then?"

It wouldn't hurt to have someone else digging. She told him what she remembered of the James Institute. "Tony King brought it up when he saw him. He didn't say anything but he seemed to react."

Preston wasn't bound by the same codes as Sanders. He had no procedures other than those which would get his story. He paid lip service to the broadcast rules which were drawn up by people who had no idea how to do the job. Maybe she would go with him on it?

"Feeling brave, Di?" he asked in a perhaps too familiar tone.

She looked at him questioningly.

"Why don't we talk to him together but don't tell him who you are? We'll say you're a friend who might be able to help."

She looked at him as if he had just crash-landed from another galaxy.

"You know I can't do that. Don't be silly!"

She wasn't even supposed to be there. Or...maybe if she just said nothing at all, just witnessed whatever took place? A thin defence to balance the rest of her career on, but she didn't come into the job for an easy life. She took a deep breath, looked Preston in the eye and said, "All right, let's give it a try. But don't you dare let me down!"

She recognised the irony as she said it but made no acknowledgement.

The youth was asleep. He was as anonymous as the day he had been brought in. He was semi-immobilised although his gunshot wounds were beginning to heal. The chart at the end of his bed still had no name above it but there was a growing list of dosage changes for his painkillers, sedatives and antibiotics. Medicine drew no line between good and bad. If they came in broken they were fixed up to go back out and be good or bad.

They approached the bed where the sleeping form lay. They looked at each other then Sanders took command. "Shake him up! Make him wake up!" she whispered.

He looked at her as if at a stranger – who was this woman? He recognised the body, but what was inside was no one he knew. She said no more but took a step back and stared hard at the reporter, then down to the buttons on her phone, one of which she pressed. Preston shook himself out of his confusion, grabbed hold of the youth by the uninjured arm and shook him strongly.

It took thirty seconds, before he came round.

"Come on son, wake up, that's it!"

The youth turned over to see the reporter staring down at him.

"Who are you! What do you want?"

"Remember me? I'm one of the people you shot!"

The youth looked at him through half dead eyes. There was a blink of recognition. Then Sanders' shadowy form formed in his vision.

"Who's she!"

"She is a friend of mine who is going to help you," Preston lied.

"How can anyone help me? I'm on a murder charge." Wide awake now.

"You might be able to tell us something to go in your favour."

"Oh sure. I've killed an old man," his eyes narrowed and his voice raised a few semitones, "Who should have been killed a long time ago. And I'm going to get it. Who's going to speak up for me, why should they! I did it, didn't I!"

Sanders said nothing but her phone took it all in.

Preston pushed him.

"There has to be a reason why you shot him. I mean there's no point in telling me I should ask the old man: he's dead. You tell me."

"I remember you now. I told you. I'm sworn to secrecy. I can't tell or I'm done for."

"You mean you're more done for than if you go down for life on a murder charge. More than that!"

The youth went quiet. He looked at the couple in confusion. The fear was back in his eyes, but it wasn't fear of them. He looked back at them again. He opened his mouth, there was a shake in his voice.

"My name's Jack."

"Jack who?" asked Sanders before she could stop herself.

"Jack whatever. I don't know my last name, or even if I ever had one."

"Everyone has a last name," said Sanders.

Preston swung round on Sanders and spread his hands as if to say shut up! Jack continued.

"I've always been called Jackie Jay, but it's not my name. We all had names they gave us."

"All?" said Preston.

"All the boys they kept."

Jackpot, she wasn't stopping now.

"Who's they?" asked Preston.

Silence.

"So you were a James boy?" said Sanders. Preston turned round on her again and looked at her furiously, but she would not be pushed around by him.

"How could you know that?" said Jack

"Lucky guess!"

"What's a James Boy?" said Preston.

The boy stiffened. "Ask her, she's got all the answers."

"No you tell me. I want to know. Was the old man part of it! What was he called?"

Sanders came in as good cop.

"Sorry Jack, we don't mean to put you under pressure. It's just that I've heard about the James Institute."

He stayed quiet for three seconds then said, "How do you know about it?"

"I was there at the time, seven years ago."

He looked at her and a snarl took over his face.

"Doing what?"

"I was one of the people who looked after the kids."

"So you know about that then."

"What did they do to you Jack?" said Preston softly.

A tear appeared in his eye as he looked first at one, then the other. He was no longer the streetwise youth, he was a little boy again.

"It's all right Jack. We're not going to hurt you. Trust me!"

Jackie Jay wiped away the tear and got hold of himself. He

was facing murder and attempted murder charges; he had a past which terrorised him; he was under threat from all quarters; and here was someone who seemed to care. Even more daft: he'd shot him.

"It might help if you told us what they did to you."

Jack started to speak. The voice was lower, he was talking in a kind of monotone which divorced him from the intensity of his words.

"I never knew how many of us there were. We didn't know much about anything. The only thing we knew for sure was that a couple of times a week the men would come."

He stopped, temporarily unable to continue.

Preston prodded.

"What men were those, Jack?"

"We were told never to say anything to anyone. If we did we would be punished, I mean badly punished."

He looked pleadingly into Preston's eyes. The youth had gone, the boy was there saying "protect me, look after me, don't tell anyone I told you, don't let them get me!"

And it all went into Sanders' phone.

Jack Jay stared straight ahead at a blank space on the wall opposite as he spoke. `His weak voice was strained making it even feebler. He hurt from older wounds than those he'd been brought in with.

"They did it in the nursery. None of us were any older than ten, most were much younger."

"What did they do?" asked Sanders.

The youth caught his breath a couple of times as he told them.

"You can't look at me now, can you!"

Sanders looked down at her phone, then up at him. Preston tried hard to keep his eyes on the youth.

"It wasn't my fault!" he nearly shouted. "What could I do about it!"

"Nothing Jack," said Preston.

Sanders said, "You were only a kid, there was nothing you could do. We know that."

"We never had any idea what they were called. They always

had a funny name when they came."

"Like what?" said Sanders.

"Like Father Christmas, or Robin Hood, or Daddy."

"Daddy?" said Simon.

"You heard."

"Not a term of endearment then, any others?"

They paused to take it in.

"What did you call the old man?" asked Preston.

"I called him the bastard", he replied bitterly.

"Why!"

Jack Jay went silent, the angry face softened, and his eyes turned down as if he were on the verge of tears. His voice turned less aggressive. "Because I was his special pet. He used to take me with him when all the others had gone."

Preston tried to look reassuring, but his reporter's neutrality was deserting him.

"Did he have another name?" said Sanders.

"We were supposed to call him Mr Jesse, but I don't think it was his real name. We never had those."

Mr Jesse? Sanders pondered then Preston turned round to her and whispered, "Jessie James?" It would have meant nothing to her outside of her police life but it was a frequent reference within it. James, Billy the Kid, Al Capone and John Dillinger; never the Krays. Maybe they were too close to home. She shrugged her shoulders and turned back to Jack Jay.

"You said something about a woman before."

"She was supposed to be the matron. She did fuck all. I think she was his wife but she never lifted a finger to stop him. Never!"

"Stay calm Jack!" said Preston.

"So that's why you shot him", said Di Sanders.

The youth regained his earlier robotic speech.

"He had it coming. What's my life worth after him! What were any of us worth after what he did!"

Preston stayed on course, "Was she the woman you were holding as a hostage in the street."

"Easy guess eh!"

"Well, was she!" demanded Sanders.

The youth looked at her. He had nothing to lose, he was going down for murder, attempted murder, illegal possession. In fact he was going down for everything anyone could think of.

"Yeah. That was her."

"Why didn't you shoot her as well?"

"I don't know. I should have I suppose," he paused, "Maybe I didn't hate her enough."

There was a sound just outside the door. The reporter and the detective looked at each other in alarm. Sanders hid her phone in a jacket pocket but left it recording.

Preston moved to the door and opened it slightly. He was shocked by what he saw, but Di Sanders was even more surprised. It was two thirty in the morning: what was Dr Paul Bowes doing there of all places?

Preston tried to close the door quickly but Bowes clearly saw something and he found it pushed open again.

"Good morning! The famous television reporter Simon Preston, I presume", said Bowes with a sarcastic air. His feet remained outside but his eyes scanned the room to reveal Di Sanders.

"And his faithful friend Detective Sergeant Sanders."

The youth started in his bed.

"What do you mean Detective Sergeant? You said you weren't a copper."

The woman looked at him helplessly. She had lied to get the truth. Now she might have to pay for it.

Bowes continued: "May I ask what you're doing here at this time of the morning, and particularly in this room!"

"You lied to me you bastards!" cried the youth, or Jack as he had become known. "You're all the same!" The rage had returned and redoubled. His face was red with fury. "And I trusted you. I told you it all!" He was so angry Preston feared his wounds might be affected.

Clearly Dr Bowes was as well. "My God what have you been doing to him! He can't be allowed to get into an agitated state. He has serious gunshot wounds!"

"I don't need to be reminded", said Preston quietly.

"Just leave. I'll see to him!" Dr Bowes busied himself at the youth's bedside checking his chart.

"You too Sergeant. I am surprised at you. What are you doing here at this time of night without authorisation!"

She was in trouble: an unauthorised interview against medical advice.

"I might ask you the same question Dr Bowes. What are you doing around here at this time of night?"

The youth had slipped into a sullen silence. Betrayal was written all over his face.

The paediatrician continued to busy himself taking Jack's pulse.

"I work in this hospital, Sergeant. Remember!"

"So do lots of other doctors, and they're not here."

"I was called in to the paediatric intensive unit. The registrar needed my help. Now, are you satisfied?"

"So what brought you here then?"

Preston watched her technique. It was abrasive without being impolite.

"It was on my way out and I heard the noise. He's still young enough to come under paediatric care, you should know that." replied the doctor. "Now just leave".

"Come on Di." said Preston grabbing at his former lover. Jack looked at them with blazing eyes then he broke his silence.

"Yeah, Piss off, bastards!"

She took out her phone once they were clear of the ward and the hospital. She didn't want any security cameras seeing it. Then she looked angrily at Preston.

"I've used a deception to get the information with someone who's already up on a murder charge."

"Why didn't you stay quiet like you said you would. Typical you, Di, bloody contrarian! I didn't make you do any of this."

She waved her phone in front of him. "No, but it's me who's got the video of him saying it all."

Will you let me have it Di?"

She thought for a few seconds; it was evidence, but gathered by deception. A half decent trainee barrister would have it thrown out of court. "OK, pair me with your Bluetooth and I'll send it."

While Preston fiddled with his phone she said, "I'm not going to tell anyone I've got it yet because I still don't know what we have here."

"What about Tony King!"

"He'll find out I was here soon enough. I was only doing it as a favour to him."

"I don't understand..."

"Never mind, Police internal politics. They're as much of a mystery to me as to you, Simon." Her phone recognised the pairing and she pressed some video icons without really looking at them. More than one went across to Preston's phone.

"Right," she said impatiently, "I've got to get back to the nick. Call me sometime!"

The radio alarm woke her. She reached languidly across the bed with her right arm. It found empty space. It had felt something the last time she had been awake; that was seven and a half hours ago. She had drifted into an unbroken, beautiful sleep very soon after. Her dry spell had ended with a thunder and lightning show.

He had hardly said a word throughout the proceedings, but he knew which buttons to press and when. He cared, he wanted to know her, to explore her, and he kept control throughout. Martin Tench was a man of experience.

The radio droned on: something about South America, something in the House of Commons; she paid little attention. Normally she would be listening carefully, aware that keeping to the narrow focus of a children's hospital ward was not wise. And she eschewed the TV in the morning, that smacked of laziness to her. But this morning she couldn't bring herself to care much. Instead she went back to the last time she had been awake. Underneath the charm and professionalism was a shy man and it had been strangely hard work getting him into her bedroom. But once they were there he became a different person; his skill left her struggling for breath sometimes.

How many other women had he made love to? Dozens? Even hundreds? Best not to dwell on that. As far as she was concerned, for their few hours together, he made her feel as if she was the only woman who meant anything to him.

She flapped her arm uselessly into the space where he should have been. And now he was gone. She was being greedy, she'd banked the sex and now wanted something on top – like breakfast, or intimate coffee, or both; or even better, more sex! Like the gameshow contestants who get a windfall but are offered double if they'll just take a little more risk – a world of possibilities opens up and the sum they'd originally won seems inadequate for the dreams being created.

The radio droned on, she picked up snippets and discarded them: "There's been a dramatic fall in the value of the pound overnight...."

Being cherished for a night – or half a night, or however long it had been - should be enough. Be sensible Louise, you wanted sex, not marriage! She squirmed a little from happy memory. Would that it could happen again, there and then. But he was gone, and anyway, she was sated. .. enough anyway, but she would be coming back for seconds.

She drifted off momentarily but caught herself in time. She didn't have to be in until ten but didn't dare risk snatching an extra 15 minutes because that could easily turn into a couple of hours. She knew Tench had to be up to attend a clinic elsewhere in the city. She had no idea when he left but he had brought no change of clothes so it must have been early.

"...Serious weather conditions in the Seychelles have hampered..."

And then she stiffened. What was this?

"...the youth shot by police during an armed siege in Oxford has died."

There had been no indication of that on the hospital grapevine. Obviously they didn't discuss every patient in the place but celebrated or infamous ones like him, they did. So everyone knew he was hurt, but not fatally.

"...he is the second person to have died as a result of the incident. Police have so far been unable to identify either of them. A statement is expected later."

Now she was wide awake. What had happened?

The phone rang at seven thirty five. The youth from the Jackson street shootings was dead. More details would follow, said Geoff Donald, there would be an inquest. Preston was not fully awake and it took some seconds to sink in.

Then the full force of the call hit him. The boy had been alive if not exactly kicking only a few hours earlier. It couldn't be right. Surely it had nothing to do with his excitable state as they left?

"When! How!"

"That's what I thought you'd like to find out," said Donald, he added, "Good riddance I reckon, he caused enough pain."

Preston did not respond instantly prompting Donald to an expletive, "For fuck's sake, wake up Simon! This is dynamite and you've gone into a trance!"

He snapped to, "Yeah, sorry, right! It's taken me by…"

Donald didn't wait for the sentence to end.

"Anyway I've got Toppers on his way to the hospital and we'll need you there as well."

"Look, Geoff"… , he knew this would be a difficult issue, "I only spoke to the kid last night."

"You *what?*"

"Two in the morning, actually. I won't go into it on the phone but he was fine when … I left him."

"*When!*"

"I'm coming in, there's something you *have* to see. I won't tell you on the phone."

"You mean relevant to this story?"

"Geoff, I was with him a few hours ago – and he was very much alive then."

"What the fuck have you been up to and are we legal?"

"Long story but, yes, we're legal. Look, there's a bad smell about this."

"All right but get a move on. You're our big advantage on this story."

Much more than he yet knew, thought Preston.

"I'm on my way."

He ended the call and dressed quickly. He would shave in the car and watch Jack's last words at the same time.

He hurried out of his home, got into his car, linked his phone to his AVsystem and brought up the video bluetoothed from Di Sanders. He idly noticed that more than one had been sent: one had the icon of a young boy, the other Jack Jay, he pressed the latter. He started the car and began driving, occasionally glancing at his dashboard screen to see if the lad's face betrayed any more than the voice. That shouldn't have been possible, the video element of his in-car system should not be operating while he drove but he'd asked a helpful techie at the studio to rig around it – rules are for the obedience of fools and the guidance of wise man he often told himself. Not everyone would put him in the latter category, but he did.

Geoff Donald was a busy man, this was what news people called a brilliant story, and he wanted his top people out there covering it, this top man in particular. Simon Preston was a frequent pain in the arse but he delivered where others didn't, took risks that others wouldn't, thought cleverly while others plodded. Donald was prepared to put up with some of Preston's unorthodoxy because it gave the programme an edge.

He paced around his desk fretfully as he waited for his star to turn up. Finally Preston strode into the office brandishing his phone.

"This is a recording of an interview I did six hours ago with the dead kid. He was alive then, and certainly didn't look like he was going to peg out!"

Donald's eyes lit up in a way that Preston rarely saw.

"Why didn't you tell me earlier?

"You don't know who's listening on mobile calls. The quality's poor but audible – I didn't have anything to do with that. I'm not certain about broadcasting it, it wasn't my recording."

Donald allowed himself to relax and enjoy the moment of triumph for that was certainly what it was. He was already rubbing the BBC's nose in it and they hadn't even started.

"Who did it then?"

"A friend of mine. We happened to be there at the same time."

Preston told the story including how he and Di Sanders had managed to be at the hospital at the same hour of the morning. The recording was a coup. But they couldn't just put it on air. It didn't belong to them and had been recorded by someone else.

They were caught in an ethical dilemma, something which rarely happened, but each had enough of a conscience to bow to it occasionally. Preston had to protect Di Sanders, yes, but he wanted to broadcast what Jack had said as well. Come on, the last words of a shotgun menace not long before he died? What hack would not want to swim around in the glory of that?

It wasn't an official police interview, in fact it had been entirely unofficial, not that Jack was now in a position to complain about that, nor about any broadcast. But Preston still had problems.

The News editor listened then pondered for a while before replying.

"If we use it without the owner's permission we could be in deep trouble. On the other hand it's of very strong public interest. We can't sit on it simply over a technical matter of ownership. This is the strongest story we've had in five years.

No doubt about that and the fever which grips hacks when dealing with an exclusive was already burning deep in them both. It wasn't just that the kid had spoken, it's what he'd said: the details of the James Institute, the so-called Mr Jesse, and his woman. There could be no sub-judice because Jack was now dead, he would never face a judge and jury. There was no doubt that the information would be broadcast and would be backed up by the recording. But what about that recording?

Donald spoke, "You know where it came from. Why don't you call this ex-girlfriend of yours and put the pressure on?"

That's what he feared would happen. She may be an ex but he had just found out she was a friend. In fact they had got on better in the last ten hours than in the entire two months of their affair. A phone rang and Donald went to pick it up. "You'd better make up your mind quickly, I want you out at the hospital now. The kid's dead remember! This is one hell of a story." He spoke into the telephone receiver and Preston turned away to his desk, phone in hand. Yes, it was one hell of a story.

He was about to call Di Sanders' mobile when Donald called out to him to approach the newsdesk.

"Yes?"

"Send me a copy of that recording, we'll probably need to legal it."

"Sure, I'll do it while I'm on my way to the hospital."

"Now would be better."

Of course it would and any other circumstance would have him immediately doing as asked. But this was different. Donald's phone rang and he turned to answer it. Preston seized his chance and left while his news editor's attention was diverted. It was insubordination of a sort, on the other hand he'd brought the stuff in, he had a right to keep some control of it at least for the time being – they could hardly sack him for bringing in the exclusive of the decade.

He called Sanders.

An alert voice answered.

"Simon! You must have heard!"

"Yes. I'm working on it now."

"But he seemed so alive when we left him."

"Exactly." Preston lowered his voice: "Do you remember what he said about being warned?"

She remembered clearly.

"Di. I need to speak to you, and not on the phone."

"OK!" Then she remembered, "What about my recording!"

"It's safe. That's something else. We want to know if we can use it."

"What! What for?"

"On air, this lunchtime."

"What! That's a private recording, I'm all over it. I gave it to you for background. I'm going to be in big trouble anyway. Don't make it worse."

"Why! I don't understand!"

"Don't be silly, you were there, my voice is all over it!"

"I'll cut that out."

"No! Anyway, it's going to be evidence. You can't go broadcasting it until we know what to do with it."

Preston saw himself being sucked into something he didn't like.

"I'm not a police officer, Di, I don't answer to your chief constable. It's not-sub judice, it could even help track down some of these people."

The misunderstandings between them, the roots of their break-up, weren't going away.

Preston cooled down a little. "But if you don't let me use it I can still say what is on it, how can I not? I was there as well, I heard it all."

There was a long pause before she responded, "I can't stop you doing that I suppose."

"Why should you want to?"

"Because we haven't considered what it might all mean."

What was there to consider? They had as much as they could get on the recording. Blowing it open could only do good.

Preston had made a career out of bending and breaking rules. He believed, like most journalists, that if rules got in the way of a legitimate story than they should be ignored or shoved aside. Di Sanders believed strongly in rules. She bent them every now and again but never broke them because she believed in them. She was a police officer and was there to uphold the law; she stood by that, it was important for her, like she supposed it should be for all police officers, to keep to the spirit, as well as the letter of the law. If there was a rule then she stuck to it.

She'd bent the rules the night before with an unauthorised visit and then a clandestine recording without approval from higher up, but she still felt she should be governed by her superior officers. That's what she was there for, that's how the hierarchy worked and she couldn't take these sorts of decisions. But, if she now went to her superintendent and told her what she'd done there'd be a warning or worse, a reprimand and that would be it for her, stuck at sergeant and probably back in uniform.

Preston faced no such problem, he would be praised not chewed out for what he had done. So far so good and every instinct told him he should broadcast the recording, but he accepted that would jeopardise Sanders' career. Anyway she had refused permission effectively.
But the content? That was different. He brought the recording up on his car device again as he drove and started to compile a detailed piece to camera from what Jack said. Di would hate it – maybe even hate him – but this way he would not betray her... much!

She was back in the real world, dressed and at her desk in the hospital. She thought again about phoning Martin Tench but decided against. Instead she sipped the triple-shot Americano she'd picked up at the hospital coffee shop and accessed her Risk file. It was buried within several layers of folders and the overarching one was still not on her dsesktop – just in case.
She turned to the David Maclean entry; a call to the social services would get this sorted out. She got through to one of the social workers she knew personally from their regular attendance at meetings and put the request through.
"This will take a little time. I'll call you back Dr Brown."
He was no less formal despite their acquaintance. She thought sitting back on titles was old school. Her parents were humble, her father was an electrician, her mother an office clerk. When she told them she wanted to be a doctor they struggled for a long time before accepting it. It was so alien to them but when the young Louise got starred A-levels and a place at the Royal Free they finally realised that it wasn't just wishful thinking and that their daughter was going to be a doctor. That's when their pride burst out and she'd had to stop them boasting about "Dr Louise" to their friends and the

family. She didn't expect them to give her a title and that carried on through qualifying and her steady advancement. Calling her "Doctor" would not make their treatment any better and it created a barrier. She was Louise to the worried parents she dealt with, and Doctor Louise to the kids because they needed boundaries.

She was sure she'd introduced herself informally to the social worker and that he had given his full name in return – Jonathan, she was sure.

She put the phone down and went over the file in front of her. There was nothing beyond her original entry. That was unusual. They normally updated her on case histories and David had been on the file for a few weeks. The Carter boy was only a recent addition so she didn't expect to see him referenced.

She took another sip of the Americano and then a swig just to get the caffeine working through her brain.

The telephone rang, it was the social worker.

"There's not much I can tell you about either of them Dr Brown."

Not so much time after all!

"But you have their complete histories there haven't you!"

The voice was patient at the other end of the line, apologetic, even.

"Normally we do but there seems to be a problem in these cases." He sounded embarrassed at the bureaucratic mix-up which had left the two boys without a past.

"You already know Maclean's natural mother's name, and you know he was fostered and then adopted by the Maclean couple."

She had a surge of frustration which sent adrenalin through her at the same time as the coffee was hitting arteries and stimulated her concentration. "It's the gap in between I want to fill in. Where did he go when he was taken from his mother?"

There's nothing on the computer, and there's nothing on his hard copy file."

"But that's a gap of three years."

It wasn't the paediatrician's job to chase this sort of thing but she needed a complete picture of the boy so that she could advise treatment.

"I can understand it going missing from a cardboard file. That happens. But how can it drop off the computer?"

The social worker was embarrassed, "I'm sorry, I just don't know."

She rapped her desk with her fingers, anger was replacing frustration. "What about the Carter boy?"

"Same thing I'm afraid. I can tell you his mother's name, and who his adoptive parents are now, but there's a two and a half year gap before he was fostered." He paused, "That was by the Maclean couple as well."

"You mean both David Maclean and Nicholas Carter were fostered by the Macleans! That's very odd."

"Why!" She realised the social worker didn't know about Nicholas Carter and the nightmare, or the condition which had brought him to hospital in the first place.

"Oh it's nothing I suppose. I'm just a little worried about the Carter boy. I can't tell you any more than that."

"Do you think he might have been interfered with?"

"It's too early to say. It's one of the reasons why I wanted to get some more background on him this morning."

"Do you think the Macleans might be involved again?"

"Well, it is a nasty coincidence that they fostered both of them." Then the thought struck her: it was also a nasty coincidence that both their case histories had disappeared from the files.

"Are you certain there's no sign of either of their histories before the fostering."

"None at all, it's a mystery." The voice took in a short breath before continuing, "You know if there's something we ought to know about this Carter boy you should tell us. The fact that he was fostered by the Macleans is alarming enough. We might have to go through every one of their children."

That was a frightening thought. They could be dealing with abuse on an epidemic scale, and all from one family. They bade each other good morning.

Dr Brown put down her phone and pondered for a short while. The tiredness had temporarily been banished. Why would someone's case history be obliterated? Why did the finger point so obviously to the Macleans. She thought of calling the police but she didn't know enough and in the end it may only be a bureaucratic mistake. She would have to give it some more thought, possibly even chew it over with Martin, he said he'd look at the Carter boy. It was a good reason to call him, but it was still too early. She would wait a little longer and perhaps see him at coffee. She'd tell Paul Bowes as well. That might make him sit up.

Preston had no time to think about the video again as he made his way to the hospital and his liaison with Steve Topping. He knew its contents well now and he was more concerned with what he was going to get from the hospital administrators. It wouldn't be much more than a statement. He parked his car and found his way to the front of the hospital. Topping was waiting for him together with the local reporter from the BBC and reporters and photographers from the local press and news agencies. He was surprised to see Topping surrounded by them looking uncomfortable. When he showed up with a cheery "Morning everyone." They turned on him and he became surrounded as well.

"Come on Simon, just a quick reaction for the early bulletin."

There was a clamour which he knew a great deal about but had never been subjected to before. He was much more used to dealing it out. He looked across at Steve who seemed relieved that he was here. He had been completely taken by surprise. Of course he was part of the story, he and Topping had been shot by Jack and their opinions would count for a good fifteen seconds each in the TV news and at least four paragraphs in the papers. There was nothing to hold them back now. Everyone involved in the case was dead or peripheral, like him. Preston stalled for a few seconds. He knew he had a certain obligation to his colleagues to say something, but he was still covering the story himself. He was in an impossible position: he was covering the story but he *was* the story. What was worse was that he couldn't do his job properly with all this going on. He would have to do a deal and hope they would buy it.

"Hold on everybody. I'm here to cover this as well you know. If you want my comments then just hang on for a few minutes."

"Don't be daft Simon!" one of the agency reporters called out, "You wouldn't accept that from someone else." That was true. He would keep pushing until he got what he wanted. The trouble was he needed to keep his conversation with Jack secret until it appeared on the lunchtime bulletin. By then he would be safely back in the office and unreachable.

He took a gamble: if he said something fairly vague about how the mystery would never be solved now maybe they would disappear to file it. He could use that few minutes to do a piece to camera with Topping.

He brushed his way through the field of notebooks and microphones to Topping and shouted, "Just give me a moment with Steve will you, then I'll give you something!"

The clamour died away for a few seconds while he told Topping of his plan. "Have you said anything to them yet by the way."

"Nothing on the record," replied the cameraman, "But I think that means precisely zero to some of this lot. We'd better say something together."

They emerged from their huddle.

"OK everyone here's what I have to say, and I think Steve will add his own comments. This case has been a mystery to me and everyone else from the day it first started. Yes I was shot and I was very angry. Another man has died after being shot and we still don't really know why. I think it's very sad that..." He stopped himself from saying Jack just in time... "the youth has died because he had all the answers." He finished then added, "I don't know if there's anything you want to say Steve."

Topping looked at the assembly and was going to say nothing when he realised it would not be sufficient. He had been a player in this as well. "I understand what Simon says, but I got shot by this bloke and I think he had it coming to him." That was all. To the point, no room for doubt, or compassion. He was a cameraman in the best traditions of British television: don't think about it, just shoot it. He was also very shy.

A chorus of questions arose from the pack. "Don't you feel bitter Simon?" "Are your wounds still hurting?" "Have the police spoken to you?" None of them meant anything, they were just trying to get their own slant on the story. He was irritated by it even though he would have done exactly the same.

"I'm sorry everyone. That's all I'm saying. There may be more after we've heard what the hospital has to say."

Most of them drifted away to quiet corners where they could telephone their offices.

Only one remained, the reporter from the BBC local radio station. His studio was quite near and he didn't need to rush.

"Not enough for you?" asked Preston.

"There's no hurry," came the reply.

Topping and Preston made their way to the hospital's front gate where the reporter prepared to deliver his piece to camera. He had practiced it in the car so he wouldn't need more than one take. The mob wouldn't have come back by then.

He could afford to be less direct in this, even emotive. After all he was the story as well.

"Camera's rolling," said Topping.

Preston looked up from his notes into the camera, "Until two o clock this morning no one knew who the youth was in this case of murder, shooting, and mystery." His delivery was deliberate, measured and sombre, he was going to squeeze every last bit of juice from these words. "I went to see him after a visit a few weeks before. His name was Jack and he said he'd been consistently abused since his toddler years. He said he shot the old man in the incident because of what he did to him and others at a place called the James Institute. He revealed to me a web of corruption and abuse which completely changed my attitude to him. Yes he had shot me, and yes, I'm still angry about it – not to mention the pain and discomfort. But I knew nothing of this lad's hopeless life. It's not a justification for shooting anyone, perhaps, but it's given me a path to understanding it."

He moved on to the old man, "The old man was known as Mr Jesse according to the boy. They never knew if that was first or last name, or even if it was real. He was a youth with deep, almost irreparable psychological problems. All I can say is that when I left him at two this morning he was very much alive… and very much willing to kick if there had been a target close enough. But this was a young man who continued to live in fear up until his last breaths and, chillingly, he told me just before our interview was ended that he'd been warned never to say anything even while he was in the hospital."

The rest he would pick up in voiceover. He looked around to see if anyone had returned and to his irritation, someone had, the radio reporter was just a few feet away.

"You bastard Preston, I couldn't get my phone running in time."

"Too bad, son." Preston smiled and breathed a sigh of relief. "You've got it going now, I expect, but don't expect anything from me."

He moved away quickly as the radio reporter gave chase, firing questions as he went.

"Mr Preston, is it true you were the last to see the youth? What did he say to you? Did you do anything to him?

The last made Preston stop and whirl around.

"I'm afraid you're getting no exclusive here, you'll have to watch our programme tonight, I'll talk after that – assuming I'm allowed to."

He turned again and walked off.

The reporter called after him, "Not exclusive any more, Will, I heard what you said and I've got a response. It'll be on air in 20 minutes."

Bastard, thought Preston, just his luck to find the first radio reporter in a generation who knew what they were doing. He'd have to do a deal and he didn't like that.

"OK, …Phillip is it?" The reporter nodded, "We'll do a deal: you get an exclusive interview with me but you don't use it until our story goes on at the same time."

"When will that be?"

"Tonight at 6pm."

"You are kidding aren't you?"

"Why?"

"Were you never a radio reporter before all this TV star thing?"

"For a short while, yes."

"And what were your audience figures at six in the evening?"

He had Preston cold. Six PM for a local radio news bulletin might as well be three in the morning for all the people who'd be listening.

"Too bad, that's the deal, take it or leave it, you don't honestly think I'm going to pass up an exclusive like this for the sake of a radio beat do you."

"Then I go with my first plan."

"Think about it a bit more: if you do the interview on Zoom you'll be able to sell it up to the network and I'm sure you're not planning on staying around here for the rest of your radio days. Right now you have nothing and they'll have it themselves after we've gone on air, they just won't have an interview – and they'll want to know why not; I would!"

The reporter went silent as he mulled the options.

Then he said: "OK, deal but we do it now."

Sure they would and then see it fly up to the network hours before his own transmission.

"Not a chance, I'll do it 15 minutes before we go on air; that gives you time to get it and send it up to London. It's a good deal, Phil."

"It's Phillip, and it's not that great a deal. How do I know you'll stick to your end?"

"Take my number and I'll give you a Zoom reference – you can test it on me now if you like."

"All right, but if you double-cross me I won't forget it."

"I won't, some of us still have standards in this business – make sure you're one of them!"

The package lasted a minute and a half, long for a lunchtime bulletin but worth it considering the story. The Graphics department had enhanced the pictures but still they were grainy and not easily identifiable. Too bad, it was all that they had, no-one had been able to get better stills of them.

The newsreader, Jenny Hunt, looked into the camera directly in front of her and read from her autocue. "The youth shot by police in the Oxford siege has died in hospital. His death follows that of the man he shot. New information is emerging about the identity and history of both victims as our reporter, another victim of the shootings, our own reporter Simon Preston, has been finding out."

The report opened on a blown-up picture of Jack from the shooting, followed by another of the old Man, the man-from-nowhere, Mr Jesse. Except that now everyone was about to know he was from the James Institute.

Geoff Donald watched and rubbed his hands in satisfaction, but not for long, there was a lot more work to do. They were bound to have stirred up a wasps nest in their competitors who would hurl everything they had at the story to get ahead, or to discredit it. It would take some doing with this one, though. Donald held all the aces, or at least Preston did, and the others couldn't get near it, but he wouldn't relax. Now they had to get on to social services and track down this James Institute, and the so-called Mr Jesse. The history of Mr Jesse that is, they knew who he was now.

Another difficult decision: Preston's exclusive it may be, but he couldn't carry it all, much as he would protest that he could; it was time to spread the story around the rest of the staff. He called over to Mike Jones.

"Jonesy, how do you fancy following in your mate's footsteps?" Jones grimaced but nodded. "Find out more about this orphanage place, and the old bloke. Get on to social services and see what they know."

Jones nodded again and picked up the phone.

Humphries had never thought that his unremarkable life would coincide with the glamour boy on the television. Preston could go where he wanted, do more or less what he liked, and be recognised for it. No doubt he was well paid too. Even when he was shot he managed to turn it into his own circus with him as the star. Now, here he was again, right at the heart of it, the last one to see the youth alive.

Statistically there are a lot more jobbing solicitors than TV reporters, the chances of paths crossing are rare. This reporter, Simon Preston, was uncovering something rotten in the kingdom of childcare, and that interested Humphries for a lot of reasons – but one in particular: familiarity! He knew the James Institute, he would always remember it; it was an early and bitter lesson in the law as a commercial enterprise. He hoped he had been better than that since.

Now he was a senior partner and settled but he could still recall this piece of work from all those years ago: it was to carry out routine inquiries on the background of a child being sent to the institute. His paymasters didn't care, they would be paid as long as they showed that the work had been done, but Humphries had always been a diligent man, even in his 20s and he saw this as important. He was a newly qualified solicitor with a year behind him in the firm. A fee earner, there to make money for the partners doing whatever they threw at him. He had gone about it the hard way, writing letters to the social services, trying to contact the institute, trying to locate the parents, he'd even tried to find the James Institute to knock on the door but his supervising partner had firmly refused that idea, she only needed to show an appropriate paper trail to justify the bill. He had explored as many avenues as he could think of to get some detail but for all that his efforts were sparsely rewarded; waste of time and resources, said one very senior partner. Decades later he could still remember it had been a charitable organisation set apart from the social services, like a religious orphanage, in this case secretive and unhelpful. He had no desire to become a television victim, but he pondered for a long time over whether he should contact Simon Preston and tell him what he knew.

His lawyerly caution held him back. He had been told that no good ever comes of association with the media and his first instinct was to say nothing, let others lead the way.

But in this case he had no clients' interests to protect, not now, twenty years later. The youth he'd been acting for would have been long gone from there. He sipped at a cold cup of tea and realised that he had been thinking about this for so long that his other work was piling up. Humphries was a lawyer, but also a family man, he knew how lucky he and his children were and that not everyone got those chances. He would call Preston at his television station. He may not have much to offer but on the other hand he might.

Conditions in the office were not luxurious but comfortably functional. There was a desk, an armchair, a filing cabinet and a small television; She did not feel at all comfortable there though, nor was she meant to be. Di Sanders stood facing her superintendent. They had just finished watching the news on his PC, less at his invitation than his insistence. She had squirmed through the three-minute report and guilt was written all over her face.

"So Detective Sergeant Sanders. This is what it's come to." There had been a time when he'd encouraged her to call him Steve, but that would be a bad idea right now. And he had always called her Di.

"The television news is further ahead on an investigation than we are thanks to you."

She squirmed some more and pulled out a chair to sit down.

"This isn't a cosy chat, Sergeant, don't sit down!" Oh, didn't he love his rank and that he could boss a woman around!

Preston hadn't used the actual video file, at least she could be thankful for that, but it didn't matter because the boss already knew about it and nearly everything else.

"Yes Sir!"

"I don't fancy your chances on this one Di…" Confusing, make up your mind! "You acted as someone else, you collaborated with the press, you made a recording and then gave it to someone outside of the force…"

"But it wasn't official sir, it was my own phone."

"How does that make it better? The contents are out in the open!" he exclaimed with frustration close to anger, "*We* carry out criminal investigations, sergeant, not the media."

"Yes Sir." she replied, quietly. No credit for the intelligence she'd gathered, no recognition of the work she'd put it, no pats on the back and warnings about sticking to procedure in future but well done, Di; none of that! That they were further forward in the investigation didn't matter at all, apparently. What mattered was that she had broken a rule.

"And worst of all you took over another officer's investigation without any reference to me. Tony King was supposed to be doing it, not you."

"Yes sir." She knew better than to argue. The superintendent sat up straight and his voice assumed a monotone.

"Detective Sergeant Sanders these are serious breaches of discipline. You are suspended on full pay until a formal hearing."

"But sir..."

"That will be all, sergeant." He turned from her and looked at his laptop screen. She had not been expecting that. She burned with fury as she turned and left the office; the flames were fuelled by her knowing that it was her own stupid fault, she knew she had done wrong. She'd broken the rules but had fooled herself into thinking she had only bent them. She'd spent too much time in Simon Preston's company and his attitude had rubbed off on her. Fuck him!

It never occurred to her now to confess, she could have not said a word, Preston didn't mention her in his piece, but Di Sanders played by the rules even when they might hang her out to dry – and here she was dangling on the line.

If they had met somewhere in a bar instead of in a café doorway under fire from a wild kid with a shotgun then it would have been a glancing blow and probably wouldn't have gone beyond some introductory remarks. Simon Preston and Louise Brown would have chuckled to themselves and gone their separate ways probably never to meet again.

But their first meeting hadn't been like that; being shot, risking personal safety and dealing with the fear cut through their personality clash, that's what the psychology textbooks said happens.

It was beyond flirtation or sexual conquest, it was deeper and would be permanent, they were bound together, as was Steve Topping. So having lunch together was acceptable for both.

Or at least it should have been according to the theory.

They were in a cafe in the city centre, not the one from the siege but a hundred metres away. Preston had unloaded his story on to the doctor and when he finished there was a short pause before she said, "So, he was an orphan locked in a hideaway orphanage run by that old man and regularly raped and abused." He was taken back by her exact and clinical summary of all he'd told her, a very good encapsulation of his story which he might use later. All the same, that was supposed to be his job, not hers, she was a doctor. But she hadn't finished, "...What it must be to live in your world!" It didn't sound like she meant it admiringly.

Preston responded with a louder voice than he intended, "It wasn't just me who was there. I met up with Di Sanders...Detective Sergeant Sanders... you remember her?"

Yes, she remembered her but with no great pleasure.

"Your ex!?"

"Yes." He heard an unvoiced question and answered it: "We happened to be there at the same time."

"At two o clock in the morning? You don't need to lie to me, you know."

"It was a coincidence; I was only trying to do my job; and so was she. Anyway, we weren't the only ones. Your boss was there as well, in fact he blew the whistle on us."

"My boss? Blew the whistle? Who do you mean?"

"What's his name? Bowels? He smirked and instantly regretted it.

She sighed loudly so that he wouldn't mistake her.

" Paul? Paul *Bowes*?"

"Paul Bowes, yes. He was passing by and had a go at us for exciting the youth... Jack."

"Passing by? Was he,at 2am? That's weird, he didn't have any of his own cases in last night."

"Why?"

"Consultants leave it to us overnight... we do the hard work, they come in and tell us what we should have done in the morning – maybe less so now I'm a senior registrar."

Preston wasn't listening to the last few words. He said, "That means he could have been the last one to see Jack alive... not Di... or me?"

"You mean you just left?" she said.

"Yes, our cover was blown when Bowels ...," she looked at

him with exasperation as he chuckled at his joke, "...recognised Di. We left him looking at Jack's chart."

"Your cover was blown? You mean you got into the hospital via subterfuge and interviewed a patient without him knowing about it and you complain that your cover was blown! For God's sake!"

"Well, yes but..."

"And you implicate a police officer and might very well have wrecked her career!"

Preston fell silent. Normally he had a coffer full of arguments about press freedom, swords of truth and all the stuff the papers bring up when someone threatens them with regulation; but he sensed no amount of argument about the truth and justice would make any impression on this woman's self-righteousness.

"So Paul didn't recognize you then? That must have hurt."

What was going on here? He took a breath to ask but she was ahead of him.

"Look... I know we shared something, I know it's supposed to bond us in some way, but I'm not at all sure that I like you."

He looked her in the eye and tried not to wince at the last words.

She continued, "Not quite a meeting of minds, is it?"

"Hardly!

Preston looked at her face slightly obscured by strands of hair and what was probably a critical glower. Another time, another woman and he'd have made a move – the glower would have meant little – but they were way beyond that. Was he really in the wrong? All he was trying to do was find out why he'd been shot, to get inside the story. He was at the centre of it, after all. Didn't she share that... that passion? She was there too!

Why was the old man killed, *why* did this kid have to die so strangely? Or did her precious procedure count for more than the truth?

"So, Louise... Dr Brown, I assume we won't be exchanging bodily fluids any time soon!"

As the last consonant died in the frosted air between them he saw he'd gone too far. She sat bolt upright, an invisible fortress wall suddenly around her. He did not know this woman, what was he doing making sex talk to her – or much more likely, no-sex talk?

"For god's sake, you are plumbing depths here. Will you stop now before I get up and walk out?"

Plumbing depths! Nice line. There may be hope. He raised his hands in submission and apology.

"You're right, I'm sorry, I haven't slept much, and I have a big story which I seem to be right in the centre of…"

"Of which you are in the centre, what happened to your grammar?"

Yes, yes, all right, he thought. When sleep goes out the window, grammar goes with it. Move on! He sighed and pressed forward as best he could.

"There's still no cause of death yet, we'll have it tomorrow morning. It might become clearer."

She nodded and took a sip from her coffee.

"Enough of that. Now that you've given me a lecture on… well just about everything, it's my turn."

"Your turn to what?"

There was an awkward silence finally broken by a customer brushing past their table and knocking over Brown's capacious bag. It was a major spill as the bag was upended: phone, purse, pack of tissues, a medical textbook, "The Mind Of The Young Child", and a couple of official-looking files.

All three of them went down at once to pick up a file and it fell open. Two sheets of paper came out directly in front of Preston. He was trained to scan anything at anytime. The words "Maclean" and "abuse" leaped out at him and lingered in his mind even though he didn't know what they signified.

"Sorry about that." said the customer as she made her way out.

"No problem," replied the doctor, coldly.

Maclean! Where had he heard that name? He took a sip of coffee and said, "I suppose I shouldn't have seen that?"

"No, you shouldn't. You could have looked away, but you didn't."

"How could I stop myself from looking at something when I didn't know I wasn't supposed to?"

"The file says Risk, that means confidential, implicitly,"

"I didn't see... anyway, I couldn't know that."

"But you don't care about that do you! You just butt your nose in wherever you feel like it."

"I just saw a name, that's all, Maclean... well, abuse appeared as well."

That was enough, her mind snapped to attention and she saw what a mistake this was. She'd agreed to meet out of curiosity but that was well and truly satisfied and dispatched now. If there was a bond between them she was about to break it because he was intolerable.

"I'm sorry I'm not enjoying this. Our special bond or whatever it may be, isn't deep enough to cut through the rest of it." She gathered her bag, checked its contents and pushed her seat back.

"Goodbye!" She got up without even attempting to smile, turned and headed towards the café's door.

Preston had hardly noticed any of it, he was still churning over the name Maclean. Then as the door closed firmly it came to him: the videos this morning, the material before his interview with Jack, he'd accessed it while trying to find the right file. Louise Brown knew who he was, so did Di, and he did not. And now Dr Brown had shut the door on him.

He stared at the closed door idly. He felt he knew less about Louise Brown at that moment than he knew before he met her.

As she walked away briskly from the café she gathered the bag closer to her; it was a useless gesture. Too late, he had seen it and she doubted if she could rely on his discretion to keep it quiet, he'd already made clear where his moral code lay.

Donald's prediction of Preston's reaction was accurate, it was his story and he wanted to dictate how it went. The fact that Mike Jones was getting in on it was of no help at all, friend though he may be. If he had looked at it dispassionately, he would know there was too much for one to do, but he wasn't and to say he accepted the decision with good grace would be misleading to the point of deception.

"All right, Simon, you've made your point. Now, shut up and get back here! I want a story conference in 60 minutes and you are it." Donald ended the call before Preston could protest any further.

A strange couple of hours, thought the reporter: metaphorically slapped across the face first by Louise Brown, then his news editor; even stranger considering that he'd been the one to bring in the biggest story of the year. Nobody likes a smart Alec, he thought, still less a successful one. Success has many fathers and they all try to kill the real one.

He made his way back to the studio complex and was greeted at the security desk by a harassed woman with a computer screen filled with message reminders.

"Hi Jan, anything for me?" She started to mouth something unpleasant but her telephone rang and she picked up.

"Yes he's just walked in the door. Who's calling please?"

She looked at him coldly, lips pursed, eyes narrowed. Her morning had been eaten up by phone calls and messages demanding to speak to Preston and she was not enjoying the pressure; she'd taken the brunt of it and as far as she was concerned it was a long way above her pay grade.

"It's the Daily Express for you. Where do you want to take it?"

"I don't. Take a message and say I had to rush straight into editing." Her eyes flared but she did as he asked. "That's the fourth from them today. And then there's all these." She swung her monitor round for him to see.

"Sorry Jan, it's big and I'm right in the middle of it."

"So am I. What do you want me to do?" The phone rang again. "It's bound to be for you." He waved his hand at her in dismissal and disappeared through the foyer and into the newsroom. The fire deepened in her eyes.

Donald collared him as he reached his desk. "We're getting calls from everywhere. Did you know you had so many friends?"

"I didn't know I had any. Did anyone important call?"

"HQ have sent down a memo from Legal, but we're clear on that... horse's mouth and all that."

Too much to ask for a herogram then! Bastards, only the sales team got that now that news was a burden. What did the high-ups think, that this might actually cost them money in legal fees maybe?

He put his phone on silent to make room to think; he checked it for messages: one from Di Sanders which he wished he'd seen sooner, and one from Tony King?

Why had he and Di called separately?

His desk phone buzzed. He put down his mobile and pressed a button to hear a frosty voice say through the loudspeaker, "Simon, it's Jan. What are you doing about these calls? I've taken five more since you just walked past me."

Donald was close and grimaced at Preston as he said, "Don't make her any more cross, she's taken a lot of flak for you today!"

Preston nodded.

"All right, Jan, send them through!"

"At last! I can't keep taking these messages, what about the rest of the office? And I've just taken one from a man who says he's a lawyer – I don't know much about what you do but I reckon you'll want to take notice of that."

Donald quickly jumped in, "Send that to me as well, Jan!"

There was a cutoff sound from the speaker.

"Lawyers, Simon? We can't ignore them!"

"I know. Let's see who it is.!"

Humphries was in the middle of a difficult interview and had turned off his phone. This was not why he'd signed up to be a lawyer. Property conveyancing and probate, yes, oaths, wills and contracts, bring it on! But not this.

He summoned his nerve and looked John Maclean in the eye – not an easy thing to do, the man had a powerful presence.

"It's difficult to know what to expect Mr Maclean. The judge could be swayed your way but you have to admit the evidence is … well, challenging."

"It bloody well is not!" There was that anger again, his wife was passive as usual. "I challenge it. It's a bloody fit up from start to finish!!"

Humphries had become familiar with John Maclean's temper,

he had even come to expect it. He saw it as a ritual now, always followed by his wife attempting to calm him down.

"Please John, Mr Humphries is doing all he can for us, it's not his fault." She was right on cue. Humphries had reached his own conclusion about Maclean's lack of control: if the man shouted and blustered enough he might drown out his guilt and persuade himself that it wasn't true. The wife was less easy to explain, it wasn't as if she was complicit or downtrodden, quiet maybe, but not cowed or bullied. Maclean wasn't controlling her. He really wished he could be rid of the whole sordid business, but in the end maybe this was a kind of quid pro quo for his prosperous life elsewhere and everyone has a right to be represented whether they deserve it or not. Sometimes he believed that cornerstone of the British legal system should not be there, he didn't feel as if the whole structure would come tumbling down as a result. Anyway, it was!

The sooner this went in front of a judge the better, then he could clear it out of his system and get back to his paperwork.

Preston was tired of waiting, he called across to Jones, "Well, Jonesy? Will they tell us anything?"

Jones looked up from his screen. "They're stalling. They say they've taken a ton of calls because of this and they're dealing with those. I suppose we should have expected that. They're trying to find it in their files."

"Trying to WHAT! This wasn't fifty years ago in some far-flung province, it was less than ten miles away and right here, in this fucking county."

Donald called out, "Easy on the language, not in here, remember!"

Preston started to say, "For fuck's sake," but pulled back. If the language flourished in the newsroom it might leak into the studio. Jones smiled conspiratorially.

But Donald was still furious, he breathed out angrily and then almost but not quite shouted, "Jonesy, take a camera, get down there and start making a nuisance of yourself! Grab the department director as he comes out, you know what he looks like! I don't mind breaking a few rules here. Go on to the premises if you think you can get away with it. Don't worry about trespassing, this story justifies it!"

Jones closed his terminal, pulled a small handicam from a drawer and nodded at Donald as he walked out.

Preston called out, "Good luck, mate." Jones raised a hand then contracted it to two fingers as he went through the door. Preston chuckled.

It wasn't enough that he'd screwed her over with their relationship, no, he had to turn that screw yet again and destroy her career! She'd never get beyond sergeant now and might even have to go back in uniform, possibly even be demoted. What right did he have to do that? And now, after dropping her so deeply in the shit he wasn't taking her calls. She had inured herself against crying over the years of her police employment and she'd been resilient before that; she wouldn't have been able to do the job if she allowed herself to be affected by every tough break. But this was a personal wounding, a double blow and she had conflicting feelings: she wanted to lash out at Preston, physically hit him, but she also found her tear ducts coming under pressure. This was akin to vomiting in her world, something she wanted to avoid at all costs because it was such an unpleasant sensation. She sought to regain her violent rage, that at least would fight back the tears.

Her phone sounded; her Nemesis.

"I've been suspended!" she said, furiously without waiting for Preston to speak. There was silence for two seconds before he responded, "What for? What are you supposed to have done?"

As if he didn't know what she ... and *he*... had done.

"What do you fucking think, Simon! The *fucking* interview you weren't going to use, what else would it be?"

"But I didn't use it!"

"That's not the point. They know about it."

"What difference does that make?"

"It's *evidence* Simon. You've made us look stupid and they're taking it out on me. Thanks for wrecking my life – my career..."

Preston formed a word but her fury was uncontained and she was in no mood to listen to him."

"You knew I was heading for superintendent, you knew how much I loved this job. Now I'll be stuck as a sergeant forever... or worse. Thanks for nothing!"

"What, just for talking about a recording you made?"

"There's no *just* about it. I broke the rules by being there with you, by making a recording without warning the boy... the dead boy, I might add. No one would have known if it hadn't been for you."

"But you've taken them much further forward, you know so much that you didn't know yesterday..."

"I know we do, but so do you. And you couldn't keep it to yourself, could you! You had to be the big reporter and let everyone know. Fuck you, Simon!"

She pushed the end icon more powerfully than she needed and threw the phone on to her sofa.

As it landed it sounded again and it was a number she didn't recognize. She was going to let it ring out but curiosity got the better of her. "Di Sanders," she said.

"Di, it's Juliet Neilson, I hear you're having a tough time."

"Juli... Guv, news travels fast."

"One of my unofficial duties is to keep an eye out for female officers. The chief is big on that even if she can't say so."

"Not much you or she can do for me."

"I don't know if that's true, Di, but we're keeping a close eye on it. Both she and I reckon the result of what you did has taken us forward. We know you were trying to help, not hinder but your super – Hawkins isn't it? I never liked him – has it tied up with the letter of the rulebook."

Sanders felt the unwelcome tears coming again and tried to fight them as she said, "You're doing a lot for me... Juliet. Why?"

"You're too good to lose over something as silly as this. The chief thinks so too."

"How does she even know me?"

"She keeps track of the promising talent, it's part of my job to make sure she does. I can't promise anything, Di, but please don't despair!"

"Hawkins still has the final say doesn't he?"

"Yes, it's his sub-division and he's got the rulebook on his side."

"Thanks for the call, Ma'am. I have to go now."

She pressed the red icon and gave up the fight with the tears.

Preston felt for an SD card in his jacket pocket and was reassured by it being there. He had backed up the interview to his cloud and his office laptop and just for an extra level of security he dumped it across to an SD card; it was already a valuable commodity, now even more so. Then his phone sounded; it was a police station extension.

"Simon Preston, who is this?"

The voice wasn't quite measured at the other end, it was just about even but there was anger there.

"DC Tony King, Di Sanders' oppo. Actually, now I'm acting detective sergeant and I think you'll know why?"

Normally when a cop told him of a promotion he would offer congratulations but he knew what a bad idea that would be right now.

"Big shoes to fill, Tony."

"I know," said King, coldly, then continued without waiting for a response, "*Mr* Preston you have information which I would like to speak to you about."

"Oh yes?"

"We'd like you to come into the station."

"Hasn't Di Sanders already told you what's happened?"

"I haven't seen her and I'm not likely to. We would like to see *you*." It was becoming more formal by the second.

"All right Tony... DC King, we'll fix something up... "

"Now would be a good time – of course we could arrest you for withholding evidence!"

Hardball it was then. No question that he had the evidence. But so did they, it was Di's recording.

"There's nothing you don't already know or can't get to."

"This afternoon, Mr Preston!"

"Look, I'm doing a big story and I need to be here – how about you come to see me?"

There was a pause, King was only a DC and even acting up

as sergeant he knew he could only go so far. The politics of police and media would get in the way if he pushed it.

"All right, shall we say three PM?"

"See you then!"

He sat down for a moment to take in what had happened: threatened with arrest for a start and a command near enough to talk to them. They were angry, or King was, anyway. He took a breath and let Donald know what was happening.

"Do we need a lawyer for you?" asked the news editor.

"Not for an informal chat."

"So long as it stays that way. Have you got the interview with you?"

Preston pulled his phone from his pocket and linked it to his laptop.

"There's a lot of stuff on here not relevant, I just copied the whole thing, didn't even have time to separate out the files. Have a look."

Donald watched then said, "We'll need some copies, just in case Inspector Plod wants to sequester it. Legal will want to see it anyway."

Preston smiled despite himself. He had one more call. He dialled the lawyer, Humphries. They arranged to meet.

Di Sanders put down her phone and sat on her sofa, her rage could only last so long, she didn't have the energy to maintain it. Now she was flattened. She had been betrayed by everyone that day, everyone. Suspended and fighting with her ex-boyfriend about a stupid video. She wished she had never left the station that night, just stayed doing paperwork, kept her head down, not tried to take the initiative or help Tony King.

She knew it made sense to trust Simon Preston, he wasn't a bad man, not by quite a long way, she wouldn't have been with him if he had been. Her head told her that was the sensible thing to do. But right then her heart wanted something to hate, it couldn't be Juliet Neilson for her adherence to the rule book because that was her code as well, so he was the easiest target. A tear appeared in the corner of her eye and quickly made its way down her cheek. She reached for a tissue and wiped the wet track which traced the route of its journey. It was pointless because her eyes welled up and the tissue became saturated.

Preston's phone sounded again, a busy night for him. It was Jones.
"Jonesy, tell me some good news for fuck's sake!"
"I wish I could, but he got away."
"You saw him then?"
"Oh yes, he's a slimy creep, isn't he! I was waiting at the main entrance and he appeared at the door. I went to fire up the camera but he must have seen me and he ducked back inside. Bastard!"
"Is there a back entrance?"
"Of course and I got round there as quickly as I could. I even asked the security bloke there if he'd come out. He had, needless to say. Sorry mate!"
"Not your fault, slippery though, aren't they?"
"Oh yes. I keep thinking that if I was better with these bloody cameras then I might at least have got the shot of him at the front and maybe fired off some kind of question."
Preston knew he couldn't blame his old friend, they trained as reporters and working a camera was a very different skill.
"I know, I'd probably would have done the same. Only Malcolm and Ken ever seemed to get that right, but even then they have to switch mindsets."
The episode had confirmed one thing, though, the director seemed to have something to hide.
"What's happened at your end," asked Jones. Preston filled him in on the latest.
"One thing, though, we've got them running scared," he concluded.
"Thank heavens for small mercies, Presto!"

His sotto voce whispers still seemed to echo around the specimen jars and pieces of human tissue, his stock in trade.
"You'll need to give me more time!"
"You're the expert, you come up with something? You didn't

have any trouble with the old peasant."

"You're being obtuse! That was easy to blame on natural causes, he was in bad health and he hadn't got long anyway. You can't do that with a sixteen year-old, I couldn't say he died of a heart attack, they'd question my sanity."

"Don't be so open on the phone, what are you playing at!"

Three days had passed since the youth's death...or Jack as they insisted on calling the brat now. The results of the post-mortem were supposed to be out and he'd been stalling.

"I can't wait any longer, the blood tests only take a couple of days, and that's up now. The coroner has been on my back but I've been fobbing him off."

The Network never met in full membership, they didn't have general meetings, and when members got together to practice their activities it was never more than five at a time with no real names used. If there was a policeman, or policemen, involved he either hadn't met them, or hadn't realised what they were. Nor was Network the kind of organisation which put out a detailed list of its members with addresses and telephone numbers: they didn't elect a leader, he just assumed the role because he deemed himself to be the fittest. It was about control. They all had it and recognised it in the others. If there was any common thought or culture that linked them it was that. No-one would say they were brought together by it, none of them was motivated by the need to belong, the very opposite, but they shared that one area of malevolence. They were held together by threat and fear of discovery.

"I'll do what I can but this has got out of hand. It started with eliminating one miserable old man; nobody cared about him, nobody wanted him. That was easy, and so was my part. I've convinced them it was natural causes. But the boy was silly. You shouldn't have done it. If there's even the tiniest slip-up then the whole bag will split open and everything will come spilling out."

There was a short silence at the other end of the line. The first speaker clearly did not enjoy criticism.

"You've spent too long down in that hospital dungeon. Have you not seen the news, the websites, anything at all? I don't like it myself but we have to go the whole way now. Once we'd started there was no going back."

"It's like trying to repair a puncture in a perished tyre: you fix one but two more open up instantly."

The second speaker, still sitting amid the detritus of his trade, felt a thrill running through him. There was a chink in the other's ice wall, enough to get a hold on perhaps and give a good tug, just to see if it would come away. That's what he lived for, what they all lived for, someone else's squirming discomfort.

Control!

She finally cornered Martin Tench in the doctors' mess but she wondered why she'd bothered. It was obvious that the passion of their coupling was not being relived. She cast her eyes quickly around the room to make sure there were no ears close by, then turned back to him; it was like dragging an unwilling dog for a walk.

"I know we're at work but you seem so remote. I haven't seen you since ... well since...you know."

The pleasure of the memory was one thing; articulating it, especially to the man responsible was different. She was shy and embarrassed when she should be the opposite. She wanted to enjoy the intimacy and share the joy, not be scared and uncertain about it.

"I'm sorry Louise. Paul has just dumped five extra cases in my lap and I'm weighed down."

He looked up at her and smiled, that smile, those eyes, that voice!

"I know how demanding he can be. But it's all right, it's only me. You don't have to be distant with me."

He smiled again: "I barely know you, you do realise that?"

That was true, of course, although it didn't seem like it. He knew a lot about her and then he knew nothing. Get a grip, Louise! The answer was to know more about each other.

The caution of the previous minutes deserted her as she was taken over by a wave of determination.

"How about doing it again Martin?"

He smiled at her again. "Whenever you like, Louise."

The thrill she wanted to get from that was tempered by the disconnected way it was delivered.

"Tonight!"

"Well…"

Her smile faded further.

"I'm so sorry, I'm committed tonight. Can we take a rain check?"

Her smile died completely.

A rain check!

Reporters mix with the rich and the poor, those who care and those who don't, the old and the new, the vulgar and the elegant. They meet everyone and everything, they are rarely shocked beyond their first year in the job. They meet life in all its variety, and often in the same day, death. They will talk to the semi-literate in the morning then lunch with the literati, and the worlds rarely collide. Through this social, cultural, divided mix they get to see what is worst and best in human beings. Often it will be the same things but dressed differently.

Preston was on the uncarpeted stairway to the office of a solicitor he had never met. He had no preconceptions, he rarely did. He might be a university graduate who wanted a quiet life in the dullness of the provincial legal system, he might be a trier who became articled in his teens and fought his way through night school to get his prized position today. He might even be a nice guy. Reporters could never tell with solicitors because they never talked to them. Barristers were different, they were another branch of showbusiness, they loved to mix with the rakish elements of the media.

But solicitors craved respectability, position and deference; they were the stuff of rotary clubs and round tables, the pillars of golf clubs.

They were The Establishment.

Robin Humphries was at the top of the stairs behind an unprepossessing office door. He did not think along the same lines as the man he was about to meet. He was a conduit through which the law passed, he knew it well where most people did not. He had compassion for his family and sometimes for his clients. He cared about what he did and he believed it to be valuable. He and Preston might share the same education, even the same values, but their attitudes were utterly different. Robin Humphries was not a flamboyant man.

That they had arranged to meet at the request of the solicitor was something which had made Preston ponder deeply. The normal way for lawyers and media types to treat each other was via official letters so what was the issue? If he'd transgressed in any way it would be dealt with by recognized channels, not by a personal meeting fixed up between the two of them.

He reached the top of the stairs, took a breath and knocked. A secretary answered the door and ushered him to a seat in her cubby hole by the side of the main office.

"I'll just tell Mr Humphries you're here."

She picked up the telephone and while he waited the reporter let his scavenging eyes run around her and the contents of her desk. She was neat, well turned out in a legal secretary's black refinery with white blouse. It was a short distraction, Humphries emerged from his office with a half-smile and an outstretched hand.

"Mr Preston, I'm Robin Humphries!"

Preston stood, took the proffered hand and responded, "Simon Preston, how can I help you?" Humphries widened his smile but not to full face and pointed the way through to his office. Preston had to move past the legal secretary who had returned to her task of typing up documents and his eye caught the name Maclean, it was unmistakable. Three times now he'd come across it when he wasn't meant to. Jigsaw deduction. He disguised his look as well as he could and tried to linger a half second longer on the name and its surrounding type – but he couldn't get anything from that without Humphries noticing.

Both men entered the office and Humphries closed the door behind him.

Back at the secretary's desk the Maclean document had reached the top of the pile and she set about dealing with it. A letter and email to John Maclean.

Dear Mr Maclean

As you will already know the date for your trial has been set and you will be required to surrender your bail to the usher on that day at the Crown Court.

You are charged with acts of gross indecency against a minor namely David Maclean, aged five. These are specimen charges and details of your history will be revealed in court.

I have spoken to you on many occasions about these matters and I am well aware of your denial. But I must again urge you to reconsider your plea on the day. You have been told of the weight of evidence and it is my duty to remind you that a guilty plea will sit better with the judge.

Yours Faithfully

Robin Humphries, Llb, Solicitor.

She took the letter and put in a pile ready for signing.

On the other side of the door from her Humphries was relaxed, friendly even.
"I imagine you were surprised to get my call?"
"Relations between the media and the legal profession can be tense, Mr Humphries. Yes I was surprised. I often feel that solicitors and journalists regard each other with mutual contempt. I only ever see you covering up or producing some form of bias for your clients. No doubt you see us as a bunch of scavengers and heedless hooligans out for whatever sensation will fill the news space that day."
Humphries' smile flickered momentarily as he considered this. Then he replied, "I would say that some of your colleagues have done a great deal to justify your description of your job." He paused for a half second, his smile recovered,

"But then many of my colleagues have done a great deal to justify your description of theirs."

Preston nodded.

Humphries continued, "The James Institute, Simon, you don't mind if I call you that do you?"

He could call him Genghis Khan for all Preston cared, The James Institute were the key words in that sentence. He recovered himself, "Please do, and I shall call you Robin."

"Of course."

"You lack nothing if not a sense of drama, Robin. What do you know about the James Institute; are you representing it?"

"No, not at all. And I know very little, but still something. This will have to be confidential of course...?"

"Of course, reporter's honour!"

"And how much is that worth?"

"Perhaps more than you have been led to believe."

Humphries studied the reporter for a few seconds, then said, "I shall take you at your word but I'm sure you understand the sensitivity of me as a source?"

"Yes, I do!" He was even more amazed that he was there. "Please carry on, you can be assured of my trust!"

Humphries waited another second and made his decision.

"I only ever had dealings with the place once. It was eight years ago when I was simply employed here as a very junior solicitor."

Preston nodded along.

"You obviously know where it is – about 10 miles outside of the city."

"Thank you, we didn't know that – any more detail on the location?"

"I would have thought your resources would have revealed that already."

"We like to think we know everything but we don't."

Humphries typed into his laptop and then turned it to face Humphries. It was an Ordnance Survey map of the region and he pinpointed exactly where the James Institute was – or had once been.

"I was obliged to make a check on behalf of a client. We were representing a family whose young boy was being taken into care. The proposal at the time was to send him to the James Institute."

"Why especially there?"

"I can't find the correspondence any more, but as far as I can remember they were a charity offering a specific kind of retrieval service."

"Retrieval!"

"It sounds awful I know. It meant they specialised in accommodating those boys who would never be returned to their families. Retrieval meant they tried to rescue what was left of their damaged psyches, at least that's what I was told by the social services."

He paused to let the reporter take it in. Finally Preston spoke, "So they took them when they were already badly abused, and then just carried on doing it!"

"That's the way it seems."

"Didn't you know!" He looked accusingly at the lawyer.

"Of course not." He spoke in measured tones, "They seemed perfect for our client. We had no reason to question them, we had already contacted the social services who appeared perfectly happy with what they did. They even made inspections of the place… at least that's what they told me."

Preston listened but said nothing. Humphries continued, "The thing is I was young, inexperienced and nevertheless determined to do a thorough job so I made further enquiries."

"Really?" said Preston.

"In the end I had to stop because I was told by my seniors that I was wasting time and money. But I tried to contact the Institute directly and then when that failed I was about to get in my car and drive out to them…~"

"But you didn't?"

"No, my supervising partner saw me leaving the office and stopped me."

"We all have annoying bosses. So you got no further than that. Was there something that you felt was wrong about it?"

"Certainly, but I couldn't get past the social services and I wasn't being allowed to. I think at this end it was simply a fee-earning thing… they wanted me here earning money for them, not out in my car chasing something which they didn't think was our job and wouldn't get us any more."

"Why bring it up now?"

"I always had a deep uneasiness about the place, I thought you would want to know."

"I do. Do you still do that kind of work?"

"Only when I have to, I avoid it and try to ensure the firm avoids it as well. Same reasons: money. And, I'll be honest, I'm not that at home with the seamy side of life."

"I understand. Sometimes we all have to get our hands dirty, though, Robin."

"I know, we don't have to like it."

True, although Preston might have been keener than most to delve into the sewers when needed.

"You realise this means the social services, or at least someone within them, is part of this as well."

"I only deal in what's known. I cannot conjecture, the law doesn't allow guesses, it needs hard information."

"You're off the record, you can spell it out."

Humphries gave Preston another examining look, then said, "All right yes, there's something quite rotten going on – or was."

That's what Preston thought. He was riding a wave of coincidences and while he was getting on well enough with Humphries he was making connections. Reporters made their own luck, he took a risk and said, "Let me try another name on you: what do you know about the Maclean Family?"

Humphries sat up, his face turned cold and stern.

"How do you know I represent them?"

"I didn't. It was a guess. It's also a name which keeps coming into my life without being asked. I'm beginning to think it means something, I just don't know what."

"I repeat, how did you get that name?"

There was no great secret to keep, he'd seen it twice on loose documents and heard it once in an extraneous video interview. There was no harm in letting him know that. But before he could start to explain Humphries' defences came up and he blustered, "You know that I can say nothing because of..." He stalled, he had been taken by surprise. This was his first encounter with the media and it was all he'd feared.

Preston finished the sentence.
"Client confidentiality?"

She had her secrets, she had spent her life harbouring secrets, she was good at it. She had even made a secret of her name, she had done it so well that not even she knew what it was, not any more. She didn't remember where she came from either. Somewhere deep within, there was a feeling that she had known people well. But she didn't know who they were. She had been practicing for a lifetime. She secreted everything she ever knew. Nobody knew what she stood for, nobody knew what she knew, and now she had done the ultimate, she had managed to hide everything that was ever known about her somewhere unreachable. Not even she could find it. She had finally managed to keep herself secret from herself.

But she still knew some things. She knew she was in a hospital, she knew some of the people were doctors and others were nurses and care assistants.

If she had not hidden so much she would know to censure the people who left her in the street. She had caught pneumonia, she had been very ill, she had been taken to intensive care when she was found by some do-gooder out on the prowl in the city streets. If she knew who they were she would have blamed them for a lot. But it was all a huge secret and she didn't know who they were. The secrets were locked tight behind a great mental door, only she had the key and she'd lost it. Sometimes the weight of them seemed to force the door and things would leak out but she was quick. She would slam herself against it and shut it tight before anything else got out.

Those little shafts of memory would sometimes seep into her consciousness when she wasn't watching, and they would sting because her mind's eye wasn't used to the light. But she always drew down the shutters in double quick time. Safe again, secret in her own darkened world.

Just sometimes, laying there in the recovery ward, safely out of intensive care, those shafts would come. They came less often than when she was lying in the bed with all the tubes and dials, and machines, and nurses hemming her in. She hadn't been well, she hadn't had the strength to slam the door shut. She couldn't get to the blinds in time. For a little while reality and memory had invaded her mind, delirious as it had been it still saw her for what she was, the secrets were out in the open, at least to her. She knew she should censure those who had left her, she knew they could censure her just as easily.

As she slowly mended she gathered the strength to close the door again and the secrets crowded behind it, waiting.

It was then that she had seen the man fiddling with the funny old man's drip. She had seen him clearly because there was some light still, there had to be, intensive care worked twenty four hours a day, the sick didn't recognise the clock, the ward didn't separate gender.

She had seen him take out a sharp looking thing, like a syringe, she had seen him push it into the drip and plunge it down. She knew what those things were, she'd been alive a long time. She had seen him looking furtively around at every stage. Then she had seen him walk out.

She had seen the nurses rushing around the old man when they saw his dials and graphs had stopped moving. But it was a secret. After all what did she know? She was just another confused old lady.

Then her rambling consciousness was interrupted by a young, unwelcome voice.

"Hello again, perhaps you remember me? I'm Detective Constable Tony King. Are you feeling better today? Perhaps we can talk?" The detective sat down by her side and smiled. The great door creaked as the secrets started pushing.

Get back! Stay where you are! We don't need *you*.

The solicitor watched as his secretary brought in the batch of letters and deeds for signing or sealing. He had spent some seconds regaining control of his temper when Preston left. Humphries had been trying to help, to direct, but instead he found he had a tiger by the tail. Preston was a reporter, he went his own way and made his own decisions and he was prepared to change the rules or even ignore them if it helped him. Robin Humphries, diligent solicitor, devoted family man, pillar of society, had just had the carpet whipped from under him. It was not the proper way to behave, not in Humphries' book. There were certain expectations in his world and Preston hadn't lived up to them. He thought he liked him; now he didn't.

He thanked his secretary, looked down at the pile of letters and saw the one for the Macleans. He opened his desk and got out the file again. Why wouldn't this man simply admit it? Denial is always the first step for anyone when they're confronted with unwelcome truth. But this had carried on for weeks, and the strength of the denial had not subsided at all. Maclean was determined and he would not compromise.

Why!

He looked again at his dictated letter. Maclean was a simple man, his wife had stood by him all the way, like so many devoted, deceived wives, yet the evidence was so obvious. There could be no doubt about the facts, and that's what he dealt in.

He picked up his pen and signed it. Maclean would go down. But while he continued to rationalise it, something ate away at the back of his mind which would not let him relax.

"They tell me you can speak now."

"Do they!"

"We need to get you sorted out."

King's task got no easier.

"None of my business what you do!"

He was too young to deal with an irascible old woman. He had neither the patience, nor the understanding; he did have empathy but his still young mind had not learned to put that to work with the more difficult. He had no idea why she wouldn't just open up and help him. She would help herself at the same time.

"You don't have to be so secretive Elsie."

"Who's Elsie?"

"You are until we find out your real name. I presume it's not Elsie?"

"None of your business!"

That would be no, then.

If she would only cooperate, he could help her.

But he didn't know what had happened in her life, he didn't know what motivated her, he didn't yet know how a life can be trampled on. He was too young and on his way up, he had no idea what it was like to be on the way down, or never even get off the ground.

"Come on Elsie, give me a clue..."

"Don't call me that!" She wasn't going to tell him, it was a secret. She had nothing else, they would have to fight her to take it from her.

"You'll have to say something soon. You're getting better, you won't be able to stay here for much longer, they'll have to put you somewhere else you know Elsie."

"I told you not to call me that!"

"What else can I call you? Doris perhaps, all right, Doris, you will still have to speak unless you want to wind up on a mental ward."

"How dare you! I am not called Doris. Stop calling me stupid names!"

"I don't have any choice. If you don't tell me your name then what else can I do?"

"None of my business. Go away."

"All right Doris, or Elsie, I'll go but I'll be back. I have to know, and I won't stop until I find out who you are."

A stern voice called out from behind him. "What do you think you're doing! Come away from there!"

It was the senior nurse.

"I beg your pardon nurse..."

"Senior Nurse!"

"My mistake, I was just trying to get her identity."

"What's yours?"

He was flustered by her brisk authority; and unnerving eyes. He realised he hadn't produced his warrant card.

"My apologies. Detective Constable Anthony King – acting detective sergeant, actually. I'm trying to find out how she came here and where she comes from."

She did not soften as she examined his card. "Mr King there are ways of dealing with matters like this. That is a confused old woman, you badgering her will drive her more into herself. It won't work."

Authority or not, and never mind the eyes, he had a job to do.
"So when did you qualify as a psychologist?"

Her response was measured and icy, "I am a qualified psychiatric nurse but if you don't believe me perhaps you would like to speak to the hospital psychiatrist."

He toyed with saying something like she looked wonderful when she was angry but one look told him that while it may be true it would also be dangerously stupid. This was her ward, no doubt about that. He settled instead for looking at the name on her badge: Mandeep Patel. Then he checked her ring fingers, empty, the ones that mattered, anyway!

"I'm sorry Nurse... *Senior* Nurse Patel, I'm not familiar with this."

Her voice softened, "Evidently not detective constable... *acting detective sergeant*. Perhaps you will be more careful in future. She is badly bruised you know."

"I didn't think there had been any serious physical injury."

"I don't mean in the body."

He knew there was something he was supposed to do at this point, but he didn't know what. A nod perhaps, a sympathetic "I see!" but he thought it would sound false and that would not work with Senior Nurse Mandeep Patel. He let it pass and tried to move forward.

"Can I ask for your help in this? I need to know who she is, where she came from and why. If you hear anything from her can you let me know?" He took a card from his jacket pocket and gave it to her. She looked at the card and pocketed it as they bade each other farewell. King made his way purposefully towards the door, he didn't look back, he didn't dare. So he didn't see Patel staring after him for a few more seconds than necessary. A smile played on her face as the door closed.

Di Sanders paced about restlessly at home then her phone sounded. She let it go for a couple of turns and then answered.
"Diane Sanders, hello."

"Di it's Simon." She felt a frosty blanket wrapping itself around her.

"Yes Simon, I know. You've already caused me enough grief. I've changed your name on my phone to Bastard, just to let you know! What more have you got to say?"

He paused half a second while her tirade sunk in.

"I know you're hurting but for goodness sake, Di, you're a detective sergeant, and you're good at your job!"

"I'm neither at the moment, remember!"

"Sorry. But I still think you'll want to know this. Let's meet! Come on Di, there are no strings attached, we're not lovers anymore."

"Were we ever?"

Preston fell silent. OK so they weren't together any more, they probably never had been. But there must have been something, otherwise why did they persevere? And that something hadn't just disappeared no matter how impossible and unworkable it was.

She broke through his thoughts, "All right we'll meet."

She still didn't know why she said it long after she finished the call.

Here she was again, settling down to another nightshift in the darkened reality of the paediatric ward. It had only been a few days since she was last there, when she had come across the Carter boy's nightmare. It wasn't much fun filling in for the registrars when they fell sick. Doctors weren't supposed to fall ill, it was a poor image for the trade. So she had been lumbered.

She was in the process of looking at everyone on the ward before going off for a cup of coffee. She asked the staff nurse about each of them as she walked past and consulted the sheaf of notes in her hand at the same time.

After the round was over she did what she had promised herself from the moment she started on the shift: she went to the doctor's mess for a coffee. It was eight o clock in the evening, there weren't many people left. A few F1s and F2s required to be on call with the registrars through the night, and some of the accident and emergency staff getting a break before the maelstrom of late evening.

And much to her surprise Paul Bowes was sitting alone at a table. She walked up and tapped him on the shoulder.

"Hi, I'm just going to get a cup of coffee."

Bowes looked up. "Hello, sorry you got lumbered. Trust Martin to get ill."

She hadn't realised she was filling in for Tench. She collected her coffee and returned to Bowes' table.

"So why are you here at such a late hour?"

"There's a girl up on the third level with acute asthma. We had to ventilate her and she wasn't taking it well. I stayed to try to keep her calm. I was just taking a break before going home."

"Do I need to know about her?"

"She'll be fine, the on duty F2 knows where you are if she needs you, but she won't."

He had always been a friend, a bossy, picky, sometimes hectoring one, but still at base level a friend. Just recently he had been distant but not completely out of reach.

"Paul, is everything all right at home?" It was a question out of the blue. She didn't even consider it before she said it.

"Why do you ask, am I behaving differently or something?"

"Frankly yes. You have been strange in the last couple of weeks."

"Sorry, things have been building up a bit."

"But you and Sarah are OK aren't you?"

He sighed, played with his cup, and then without looking directly at her he replied, "It's not great. We've had problems for a while."

"Paul I'm sorry I had no idea."

"Well I can't bring personal problems to work, there are enough here already. It's just that I don't feel like going home at the moment. The only other alternative is to go for a drink before facing it. But you know what that can lead to."

She knew, she'd travelled the same road at a slower speed. Alcohol is a proven anaesthetic. They lived to get rid of pain, why not their own!

"Is that why you were in the hospital the night this Jack boy died? You should leave it to the registrars, Paul, that's what they're there for."

Bowes looked at her in a way that she thought might have been uncertainty.

"How did you know about that?"

Of course it wasn't general knowledge. No one else had spoken to her of it in the hospital, she'd heard it from Preston.

"The reporter, Preston, told me."

"What are you doing talking to him?"

"I ask myself the same question, I won't be again, though! How come you didn't say anything about it?"

"It wasn't important, like this isn't important tonight. But I repeat why talk to that man?"

It was Louise's turn to look confused. "I can talk to who I like, Paul. In case you've forgotten we were both held at gunpoint. Anyway there's supposed to be some kind of bond between people who've shared a trauma but not so much here. Enough of that, it must have been a shock, the boy died after you saw him. Have you seen the police?"

Bowes looked at her quizzically and the pause suggested he was going to pursue the Preston issue, but instead he said, "Yes, they needed to speak to me straight away. And yes, it was a shock, he was getting better, he was young and everything about him seemed to be healthy apart from his wounds."

"Sepsis, perhaps?"

"No sign of it anywhere. I want to know what the post-mortem has to say because this happened on my watch and I came into this to make kids better, not kill them!"

"So, no ideas?"

"None, I heard the commotion and saw the reporter and detective Sergeant Sanders so I put a stop to it. I left shortly after the boy had calmed down."

"So, you're not under investigation or anything like that?"

Bowes looked at her bemusedly. "Good lord no! Should I be?"

"Why not Paul, you're a witness, you might even be a suspect."

He looked at his coffee and then back at her, uncertainly.

"Don't joke about it, Lou, I can't find anything funny in it."

Paul Bowes, dedicated to kids, ignorant of the ways of the world.

"So what did you do to the boy when they had gone?"

"Absolutely nothing. That's the point, there was no need. I thought there might be some danger he was getting overexcited and that could damage his wounds. But apart from that there was nothing I felt I needed to do."

"You're absolutely sure, Paul!"

His eyes narrowed and his voice cooled.

"Yes, I'm absolutely sure and now I'm being questioned by my own senior registrar. Thank you very much Louise, that's all I need!"

Didn't he see how serious this was!

"Paul you can't keep quiet about this, at least two other people believe you were the last person to see Jack alive; a reporter and a police officer at that. The light is being shone straight at you, don't you realise?"

Bowes stared down into his coffee cup again.

"You might take up poetry if medicine gets too much!"

Exasperating man! There was a time when she harboured more than friendly feelings for him. But it had been impossible. He was married and dedicated. She would not compromise that. But she felt for him now, staring into a coffee cup not wanting to go home with suspicion beginning to gather. She reached across and patted him on the arm. He looked up at her and smiled ruefully.

The nightshift on a children's ward was always active, sometimes busy but rarely boring. Unwell kids had a way of continuing to be unwell in darkness; adults often had learned to sleep through their discomfort. So, Dr Brown was kept engaged enough to stay awake and alert.

In a rare respite she sat in the staff room with a livening coffee and started on the night's paperwork. Then she noticed something missing: where was Nicholas Carter? She wouldn't describe her memory as encyclopaedic, but it was certainly very good and accurate. He was there a couple of days previously and his nightmares still burned her memory. There was nothing unusual in patients disappearing from wards, there was a high turnover. But the Carter boy had only just been brought in and there were a lot of questions hanging over him. She had alerted her whole department to his potential risk, and he still had bowel problems, at least he ought to have, they were unlikely to have cleared up in a couple of days, especially in his state of nervousness.

So where was he.

She got up from her desk and walked back into the ward to check. After all she might have missed him, improbable as it was. There were twelve beds occupied and she walked past every one checking the names, just in case he'd been moved from his previous spot or there had been an administrative mistake.

But he wasn't there!

She went to the staff nurse.

"Jane can you remember what happened to the boy with bowel problems? His name was Carter."

"Sorry, It's my first shift for five days. I remember him coming in, but I assumed he got better."

"I'm just surprised to see him discharged so soon."

"His details will still be in the weekly file."

"Thanks Jane. Everything else all right."

"Smooth as a baby's bottom."

"Very funny!"

She headed back to the office and dug out the file on the desk laptop

Nicholas Carter had been discharged two days after she had alerted her colleagues to his condition.

Yesterday.

But what opened her eyes wider than anything else and forced her to stifle a small gasp was the signature on the discharge note.

He had a list which if it grew any bigger would need a stone monument. Not that he wanted that, he wanted them all to just *go away*. They had been nobodies counting for nothing. What was an orphan kid? What was an old man?

But it should stop there because once they went beyond nobodies and started killing the somebodies to protect their skins questions would be asked by people he couldn't control.

It was bad enough: a nosy reporter, a nosy doctor, and a nosy policewoman, all of them somebodies. He liked to think he had it all covered but things kept happening and something needed to stop one of them to halt the momentum.

Crown courts have a different flavour to magistrates' courts. The lower courts deal with the less significant infringements of the law, so their bleak aspect reflects the ceaseless grind of daily small-time lawbreaking.

Crown courts have a more serious atmosphere often reflected in dark and austere surroundings dating back centuries to the old assize courts. The difference is also in the accents heard in and around the waiting areas, and in the courts themselves. Cut glass public school barristers mingle with well-healed middle class solicitors. For the most part the defendants are kept away from this club because they're behind bars, in the company of a police or prison service jailer.

Humphries sat with John Maclean, waiting. Maclean's wife Pauline was with him as ever, even though she would be a witness in the case. The Macleans had no criminal record, nor any dealings with the police before now. This was their baptism, and if Humphries hadn't been so disgusted with the nature of the charges, and hadn't already found them guilty himself, he would have felt sorry for the simple man and his devoted wife. But he was frustrated by Maclean's pigheaded persistence. It was hard to deal with people if they would not recognise and confront themselves. Denial was all very well, but this refusal had gone on for too long. Maybe it was by the immensity of what he had done? Perhaps he couldn't bring himself to admit his actions to himself. Maclean would plead not guilty today as he had done throughout. Humphries had little experience of this kind of case and he was praying that this hearing would end it for him and he could wave the Macleans goodbye.

Maclean was not being kept in custody, he was due to appear in Court Number One. It was a full day by the looks of it. Police, lawyers, witnesses, and members of the public filled the functional reception area which gave directly on to the courts. All of those were expected, but it was rare to see a reporter at Crown Court these days so when Humphries caught sight of Preston he was surprised and suspicious.

Maclean saw him as well but his reaction was different: he caught the reporter's eye and gave him a nod. Preston returned it with a smile. Humphries witnessed the exchange and put his hands to his temples.

"Do you know that reporter, Mr Maclean?"

"I do, we met the other day."

Humphries' anti-media caution nearly made him shout at Maclean but he managed to hold it back. Instead he stared at the reporter and prayed that the judge would maintain anonymity.

Preston was there because he thought he should be and it took some convincing Geoff Donald, but he gave in. The set of circumstances which had led him to hear about the case in the first place had made him curious enough to look up Maclean on the internet and pay him an unannounced visit. He had taken the time to watch the David Maclean video Sanders had accidentally blue-toothed to him. He had been curious enough to listen to the Macleans tell their story while he sat back and didn't interrupt. He had also been curious enough to have a glance at the Maclean's personal records, kept in a separate file and backed up, thanks to Pauline, on a USB pen drive.

And curious enough to drag off a copy because he was beginning to think there was more to this than met the eye.

The one thing he had not done was contact Di Sanders. She was still suspended and he couldn't bring himself to do it after their last exchange. But he knew she had interviewed Maclean, and he wondered why the case was going ahead without her being there.

Defendants not in custody tend to wait outside the courtroom for as long as possible before going in, no matter if they're eventually found guilty or innocent. The ushers, clerk and prosecution lawyers had been inside for at least ten minutes before Humphries brought Maclean into the chamber and the usher put him in the dock. Maclean sat there quietly, looking dignified.

The usher called for silence in the court and demanded that everyone stand as the judge walked in, bowed to his clerk, and sat. The rest of the courtroom sat on cue. Preston had taken a seat in the public gallery to avoid attracting attention.

"Mr Maclean will you stand please?" came the quiet voice of the clerk, a woman in her mid-forties who had seen most kinds of defendant in her time.

Maclean rose awkwardly.

"Are you John Maclean?"

Maclean looked to his lawyer for guidance, then quickly answered, "Yes."

"Mr Maclean you are charged with acts of gross indecency against a minor namely David Maclean, aged five years, and your adopted son. Do you understand the charge?"

Maclean winced slightly as the words filled the courtroom.

"Yes, I do."

"And how do you plead, Mr Maclean, guilty or not guilty?"

Maclean hesitated. He cleared his throat and the words seemed to struggle out.

"Not guilty."

The clerk noted down the response. "Very well, Mr Maclean." Then she looked up at the judge who confirmed her next action, "Proceed with swearing in the jury."

The judge directed his gaze towards the empty press bench, then caught Preston's eye in the gallery.

"I presume there is an identity issue here!"

The counsel for the Crown Prosecution Service responded in a stuttering public school accent, "Yes M'lud. The boy is a minor and should not be identified."

"The defence concurs, M'lud," added Hoskins.

The judge addressed the lawyers and public.

"I am aware that there are members of the media here even if not seated at the normal station. I hereby make an order that the name David Maclean shall not be published nor anything which might lead to his identity being disclosed."

The clerk again spoke to John Maclean, "You may sit down Mr Maclean."

The process of swearing in a jury commenced. Preston relaxed back in his seat. It would take time. Out of any twelve there was a good chance one of them could not read or was too simple to understand what was happening; there would always be someone who was unsuited to the task, they had to be screened.

Preston pocketed his pen and made his way into the general concourse. It was still busy although many had now been syphoned into the courtrooms. As he walked towards the coffee shop he passed a dapper looking man in a suit with a concerned look on his face. He thought he ought to know him but he had no idea why. The thought passed and he walked through to the cafe where he ordered a coffee and sat with it.

His meeting with Maclean had been cordial but stiff. Maclean was a simple man who resolutely denied any form of abuse against the children who had come into his care. He and his wife were suspicious at first; how had this pushy television reporter got hold of their address in the first place and how did he know about the case? But slowly they had warmed to him. The man was living on the edge and gave Preston the feeling he was being pushed about by events of which he knew nothing. And there was one other thing. Sergeant Sanders was no longer on the case and it had been taken over by a Detective Inspector from CID. Not a family specialist, just an ordinary copper.

"Any idea what David was doing before he came to you?" he asked at one stage and had been surprised by the answer: of course they knew, they had records of all the children in their care! They kept the digital files and hard copy back-ups.

If Maclean went down he would have to be given Rule 43 protection inside the jail. Other inmates hunted down sex-offenders and thought nothing of mutilating them. Child abuse was the worst offence of all to those inside who carried their own code of honour. The nonces weren't always helped by the prison staff. A careless shift change, an accidental turning of the eye while the rule 43 prisoners mixed with the rest during a football match or a work detail. If Maclean went down he would be in trouble.

But such was the simplicity, and dare he say, even innocence, of the man, that these things would not have occurred to him. It took time to get their confidence but finally they told him what the case against them was supposed to be: the evidence of a doctor, a social worker, the boy's interview and a police interview.

Preston could afford to be doubtful, it was his job to ask questions and not accept the answers. He thought there was doubt over Maclean, because of the intensity of his denial. Some people can act that, but Maclean was not that kind of person, he was too uncomplicated and lacked the skill to deceive.

Preston returned to the public gallery. Time dragged in the courtroom. The jury was taking its time, not everyone was keen on the idea of having to witness what could be several days of harrowing detail about child abuse. He overheard the judge in an aside to the clerk and for the benefit of the two counsel.

"I don't think we shall be ready to make a proper start until after lunch". Preston pocketed his notebook and left the court. He checked his phone and called the newsdesk to explain the progress or lack of it. Donald was not pleased.

"I can't tell a judge to get on with it, Geoff," he said. Donald knew that was true despite his protestations.

"All right, but before you go, Simon, there's a development on the Jack business."

"What's happened?"

"Somebody phoned in half an hour ago and wanted to speak to you. He sounded quite young and of course he wouldn't leave a name."

"Where's the Jack connection?"

"This kid mumbled something about knowing Jack and everyone else at the James Institute. He was there himself."

"And you let him go!"

"I didn't have much choice. I offered to put him on to someone else but he wouldn't have any of that. He wants to speak to you and no one else. It sounds brilliant if we can get to him."

"Oh boy are you not kidding. Listen if he calls again give him my number. We don't want to lose this."

"All right, but don't forget what you're supposed to be doing today. We need it for tonight's lead."

He knew his job. Today was always more important than tomorrow in the news game and yesterday never happened.

The trial finally got under way at 2pm and, as the prosecution laid out its case, it became clear that Maclean was in trouble.

"Ladies and gentlemen of the jury you will be required to see and hear distressing matters in the coming days. Matters that all of us would rather not have to confront, but nevertheless we must. It will be my duty to bring out details which you may find depraved. Sadly, that is the nature of this prosecution.

"We shall prove that the accused, John Maclean, wilfully abused the trust and responsibility placed in him as the custodian of an adopted child. It is our submission that this abuse of the boy, namely David Maclean..."

The judge interrupted, "let me remind any members of the media that any public naming outside this courtroom will be a serious contempt of court!"

"Of course, M'lud. We will say that David Maclean was subjected to regular physical abuse since the time he entered the Maclean family home."

Preston looked at Maclean in the dock. Was there a nod of the head, or was it a shake? The barrister's public school tones broke in, "You may hear from the defence that the defendant denies any association with these activities. We shall say that the proof of abuse is there, and we ask, who else could have done it?"

He went on to outline their case and then said, "The prosecution calls Mrs Valerie Jenkins."

A petite woman verging on middle age told the court her name and profession; teacher.

"Mrs Jenkins do you know a boy called David Maclean?"

She did.

"Will you tell us what you know of him?"

"I had always thought him a listless boy but I took that to be his nature."

"When did you begin to feel there was more to it than simply a disrupted childhood?"

"David never said anything but his friends in the school started mentioning things."

She paused, uncertain of her next step.

"Please go on."

"They referred to parts of the body and certain activities which seemed wholly inappropriate in children so young. It became clear quite quickly that they weren't talking about themselves, but they had heard it from someone else. It was David Maclean. A few questions was all I needed to identify him."

"Did you talk to him about it?"

"Yes, I started straight away."

She told the court what she had learned while it sat in silence. A couple of women on the jury turned their heads, a man appeared flustered with his face turning red and contorted in a rage he was trying to suppress.

"Did you ask David who had done this to him?"

"Yes I did. He would not tell me. He said if he did then they would get him."

"Who would get him?"

"He only ever said he had been told never to say anything to anyone."

"And yet his playground friends found out?"

"He probably thought they were safe to tell."

Preston's hand stayed in mid-sentence. His pen remained poised over his notebook.

Isn't this an exact copy of what the late Jack had told them?

Humphries watched the teacher give evidence and made notes. Every now and again he thought of his own two children then looked at Maclean. There wasn't much their counsel could do with Valerie Jenkins. When it came to his cross-examination Hoskins went gently, he started by complimenting her on her sense of duty; she lifted her head in response as she gave a perfunctory, "Thank you".

"Mrs Jenkins, is it possible to be overcautious perhaps?"

"It's difficult to see how you can be overcautious with the

welfare of children."

"But is it possible that in your concern for his welfare you might have been too zealous. For instance, regrettable though it may be, children do pick up language and habits in the playground which they freely exchange."

"I am well aware of the nature of young children. There is a considerable difference between what I heard and what you imply."

"But could it have been the workings of a precocious imagination, Mrs Jenkins."

"No, David is an ordinary pupil with no great imagination, what I got, or at least sensed, was fear."

Humphries caught the hesitancy in the barrister's face, so did the jury.

He recovered, "Would you accept that he may simply have been playing games. After all he named no one?"

"Fear is something you can smell sometimes. David was afraid. All things are possible but I doubt it in this case."

"Smell, Mrs Jenkins, are you sure of that? It sounds like the sort of thing you see in gangster films."

"Very well, to say I literally smelled it may not be accurate, but I have no doubt at all that I sensed it."

Preston felt his phone vibrate in his jacket pocket.

He got up from the public gallery and went to the foyer, where he checked the number and called the newsdesk. Geoff Donald answered.

"He's contacted again and will call you on your mobile."

"Christ!" spluttered the reporter, this court case would have to wait, he needed to be with his telephone, and that could not operate in a court of law, not without being done for contempt.

"Ok, this will finish for the day soon."

"What's it like by the way?"

"Grim, you wouldn't want your kids to hear it. I'm not sure you'd want to hear it yourself."

"Will he go down?"

"Not much doubt if today's anything to go by."

He ended the call and left the court precincts. He did not see the Ford driving towards him from the car park, nor did he see the driver's face when the car mounted the pavement directly in front of him and caught him a full blow on the hip. He saw the car speeding and an inexplicable instinct told him to get the registration number but he couldn't make one out, it looked like the plates were masked. Clever, dodge the court CCTV! Then he was overcome by pain and fell to the pavement. There was no one else around. He tried to stand, but it was hard work. His hip wouldn't support his leg. He stumbled and fell. Gradually control returned to the hip, and with it more pain. Was it broken? There was no help in sight. He grasped the phone which had fallen to the ground with him and was about to dial the emergency number when it sounded. He answered automatically and was about to gasp out his name but was interrupted with a voice disguised by a very poor southern Irish accent. "You got off lightly this time but we're not joking, Preston.."

"Who is this?"

"Get out of this while you still can! You've seen what we can do."

"Who the fuck are you?"

"Stay away from Maclean, stop looking at Jack. That's a final warning."

The line went dead again. Despite his pain he tried to see the number of the last caller but it had been withheld, of course it had. No phone number, no number plate, they knew what they were doing.

He called 112

In all the time he had been lying on the pavement no one had passed in one of the city's busiest thoroughfares.

"Emergency which service do you want?"

"Ambulance!"

The pain started to affect his consciousness, he was going into shock.

Stay away from Whom?

Maclean's barrister, Hoskins, seemed to be making matters worse, but that was not hard. It was child abuse and no matter what the judge may say or instruct, the jury will often make up their minds from early on. Humphries had been in courts enough to know that at least and a study of their faces after the first hour told him which way it was going.

By then it was established that the boy had been abused, the only issue in contention was whether this man, John Maclean, had committed the acts they had been forced to hear about.

There would be wise heads on the jury, of course, there always were. But the flow of feeling was against the man in the dock.

Humphries carried on mechanically taking his notes. Valerie Jenkins had been a proper witness. She had been outraged by what she had heard. But she was dispassionate in giving her evidence.

The prosecution continued, "Sir we call Dr Martin Tench."

A dapper man in his thirties walked into the court and entered the witness box, the man Preston had seen in the court concourse earlier. He looked at ease as the usher asked him to take the oath.

"Take the Bible in your right hand and repeat after me!"

Tench did as he was told holding the book firmly.

"I swear by Almighty God."

"I swear by Almighty God."

"That the evidence I shall give."

"That the evidence I shall give."

"Will be the truth."

"Will be the truth."

"The whole truth, and nothing but the truth."

Tench completed the oath confidently, a man perhaps familiar with this sort of procedure.

"Your name and profession please!"

"Martin Tench, senior registrar paediatrician at St Giles Hospital."

"And as a paediatrician you specialise in the treatment and care of children.

"Correct."

"Dr Tench does that work include the examination of children for evidence of abuse?"

"Unfortunately, yes, it's not a part of the job that any of us looks forward to."

"Understandably doctor, but no doubt a very necessary one."

"Sadly, yes."

"Doctor were you responsible for the initial examination of David Maclean?"

"Yes I was."

"Can you remember the circumstances in which he was brought to your attention?"

"I believe it was a referral from the social services. I carried out a formal examination."

"Now members of the jury you may find this uncomfortable but I must ask you to bear with me: doctor what was the result of your examination?"

"I found the boy had been abused on what seemed to be several occasions. He also carried some quite recent bruising."

"What was the nature of the abuse?"

Humphries paused his pen. Why did the details need to emerge if they had already been accepted by the defence? Were they trying to turn the jury even further?

Tench revealed the results of his examination and what it meant. He spared nothing

"Doctor, did you ask David Maclean who had done this to him?"

"Yes, I did. He would not tell me. He said it was a secret and he wasn't allowed to tell."

"Did you get any indication of who it might have been from your examination or from the boy himself?"

At this point, and not before time thought Humphries, Maclean's barrister rose and spoke firmly, "My Lord I must object to this. The doctor is being asked questions beyond his level of competence. Surely we cannot allow his evidence to become hearsay or nothing more than uninformed opinion!"

The judge looked down sternly and cleared his throat. "You are right, Mr Hoskins. Doctor, you will disregard that question, jury you will ignore it."

"In that case that is all, M'lud."

Hoskins rose and looked at his notes for a few moments.

"I wonder if we could go over some issues which I feel need clarifying."

Humphries studied Tench. He had remained cool and

professional throughout, as would have been expected, he was not on trial after all. His answers had been clinical and to the point. He was dressed smartly as all doctors seemed to be. It never ceased to surprise Humphries that medical people remained so immaculately turned out when they were dealing with sick and ailing people all of the time.

"How long have you been practicing Doctor Tench?" continued the barrister.

"I qualified twelve years ago."

"And have you studied any other specialisation in your career?"

"No, I did the required time on the rotation system, but I specialised in paediatrics almost immediately after."

"Would you describe yourself as an expert?"

"I have been doing the job consistently for nearly five years, I think I can call myself that."

"Would you accept that there are still areas of your specialisation which are unknown or sketchy to you."

Humphries looked at Tench to see if this openly provocative question would get under his skin. But his face remained impassive.

"I would have no trouble accepting that. Medicine has become a vast area of knowledge. I would say it was impossible for any one person to know even all of their own specialisation. I should also add, if it helps, that my position as senior registrar means that I deputise for consultants and the title is a matter of appointment when there's a vacancy, the level of work and responsibility is the same."

"But there are people more senior and more expert than you?"

"Of course, we have an upward referral system. If I cannot deal with a particular issue I will refer the patient to a relevant senior consultant. If they cannot deal with it then it goes further up to a department director or professor. All it means is that I would not presume to try to treat something about which I do not have enough knowledge."

Humphries noted the exact use of language, no shortened forms, everything was being meticulously spelled out, as if every single word was crucial.

"I am sure we are all reassured by that doctor. Can you tell me if you are an expert in the abuse of children?"

Tench had stayed calm under fire but he was clearly more wary now than before.

"It depends on what you mean by an expert. I have experience because of the nature of my work."

"Would you, for instance be able to tell from an examination quite how often a child has been ... preyed upon, and whether it was recently or took place a long time before."

At last, thought Humphries, he'd taken his time getting to it. Tench paused.

"Is there a problem doctor, you can answer the question I presume!"

"Yes, I suppose I can but not very helpfully."

"I would be grateful, Dr Tench."

"I would say that abuse could have taken place any time in the previous eighteen months."

"And can you talk of frequency?"

"I am afraid not. The test only reveals that abuse has taken place. We look at tissue recovery to gauge how long ago it will have been."

"So to sum up doctor you are not an expert in this field and you cannot be sure if the abuse took place any later than eighteen months before your examination."

Tench's face twitched. "That's not what I said. I told you abuse could have taken place in that eighteen months but I cannot say if it happened any earlier."

"Nevertheless, your evidence clearly says that David Maclean was abused eighteen months ago, and quite possibly no later than that?"

"That is your interpretation, not mine!"

"Come now doctor, you either say it or you don't. You have told the court you cannot categorically say when and how often he had been abused except that the last time it happened was in the eighteen months previous to your examination of him."

"That is true!"

"Therefore it is quite possible that young David Maclean, the sad victim in all of this, was abused by someone many months before he even came to the Maclean household."

Tench paused again. Humphries looked at him and then the jury. There had been a shift in facial expressions, Humphries read genuine doubt now. This had gone well.

He also questioned himself: was it possible that Maclean had not done it?

"I suppose it's possible....but unlikely. The eighteen months is the maximum allowed under the guidelines."

"Thank you, doctor, we are grateful for your help."

Humphries noted the professional sarcasm in his barrister's voice. The jury looked thoughtful.

The judge spoke, "If that is the end of the cross examination I propose that we adjourn for the day. We will resume at ten thirty tomorrow morning."

The pain had subsided to a dull ache thanks to a painkilling injection from the paramedics. It allowed his mind to move on from the all-encompassing pain. What should he do, go to the police? He had no confidence in them at the moment. Di Sanders? She was still suspended and would not welcome him. Tony King perhaps? They hadn't exactly hit it off but he seemed all right.

As he lay in the hospital, doped by the painkillers, a grinding wheel of coinciding events was turning and getting wider as it did. They knew his phone, they knew where he was, for all he knew they'd been bugging and dogging him for days. Why?

His mind went into overdrive and fought its way out of the haze. The series of coincidences surrounding the death of Jack Smack, The James Institute, Louise Brown and the Macleans kept forcing themselves into a theory that he could not quite grasp. Somewhere they all came together but his mind wouldn't let him make the connections.

Or maybe they weren't there to be made. He tired himself, he fought to stay above the haze but was running out of energy. Slowly he sunk back into it again and consigned it all to his subconscious.

She rushed through her food for no other reason than there was nothing else to exercise her mind. She lived a life of daily boredom where she read the websites, did the household chores, took a bit of exercise and maybe read a book. The sense of injustice burned brightly and deeply with her. Why had she been singled out? All right, she had not stuck to procedure and her actions could have compromised police activities, but to suspend her indefinitely when she had actually brought in a result was just unfair. She had heard nothing from her senior officers, and a block had been put on her going into the police station. And the worst part was she couldn't speak to anyone about it, least of all to Simon Preston. If she was even suspected of talking to him again that would be the end. Tony King had rung a couple of times but it had been quick and covert. Just a general enquiry about her welfare and made from home, not the station. At least it showed he cared, there didn't seem to be anyone else who did, and certainly not the glamour boy from the TV station. He might at least have tried to call her even if she wasn't able to speak to him. She needed friends right now and she didn't have any.

A woman on her own, rising too fast within the force, being brought down a peg or two and with no one in or out of the station to turn to.

She scraped the last few scraps of food from her plate as she watched the tablet. Then she stopped as she saw a picture of the crown court and heard Preston's voice. He gave no names but was telling the story of a man being prosecuted for gross abuse of his adopted son. She didn't need to be told who it was, she could tell from the opening. She could even remember the names: John and David Maclean.

How could they be going ahead with this case without her evidence! She had carried out the initial investigation, she had even done an interview with David, such as it was. The real evidence had come from the doctor and the teacher.

Then she snapped. She put her meal tray to one side and picked up the telephone. She knew the direct line to the superintendent's office and she didn't stop to think as she dialled it. What were they playing at!

The phone rang once before being answered.

"Sir, this is Diane Sanders and I know I'm not supposed to

call but why is that abuse case going ahead at the crown court without me?"

The soothing voice at the other end made her all the more frustrated.

"Di, you're under suspension, the matter was handed to Detective Inspector Spencer."

"Sam Spencer!" she almost choked as she spat the name down the phone, "He doesn't know a child abuse case from a giraffe."

"I shouldn't say any more, you're already in enough trouble."

"At least tell me if my evidence is being used."

"I'm afraid I don't know Di. Spencer carried out the investigation and he no doubt put forward whatever he thought was necessary. Now you had better get off the line!"

She didn't bother with the proprieties, she just slammed down the phone. Now she was mad, very mad, and she needed to know a lot more. Was it worth calling Tony King, was it even worth calling the glamour boy? One thing was certain, doing nothing was no longer an option.

The doctor's voice broke through

"Are you feeling better, Mr Preston?"

"I feel no pain."

"Good. We've had a look at the X-rays and nothing seems to be broken but you are very badly bruised."

"Does that mean I can go?"

"It will be painful for a while and you'll need supervised medication."

"You mean morphine-based pain killers!"

"You're very well informed, Mr Preston."

"I've been down this road before Doctor, in this very hospital."

"Of course you have. You are something of a celebrity aren't you!"

Preston's phone sounded.

"Excuse me please Doctor!

"Of course."

Preston answered but the medic stayed.

"Simon Preston, who's that?"

It was a thin voice, young, Preston realised who it was.

"Don't tell me who you are, even less where you are. I am in the hospital at the moment and I can't make any arrangements. Do as I say!"

The doctor looked on quizzically.

"Write me a note saying who you are and where to meet, then bring it to the hospital and give it to the reception area. Don't bring it to my ward or you'll become known. No one will know if you just deliver an envelope to reception - it happens hundreds of times a day, You could be anyone."

He waited for a response. There was a pause of about four seconds.

"Why?"

"I can't tell you. Please just do it!"

Another pause, then, "All right".

The line went dead and the reporter put down the phone.

He looked up at the doctor.

"Mr Preston, You should try to rest."

With that he turned and walked off. Preston did as he was told and tried to relax; he was helped by the meds.

As his mind drifted and he stopped thinking he realised that the link was already there, they had provided it themselves. Thankyou!

A threatening call and an attack, but they had made the connection: "Stay away from Maclean, stay away from Jack!"

Whoever and whatever it was, it was the same outfit.

King no longer had any idea for how long he had been trying to get any sense out of Elsie. The days merged with the weeks and hours into a grey sludge. He trudged wearily through the hospital corridor to the geriatric ward where she was still being kept. It had been weeks now and under normal circumstances the unit manager would have farmed her out somewhere else. But here there was nowhere else to take her. She appeared not to have a home, nor even a name. Furthermore she refused to get completely well. At least that was what Senior Nurse Patel had told him.

"It might be the first time anyone's ever looked after her," she'd said, "She wants more of it."

More of being on a cold, clinical hospital ward with no visitors or friends?

"Not everyone gets lucky enough to take these things for granted, DC ... Sergeant King."

"Tony, please, and it's *acting detective sergeant*!"

"Tony," she'd said less confidently than the rest of her speech.

He had made two visits since his first encounter in the ward and each had been unproductive. It was true that he had spent more time on this inquiry than it warranted; Nurse Patel had a lot to do with that.

He approached the ward reception area and looked around. It was depressing. To think that a life ends up like this, coughing and groaning in a bed with no other company than other people doing the same.

DI Spencer had at least taken some of his load off but he didn't feel as relieved as he hoped he would. One lousy file, the Maclean abuse case, although admittedly he was glad to be shot of it.. Spencer had taken it on and King had been secretly pleased. He had not felt up to it. Detective Inspector Sam Spencer was just the man: plenty of experience and a safe pair of hands.

All the same, there was still a ton of work to do and his tentative request to offload more had met with a firm putdown.

"Just be grateful I'm doing this, King. The rest of it you can handle yourself. Look upon it as character building."

Spencer was old school in every way, especially in dealing with underlings. He was an effective copper who got results because he knew how bad people worked. He didn't always care for the modern ways of counselling, management and especially not computers, phones and IT. As for just what sort of character King was supposed to be building, though? He tried to beat down the resentment but some still got through. He was a tired detective who was close to throwing in the towel and admitting that police work was not for him. Is that what they wanted?

"Tony, hello again!" Mandeep Patel was warmer around him now; there was hope.

He wanted to be warm in return but the weight of it all pulled him down.

"You look tired, Tony," she said quietly so that no one else in the ward could hear.

Never go towards a woman who hasn't already come halfway towards you! King estimated that Nurse Patel had covered the required distance and he would do his part.

"Tired, yes!" then the big step, "Seeing you has perked me up." He hung on the last word hoping it was all right.

"Flirt!"

Thank god, yes.

"Guilty as charged, is it working?"

"I'll let you know."

It was.

"Is she still in the same place?"

"Same place, same face," she smiled back.

"No change?"

"Not a thing!"

He did actually care about this obstinate old woman, why, he did not know. After all there were hundreds like her and it was professional idiocy to become involved. But there it was.

"I wonder what her story is. It must be something to go to all these lengths to hide it."

"I think she's not just hiding it from you Tony, there's every chance she's hiding it from herself as well."

"That's deep."

They spoke as they strolled slowly to the woman's bedside.

"Not really. Once you've been doing your job a little longer you'll get a bit more insight into the way humans think...or not."

"But you're the same age as me..."

She faltered in her step and looked at him. They reached the bed before anything could come of his outburst. The woman lay there oblivious to everything.

The nurse spoke again.

"You do a different job to me. You only see the bad side and most of what you do requires thought, not feelings. We're different, nurses are meant to care."

King stood and listened.

"When people come in here they're at their weakest, not their worst. Their barriers tend to be down and you can see them better for what they are; better than most doctors because they're so tied up with their clinical observations and treatments they don't have time to just look and feel."

"But no-one has time for that these days?" He saw the inadequacy of the response even as he said it. "Anyway, what's all this got to do with her? She's tough as old boots."

"I think she's hurting but nothing will get her to admit the humiliation she's feeling."

"What humiliation! What for?"

"If we knew that we might have a key to unlocking her cage. The thing is I don't think even she has got that."

He wasn't stupid, nor was he shallow... not much, anyway.

The nurse smiled at him.

He relaxed and smiled back.

"Hello, this is Dr Tench."

Louise Brown's heart leapt into her mouth. She tried to avoid gabbling.

"Martin", she paused for breath, "It's Louise."

"Louise, is something wrong?"

Of course there was something wrong you stupid man. Tench's voice was clear and confident but had an air of fake concern, like he was laughing at her.

"Martin, I must speak to you."

"Evidently. What seems to be the trouble?"

Ha ha, very funny.

"Please Martin, not now. I need to find out what's going on."

"Going on where?"

Infuriating man!

"Going on between us for goodness sake." Her heart was pounding.

"I'm sorry Louise, I had no idea there was something going on between us."

She gasped loudly, the phone went loose in her hand.

"What's the matter Louise. Tell me what's on your mind."

She took a breath and tried to recover.

"Martin..." there was an involuntary pause while she fought for control of herself, "How can you say that?"

"Louise, how long have you been feeling like this."

"Ever since the night you... made love to me."

It was Tench's turn to pause.

"Oh dear, you didn't read anything into that did you?"

"Yes I did!" she mouthed but didn't say.

"I thought it was just a bit of fun for both of us. I mean you did enjoy yourself didn't you."

Oh yes I enjoyed myself, she thought..

"Louise you've gone very quiet."

People often do when they have just been kicked hard in the stomach. She gathered herself together.

"So it meant nothing to you? It was just a one night stand?" She felt weak.

"Oh god, I am so sorry. It was – it *is* – nothing more than friendship, Louise, really! I had no idea you thought differently."

Idiot woman, what had she done to herself – because it was surely her. Her grasp tightened on the phone, she gathered herself and tried to brazen it out.

"Silly me, I just thought it was too good to be just another night in the sack."

"I'm so sorry Louise," he was less false now, "But I'm sure I did nothing to lead you on did I? Please forgive me if I did, I really didn't mean that to happen!"

In a way it was a relief. No, he had done nothing to lead her on. She had made all the running on the night and he had done nothing since to nurture it. She felt foolish and wanted to end the call as quickly as possible.

"I'm sorry to have bothered you, Martin. I've obviously got hold of the wrong end of the stick."

"I feel bad now. I had no idea you lay such store by it. What can I do ....?"

"I have made a teenage mistake and I only have myself to blame. I'll see you later in the week. Goodbye now."

She ended the call hurriedly without waiting for his final acknowledgement then took a deep breath and started to cry quietly.

Alone again.

"Hello again Elsie."

"Who!"

"Doris then."

The old woman sighed, "Oh, it's you!" Her face was unrelenting.

"Do they teach you to be so rude in the police or were you born like that?"

Nurse Patel shot a look at King and moved to cut off any sharp-tongued response.

"You're feeling better today?"

"What's it got to do with you, girl?"

Two steps forward, one step back.

"Nothing and everything," said the nurse.

King wasn't experienced but he was quick on the uptake. He could see they were getting through. Just a chink but it was more than they'd had before.

"Why? I don't care. Why should you?"

King's unvoiced thought was that if he had his way he would not give a damn either. He was trying to get this safely dealt with. But if she couldn't be bothered why would he? He looked up at Patel and shook his head. She nodded.

"I just don't get it Elsie.. '" her eyes narrowed but her lips didn't move, "Do you want to stay here forever, because you can't you know. You'll have to go soon. I need to know where."

She stayed silent. King and the nurse walked from the bed and conferred by the nurses station.

"What am I doing wrong, Mandeep?".

"Probably not you – although you have a way of putting your size 9s in sometimes," he didn't miss the hint of a smile around her eyes, "Opening up for her now would be as hard as breaking out of a rusted cell after sixty years inside."

"You mean she's trapped inside."

"My but you learn fast DC King."

"But surely she can give me her name. What's secret about that!"

"Nothing to you and I. It could be everything to her. Maybe it's the only thing she knows for sure."

King looked uncertain, the nurse carried on..

"She may have had an incident in her childhood which forced her into thinking that everything is a secret. It must be kept, nothing must be told. By the looks of her, her entire adult life has been spent saying nothing. She would have covered it up well when she was younger, by creating another world around herself, lying to people, saying only platitudes instead of opinions."

This was getting further and further away from nicking villains, which is why King had joined CID.

"Where does all this lead us?"

The nurse withdrew a little. "Tony, I'm only trying to help. If you don't want it just say so."

His fatigue and impatience had got the better of him, he rowed back.

"I'm sorry, but this should be easy. Instead it's the toughest of the lot, and for no good reason that I can see. How do we get inside this rusty cell of yours?"

"It's hers, not mine and I'm afraid we don't. She has to come out of it, she created it, and it's her life locked inside."

"No one can stay that isolated for a lifetime."

"You would be amazed how many people can do just that. People you meet everyday. Elsie is a more extreme case than most, but you already know loads of others."

"So there's no short cut."

Nope. She shook her head then looked him straight in the eye and smiled fully.

Sanders had a feeling that no matter what she did in future, no matter if her name was cleared, she had gone as far as she was going to go in the police. She thought she'd had a chance. She at least expected to make senior rank before bowing out.

But the last few weeks had finally shown her where she really stood. The suspension would be on her record no matter which way it went. She might make it to inspector because she had passed the exams and she couldn't do much harm there. But any more than that she might as well forget and start planning for an early retirement. The writing was on the wall in big graffiti: YOU'RE WASHED UP SANDERS!

Every now and again she would try to cheer herself up by saying: It can't be as bad as all this. It's just a mistake, soon I can go back to what I was doing. But no-one had spoken to her, no-one dared. Tony King tried every now and again, but he was so furtive about it. She was on suspension and in Purdah.

She toyed with the idea of calling King just to talk if he could manage it. The hell with it. She wanted a shoulder to cry on and the only one she could think of was his. That was stupid, how could she maintain any authority and do that? But what authority? It had been blown to pieces in the last few weeks. She might as well call him anyway.

She scrolled and tapped on his contact.

King was quick to answer. He was at home on a brief visit between duties. He was only there to change his shirt, there was not much time, he had to get on. It was probably the nick trying to find out where he was.

"Tony, it's Di!"

"Hello Sarge. Should you be calling me?"

"Any reason why I shouldn't?"

He heard the hesitation in her voice. This was not the Di Sanders he knew.

"I've been told to stay away from you by the guvnor. And you shouldn't be trying to contact me by rights."

"Who told you not to see me?"

"The super."

"Why!"

"Because you're suspended, I suppose."

"Tony..." she tried to stop herself from crying but she could not do it. "...It's just not fair!" the last was forced out in anger which failed to mask her sobs, "I have to talk to someone, Tony, and I just don't have anyone. This is awful, and I don't see how it will get any better."

She was a strong woman and had only lost control for a moment. But it was a crucial moment for Tony King.

"Look ...Sarge...Di, Shall I come round for half an hour?"

"You're taking a risk if you do."

"It can't be that much of a risk can it. I'm not breaking any laws. I'm not even breaking any rules as far as I can see."

"No but you're disobeying an order."

"Well you always cared more about that sort of thing than I did. That's the ironic thing about this whole business: you've always been the one for sticking to the rules and you're suspended for breaking them."

"You don't need to remind me, Tony."

King looked at his watch. He was still in the middle of a double working day. He had to get on.

"I'll be free about nine. Why don't I give you a call then?"

"It would be easier if you just came around."

"OK, I'll see you then."

"And you can bring a bottle of whisky. I want a drink tonight."

King laughed. At least she hadn't lost all her CID training.

"Done!" He put down his phone.

Sanders put her phone down on a coffee table.

Why would they order King not to see her?

Louise Brown had enough self-awareness to recognise what she was doing: she had volunteered to work an extra nightshift. Anything to stop her being alone with nothing else to think about because those are poisonous hours. How many millions of people have tried to counter one obsession with another over the millennia? So she was at the hospital again concerning herself with other peoples' tragedies to stave off her own.

She pored over a set of notes handed to her half an hour before. A six year old girl transferred from Accident and Emergency with head injuries. She had been in a road accident but did not need intensive care. She was kept in to make sure there were no complications. The parents were still worried of course so she might do some good there. They were waiting by the girl's bedside. The girl looked miserable which wasn't surprising for someone who had been knocked off her bicycle by a motor car. She had cuts and bruises on her face, arms and legs and a bandage swathed around her head.

Brown looked at the notes again: no fracture but the concern was for the brain which might have been jolted by the knock and something could have come loose

She approached the parents.

"Hello, I'm Doctor Brown. I'll be keeping an eye on..." she glanced down quickly at the notes, "Jennifer tonight."

She looked up again as if to make it look as if she was checking on her condition, not trying to remember the girl's name. But she had not taken it in when briefing herself; bad sign! She would have chided a more junior doctor for doing the same thing. The patients want reassurance, so do the parents. They don't get that if you don't even care enough to learn their names.

She told herself off mentally but the two worried parents standing over the hurting child had not noticed. Nevertheless, she repeated the name Jennifer to herself silently as she bent over the bed.

"We don't think there's anything serious, and she's not showing any signs of concussion or internal damage. But we just want to be sure."

The parents mouthed their acknowledgements. She smiled at them and moved away.

This time she whispered it to herself, "Jennifer, Jennifer".

Tony King walked up the stairs purposefully. He had an off-license bag in his hand containing two bottles, whisky and Sancerre. Whatever his erstwhile sergeant wanted to have, he would stick to wine, and not much of it.

Di Sanders had made an effort to look good. Nothing special just a shower, a clean blouse and a little makeup, to keep up appearances. The bell rang and she picked up her security phone.

"Hello"

"It's Tony."

She pressed a button to release the main lock, "Come on up."

She had pushed open her door so all he had to do was go in. He stepped over the threshold with his bag and Sanders smiled from in front of the sofa.

"I come bearing whisky and wine and all manner of treats from the east."

She smiled again and took the bag.

"What have we here? Johnny Walker… and Sancerre. I also have a bottle of Sainsburys red opened and ready to go."

She poured a large glass each. He took a sip and got down to the real reason for his invitation.

"What's up, Di. You're not supposed to go flaky, even with me. I'm still your junior."

She paused for a second and then asked, "What are they all saying about me at the station?"

"To be honest I haven't heard you being mentioned."

It was the truth. Tony King was one of the lads but still reckoned to be close to Di Sanders. If anything had been said it had not reached his ears.

"That's strange in itself isn't it."

"I haven't had time to think about it. But I suppose you're right."

They both sipped at their wine, Sanders drinking more than King.

"What do you think Tony?"

"I can understand them getting het up about a few rules being broken and you went a bit far in passing the video to Simon Preston. But suspension? It didn't seem to make sense. Especially when you took the investigation further forward."

"It still doesn't, and even less that you should be warned off speaking to me."

"Yeah, that's weird. I wondered if there was more to it."

"And you're my friend. What do the rest of them think down there?"

King sat down.

"I know you're upset, Di, but why the tears?"

"I just haven't had anyone to talk to. I've made my life the police and that means that just about everyone I know works there. Any other time when you need a shoulder to cry on you go to a colleague. That's what the teamwork is supposed to mean. But when they take the team away from you it's so lonely."

She took a sip from her drink to cover a sob. It didn't quite work.

King got up and put an arm around her shoulder.

"No it's all right, Tony, I'll be all right."

She regretted saying it instantly. The arm, King's warmth, her need, said bring him back! She put her drink down on a small table, returned King's arm to her shoulder then buried her weeping face in his chest. King stroked her gently and let her cry.

"It's so bloody unfair! I'm a good police officer, why won't they let me be! What have I done that's so wrong!"

King tried fought to find the words which would explain it to both of them.

He gave up because there were none.

The coffee was disagreeable but all that was available. Louise Brown stared into its murk and forced herself to think, "Jennifer, Jennifer." She would not forget that name. "Jennifer, Jennifer." She sipped the coffee and grimaced. For the next night shift, she would bring in her own jar of coffee, a pint of proper milk, and her own mug. That would be more palatable than this stuff.

Keep busy, "Jennifer, Jennifer."

Sitting alone in the mess, her shoulders relaxed and her frown lightened. She was like someone finding a ledge on a mountain: temporary safety, but still a long way from home.

"Jennifer, Jennifer, Jennifer..."

But she was still needed, still wanted. those children depended on her, they might not live without her. They had to love her. It was a consolation.

She closed the door behind her and did not look back as she strode out towards the main corridor.

He moved his hand gently through his sergeant's hair.

"Is that better?"

"Yes," she breathed.

To be held, to be comforted, to be told everything was going to be all right. She let herself forget that this caressing was only an aspirin. It made the ache go away for a while and no more. But it was relief, she was calm.

He held her and told her that she shouldn't worry and then she became someone he had not seen before. She had to put on a stiffer mask than any of the men and she had hidden the human being behind her ambition.

"Tony."

"Yes, Sarge."

She spoke softly, "I know you're joking but it's Di tonight, or even Diane."

"All right... Diane."

"Thank you for being here."

"I thought I ought to come."

What he wanted was to take her in his arms and make love to her, but the barrier of rank was in his way.

Not in Sanders' way, though, she whispered, "Kiss me, Tony!" The barrier meant nothing to her, not tonight; very well then, it would mean nothing to him. He put his lips on hers and pressed, gently. Their tongues touched and ran and touched again. She broke off.

"You're a healer, Tony."

Any lingering doubts melted with her smile. He could do some good. He could enjoy himself. It was new. She was using him but what the hell, there are worse ways of spending time! He broke into a smile and joined his lips with hers again. This time she felt him relax fully and give himself to her.

She did the same. They broke off again and she led him through to her bedroom.

Preston's body was recovering, less so his bruised pride. He glanced again at his mobile phone; it had remained silent for several hours. The envelope hadn't been delivered yet. What had happened? He eased himself from the hospital bed and attempted a few steps. He was stiff and pain returned but he was not immobile. He still winced as he forced his hip joints into use. He set off across the ward at more of a limp than a walk but at least it was better than sitting on a bed. He had become used to most things in the hospital, it was his second visit after all. He lumbered past the empty nurses' station, through the ward door, and then with gathering speed and confidence, into the corridor.

Then he pulled himself up short.

"Simon Preston!"

"Louise... Doctor Brown!"

"What are you...".

"Doing here?"

"Are you here for a very good reason Mr Investigative Television Reporter?"

She hadn't softened since their last encounter.

"I have a season ticket, it comes with the job – get shot, get run over. We thought we'd go for economy of scale."

She didn't laugh, nor even smile.

"What are you talking about?"

"I was run down on a pavement outside Crown Court. It was made clear to me that worse will follow."

"Why?" Her question had urgency.

"Too curious about something. Do you actually want to know what or are you passing the night time hours until something more interesting comes along?

"So who ran into you?"

"It was hit and run."

"And you think you're a target?"

"I know I am; why all the questions? Have you developed an interest in me now?"

"They'll find a cure for the common cold before that happens."

"I am reassured."

"I am comforted by that."

He smiled, and to her annoyance, so did she.

She relaxed, "Is this karma? Are you paying for your sins as a reporter?" No mistaking her smile this time, she gave in to it.

"Funny! I'm paying for someone's sins, certainly." He grimaced as he forgot to keep the pressure off his hip and it told him.

"Sit down, that's not doing you any good!"

"Yes, Doc."

She found a blue plastic chair a few feet away and brought it to him.

"Thanks! Now you're caring?"

"Let's not go too far. So why would you be run down?"

He told her.

"Have you described everything to the police."

He studied her. Just who could he trust in this world at the moment? No one! But he had to make a judgement somewhere, and Louise Brown was one of the people less likely to threaten him.

"No I haven't, And I don't want you to say anything either."

She looked at him questioningly.

"Me being an annoying reporter again, I've unearthed something and I wish I hadn't."

He heard his words echo down the corridor and lowered his voice to a whisper.

"It's the care children. You know who they are?"

Her smile faded.

"I do. What's the big deal?"

"The boy who got killed, Jack, was part of it, and that young lad you were looking at, David Maclean. I've been told and warned."

Her face frosted over, "You used the information from my file!"

"Did you hear anything else from what I've just told you? Did you hear that I was run down… threatened … told to stay away from those areas?"

The faintest hint of a smile played on her lips, but not her eyes. "Of course, I heard it!" then without missing a beat, "I wonder if your meds are too strong!"

"You think this is paranoia! For fuck's sake!"

"Stop that! Swearing is violence, don't do it to me!"

Her eyes narrowed, her folded arms rose to her chest.

"Jesus Christ you're hard work!" Her stance didn't change. "Don't tell me, you're a committed Christian as well and I've just blasphemed!"

"Nowhere near, send it up as much as you like, just don't swear at me… you can swear *with* me, though!"

What was the difference, he was going to ask, but thought better of it.

"Is there just a *chance* that your imagination is running away with you? I mean it sounds fanciful to say the least – the sort of fevered stuff that fills your papers."

"Great, the evidence is staring us in the face and you're saying I've made it up as if I was some tabloid reporter. I'm not, never have been, I work in TV, different rules entirely. You'd do well to note it!"

Her face hardened and what little there was of the smile disappeared.

"Thank you for the lecture, I stand corrected. If you'll excuse me, I have patients to attend to. Good luck in limping back to your ward."

He felt his phone vibrate with a text but ignored it.

"Nice, you're sure you're looking after them, are you? From what I've learned they're no safer here than in a Dickensian Workhouse."

She turned on her heels and walked away briskly.

"Good night, Mr Preston. Get well soon, for all our sakes."

He watched her as she diminished into the night. She had a poised elegance which held his gaze until she took a right at the end of the corridor and was gone. But he still seethed and in doing so lost concentration and stressed his hip again. Without thinking the searing pain, barely masked by the painkillers, made him yell much louder than the time of night warranted.

"FUCK!"

It echoed off the walls of the empty corridor and he remembered the text. He got out his phone. Yet another from Mike Jones.

"Fuck, Presto! I'm picking up your dirty washing again. I'm at Crown Court with this Maclean thing because of you. Do you LIKE it in hospital or something?"

He quickly tapped out a reply, "The diseases not so much, some of the nurses make life easier, though!" He tapped Send then remembered the true ugliness of the Maclean case so added, "Gruesome stuff in court, try to keep neutral, but it won't be easy. Sorry you got lumbered." He pressed send again and almost instantly got a droopy face emoji back. He'd be all right, it was Jonesy after all, he'd seen pretty much all there was to see.

Tony King smiled down at her, she raised her eyes and forced a smile in return.

"Coffee or tea?"

"Tea, no sugar."

"Coming up."

He turned and went from her bedroom to the kitchen. She heard the sound of a kettle being filled, then cups being taken from a cabinet. What had she done! She lifted the duvet and looked down to confirm the evidence: yes, it had happened, willingly, wonderfully, wrongly, and now she thought, regrettably. King continued his business in the kitchen, she hurriedly found some underwear and a t-shirt for when he returned. It could not happen again and her naked state might encourage him.

He came back in carrying two steaming cups. He put one on the small table by her bed and held the other close to him.

"You got dressed quickly."

"I thought it best. Thanks for the tea, just what I need."

"Right!"

There was an awkward pause before she asked, quietly, "Are you going straight to work?"

"I'm going back to my place first, I need to change."

Then a wave of panic swept through her and she nearly spilled her tea on the duvet.

"Tony you won't tell anyone about this!"

"Who particularly?"

"Absolutely no-one particularly. I don't want this being chalked up on the Intranet notice board."

King looked crestfallen and she hated herself, but she knew she had to do this.

"Are you sorry you did it?" he asked.

She took a sip of tea while she pondered her response, then, "Yes, I am. It was a big mistake."

He turned half away from her, "Thanks a lot."

"And, no, I'm not, it was lovely."

"Er…"

"I'm sorry, Tony, but you know how this could seem. If I'm ever allowed back we'll have to work together."

"You will be allowed back, you'll stay a sergeant and you'll carry on being promoted. So will I."

"Tony, I'm your superior in rank, this is against the rules. I'm already in deep enough as it is."

"First, you're not my superior, not right now, technically you have no rank; second, that's why I came round, because it's hurting you. When you return to work, who knows where I'll be and what rank I'll have – I passed my sergeant's and inspector's early, I might even overtake you."

His energy stopped her for a moment. Logical? Yes. Sensible? Probably not!

He pressed further, "Did you ever see anything like that from me before?"

She relaxed. "No, I haven't." Then she realised what he had said and raised herself up on the duvet: "Who else have you done this with then?"

"Does that matter. If you never heard anything, then nobody else did: and they won't."

She became bold. "Is that how you kept Juliet Neilson a secret?"

King went silent for a few moments, a chastising look filled his face, but Sanders did not back away. "You're not responding, Tony, so it's true!"

"I don't know what to say, Di." He stopped as he considered how best to respond then continued, "She'd only just joined and came from outside the force…"

"I know all that, straight in as inspector, future commissioner, who knows, even Prime Minister!"

"All right, that's enough. Yes, we had a bit of fun together in her early days. She wasn't that bothered about rank and hierarchy, and we liked the look of each other. So, yes. Satisfied?"

"Are you still doing it?"

"You're kidding, she's a chief superintendent now and I don't want to piss off the Chief constable… you get my drift?"

Yes, she got his drift and already she was annoyed with herself. One night at her invitation gave her no grounds and she did not want any more than that.

"I won't tell anyone Di, don't worry."

She lay back on her pillow and sighed. "I've never heard anything about you at the nick before so you're discrete."

"Some people call it being a gentleman."

Don't push it, she thought.

"I'll go now then. Will you be all right."

"Yes. Go now, Tony."

She looked at him with a mixture of firmness and regret.

"Any time, Di."

"No Tony, just this once, but thank you."

Robin Humphries walked alongside John Maclean through the court security corridor and up to the chambers area. This day was different, the solicitor had softened his view of Maclean and was even entertaining doubts.

"I think we can take some consolation from yesterday, Mr Maclean."

His client didn't feel the same.

"I didn't like that doctor. He said I did it, more or less, and he's never even met me."

Humphries did not respond to that but moved on.

"We still have police evidence today, Mr Maclean."

"I know! And what do they know about me or my wife?"

"I have tried to tell you what they will say, Mr Maclean, it won't be easy for us today."

"But it's all lies. It's wrong, it's not fair."

"Mr Maclean, but you must understand..."

Maclean cut him off. There had been a change in him. He had always been deferent, but not any more.

"I understand well enough. I understand that you don't give a damn about me or my family. You're just picking up the money now aren't you!"

That stung.

"Mr Maclean I can assure you I am doing no such thing. You must believe I have done everything in my power to ensure you have as good a case as possible."

Even now there was respect for his position – the continued use of Mister before the solicitor's name.

"Save it, Mr Humphries, we both know how you feel. You believe them."

Humphries choked back an automatic denial because, no matter the softening of his doubt, Maclean was right.

Preston was discharged, he moved as quickly as he could off the ward and down the corridor. For once he was not alone. It was the middle of the morning and there were people about. The empty echo of the middle of the night was gone. He walked stiffly to the hospital reception and straight to the desk where an officious looking uniformed security guard was sitting behind a counter. The woman peered through prohibitive glasses as she looked up from her phone.

"Can I help you, sir."

"My name is Preston, has a package or envelope been left for me?"

The guard's manner remained officious, but she recognised the reporter.

"You are the gent on the TV I think, Sir."

"Yes, that's right. Has there been a message?"

"Not while I've been here, Sir."

"Thank you very much."

"Not at all, Sir."

Preston turned to go but the guard stopped him.

"There was one other thing sir. Someone was asking about you."

"What did they want?"

"To know where you were being kept, when you were coming out, that sort of thing."

A shiver ran down his spine as he thought, not again, where can I run to.

"What did you tell him?

"Nothing at all sir, you know we can't do that unless it's a relative."

"How did you know it wasn't?"

Preston was well aware it could not have been because neither his parents nor his brother knew about the latest accident.

"I asked him, sir."

"And he said he wasn't?"

"No, he said he was a friend but he had no way to prove it and we can't just let people through on their own say-so.

Now there was a surprise. A security operation which worked. Of course it might have been a friend.

"Thank you for your help again."

"Goodbye, sir, get well soon."

Preston moved out of the hospital entrance and looked around. So the envelope never got to the hospital which meant it had never been taken in, or the lad had been stopped before he'd had a chance to do anything. It was difficult to know how though.

He moved increasingly less slowly through the hospital car park and on to the street. Once there he realised his car was still in the car park two miles away. He cursed and thought about taking a bus.

Then he jumped, painfully, as he reacted to a tap on the shoulder. He was expecting another car to come for him, or a cosh on the back of the head, or even a knife in the ribs. He was paranoid, but with good reason.

"Are you Simon Preston?"

"Yes!" he forced the word out while his heart thumped hard.

"I think you want to see me."

Preston turned around slowly, the adrenalin still pumping, and saw a willowy young man of about seventeen. He was nothing exceptional, the voice lacked confidence, but it had depth. He had the same haunted look he remembered Jack having.

Then he realised..

"Are you the one who's been trying to reach me? "

"That's me."

Preston's heartbeat began to calm. He relaxed his tense shoulders to look at the lad who could be the key to so much of this sorry mess.

"Call Detective Inspector Spencer!" The usher fetched the besuited man waiting outside the court. Humphries watched him take the oath knowing more or less what was going to come out in the next half an hour.

"My name is Samuel Spencer, detective inspector stationed at Castletown Central Police Station."

"Inspector is it correct that you have carried out interviews with both the defendant Mr Maclean, and his adopted son."

"That is correct."

"Can you tell the court the substance of Mr Maclean's responses?"

"Yes sir. This was a recorded interview at the police station in the presence of myself and another officer."

"Thank you Inspector, I'm sure the defence will accept the normal procedure."

Hoskins rose to acknowledge.

Humphries listened unsurprised. He had been at the interview as well. There were no shocks expected here.

"The interview was carried out over a period of two hours. The actual questioning took a total of about twenty minutes."

"Just wait a moment please inspector." The prosecution barrister turned to the judge, "M'lud there is a transcript of the interview available. But I only wish to refer to certain elements of it."

The judge looked down. "Very well."

"Inspector, is it true to say that the defendant has steadfastly refused to admit these offences."

"Yes, sir, he denied them from the outset."

"And this in direct contradiction of the evidence before him."

"That is also true."

Humphries looked at his counsel expecting him to jump to his feet. He did.

"M'lud I must object. This so-called contradictory evidence has yet to be proven. So far all we have heard is hearsay and inexact medical evidence."

The prosecution rose alongside him.

"M'lud the evidence will soon be available, as I am sure my friend knows."

"That may be so, but not at this juncture. I ask that any references to my client's denial of evidence wait until they are appropriate... if they are appropriate."

Humphries maintained his detachment. He knew Hoskins was trying but he was really pissing in the wind. The prosecution had been underhand, but so what. The implication for the jury was that John Maclean had put his adopted son through unnecessary suffering by not admitting to everything straight away.

It was too late to change anything because the idea had now been planted in the minds of the jury.

Spencer read from the transcript the list of questions and responses. Maclean had resolutely refused to admit to anything.

The defence had to sit through it all. Denials were all very well and they in themselves did not incriminate Maclean. But the previous exchange was already doing its work with the jury.

"Inspector, let us now turn to your interview with the victim in this case David Maclean."

There was a rustling of pages as documents were rearranged.

"What were the circumstances of this interview?"

"This was carried out in a social services home in the presence of a social worker."

"And is there a video available of this interview."

Spencer's stance shifted, He drew himself more to attention and took a slightly deeper breath.

"No, sir, it's in note form only. There were no facilities at the home and it was thought potentially harmful to the child to transfer him somewhere else."

The judge intervened.

"This is quite unusual in these times inspector. Was it not possible to take a video camera to the home, or even your mobile phone?"

Spencer remained at attention, his responses became more clipped.

"M'lud it was thought to be disruptive to both the boy and the other children at the home."

Humphries had not challenged this before it came to court. It seemed reasonable, the children had to be protected, after all.

"And to my shame, Sir, I find modern technology a problem. I prefer to rely on my notebook and pencil."

"Proceed!" said the judge, wearily.

"Does David Maclean substantiate in any way Mr Maclean's denials?"

"Not at all sir."

"What did the boy say to you?"

Spencer looked down at his notes.

"I asked him if his father had ever touched him. He said, 'Yes, a lot.'"

He added the details.

Maclean shifted in the dock. Humphries looked at him fearing an outburst; he was right. Maclean leapt to his feet and roared to the court, "This is a lie, it's a bloody lie!" Humphries could not judge if it was faked, or whether Maclean had truly lost his reason. Whichever it was he had ruined what slim chance he had. The jury was already against him. The rage would set the seal.

The judge demanded silence.

"Mr Maclean, unless you control yourself immediately you will be removed from the court!"

Maclean heard the stern voice of authority, he quietened but continued breathing heavily.

It was a false dawn. Humphries told him to sit down but instead Maclean took a breath and renewed his attack. This time it was controlled. He knew what he was saying and he addressed himself directly to the judge.

"Sir", and there was no sarcasm in his voice, only fury, "It seems to make no difference if I am here or not. No one believes me, everyone is lying and even my lawyers think I'm guilty."

Humphries squirmed at the accusation. Maclean was imposing as he stood in the polished wood panelled dock.

"Mr Maclean, sit down!" ordered the judge.

"You might just as well sentence me now and forget this bloody jury nonsense."

Humphries winced. The judge would not like that, nor would the jury.

"You leave me no choice. Take him out until he has calmed down."

A uniformed arm reached out to take Maclean, none too gently, out of the dock and back to the court custody area. As Maclean was led away Humphries heard the sudden and unexpected sounds of him sobbing. He looked for Pauline in the public gallery. She was transfixed, uncomprehending. The door closed and the judge adjourned the hearing. Humphries looked at his watch and began to tire of the whole thing. He would be glad to be rid of this client. He had done his duty but his patience was being tested to the limit.

The press bench still had few representatives there, most outlets these days relied upon police handouts for trial reports and couldn't spare the staff for full coverage. Mike Jones was there, though, and he wrote furiously in his hardly-used, skeletal shorthand. When he'd finished he sent a summary text to Preston and added at the end, "What's up at your end?" He received a reply a minute later saying, "Hush, big development. Major new source. More follows." He wrote back, "Give me a clue, I need some relief from this shitshow!" but there was no further reply.

Preston still moved stiffly but was feeling better. His companion at a city centre coffee stall eyed him warily but remained.

"I thought they'd got to you," said Preston.

The young man had remained closed since their initial meeting 45 minutes earlier. He did not present physically as a victim, but his eyes evaded.

"Who's They?"

"Never mind, I'll tell you later. Why didn't you contact me in the hospital. I was worried something had happened to you?"

The young man toyed with his teacup and raised his eyes as he thought about his reply.

"Your voice on the phone told me something was wrong."

Preston nodded.

"There was some sort of danger, you wouldn't let me speak. I had to listen."

"Yes," Preston grunted and took a sip of tea.

"You were right, I'm not sure we're safe now."

"What's your name?"

"William. Call me Bill."

"Family name?"

He laughed, then replied," James Hyphen Institute!"

"You're the first one I've come across who's prepared to have a laugh in recent days."

"You can laugh or you can cry – it would have been easy to break down and be a loser, plenty did, but I didn't."

"Are you sworn to secrecy as well."

Bill took a doughnut and delicately sliced it with the throwaway wooden cutlery provided. Then, much to Preston's surprise, he picked up a wooden fork and delicately took a chunk into his mouth. Why he should be surprised he did not know, he was comparing Bill with Jack probably. Jack had been a down-at-heel lad, ill-educated, ill-bred as well. None of it his fault but of a definite type. He had expected Bill to be the same.

Bill replied, "Yes, I was sworn to secrecy. My name's Cooper."

Preston looked askance across the table.

"I don't think they'll remember me, and I didn't care a lot for their oaths of secrecy."

The youngster's composure surprised the reporter.

" Why won't they remember you?"

"I shouldn't think they'll remember anyone. It's not what they do. They just used us, we could have been anyone, they wouldn't have noticed."

Preston braced himself for the next question.

"What did they do to you?"

Bill paused the movement of his arm as it delivered the fork to the doughnut. He looked up assessing the man opposite.

"They beat me."

"Anything else?"

"No, I never had it as bad as some of the others," then he stopped. It wasn't a pause, it was a gap.

Finally he spoke, quietly, "Especially Jack!"

"Why didn't you get the same treatment?

"I never really understood. It might have been because I was too cocky for them. I've never been the best looking of blokes.

"They used to slap me around but I always resisted."

The fork went down and back to his mouth. They waited while he chewed and swallowed.

"I don't think they liked that."

Preston's own childhood was privileged by comparison. Here was a young man, abused and humiliated, saying he had got off lightly.

"Why have you contacted me?"

Bill looked up from his plate.

"Because you already know a lot of it. I wanted you to know it all. Just keep me out of it."

"All right, but you know what's happened in this affair so far?"

He had his work cut out protecting himself, how he could look after Bill he didn't know. He hid his thoughts.

"Where are you staying, Bill?"

"I have a place!"

"Where?"

"It's best that you don't know."

It probably was, thought Preston.

"Are you sure you're safe?"

"I'm safe enough as long as you keep your word."

Preston shivered at the trust being put in him. He did not know why, it had happened hundreds of times before and had never worried him. This was different.

"Why me; why trust me?"

"Because you're not one of them, you couldn't be. You wouldn't have done the reports if you were. You don't know how much you were risking your neck by doing them."

Yes he did, his hip told him the risks he had been running.

"But why not go to the police?"

"Mr Preston," again that unexpected civility, "It's as dangerous there as anywhere else."

"How do you know?"

"They let a few things slip. When they were off their guard they'd sometimes refer to playing cops and robbers. Once I can remember one of them saying 'Sir' and later 'Guv' to another one".

How could one so young have known those police familiarities!

"How old were you?"

"Nine or ten, I can't remember."

"When did you learn about those words?"

"I watch television, same as everyone else."

"Did you understand at the time?"

"No, I learned it later, when I was older."

"But how could you remember details like that from such a young age?"

"Mr Preston there is very little I don't remember from that time. It's not the kind of thing you forget, no matter how much you try."

Preston reflected again on his own innocent childhood. He had nothing worth remembering from it. It was too ordinary, too loving. Nothing stood out.

Bill finished the doughnut. They were silent for a few minutes.

The judge looked down wearily at the reconvened court.

"Has your client calmed down, Mr Hoskins?"

Hoskins stood, Humphries sat behind him, Maclean was back in the dock, apparently quietened, but with a security officer on each side.

"I am assured by my client that he will observe the proprieties of the court M'lud," said Hoskins.

"Perhaps we can continue, then?"

"Yes, M'lud, quite so."

Only the police cross examination remained, before Maclean himself, then the jury would go out and everyone could go home. The parent in Humphries briefly surfaced but he made the solicitor suppress it. He could not take on the problems of the world, could he!

"Recall Detective Inspector Spencer."

Spencer walked through the court again and to the witness box.

"I'm sure I don't need to remind you, Inspector, that you are still under oath," said the judge.

"No M'lud."

"Proceed!"

"Inspector, is there any doubt that David was referring to his adoptive father."

"None at all, sir."

"Could there have been a mistake? Could he have been talking about someone else?"

"Not to my mind, sir. He referred throughout the interview to 'Daddy'."

"Could that possibly have been his real father, his biological father?"

"I don't believe so sir. As far as I understand he never knew his real father, and these incidents happened at the Maclean household."

Humphries turned anxiously to look at Maclean in the dock. He stirred but did nothing. The guards looked nervous as they flanked him. Maclean was a big man.

"There can be no doubt of the location?"

"I don't see how, sir. The boy told me it happened in the family living room."

"He did not say where this family living room was?"

Spencer looked at his notes.

"I asked, 'Where did this happen?' he said, 'At home.' I said 'You mean your new home?' he said, 'Yes'. I said, 'Where in your new home?' he said, 'The living room.'"

"You see my client, Mr Maclean, says this is simply not true. No such events took place under his roof or in his presence."

"With respect sir, I took these notes in the presence of a highly experienced social worker, and they have been properly witnessed."

"Yes, thank you, Inspector,"

He looked at the judge. "I have no further questions M'lud."

It was time for Maclean himself to come to the witness box. Or it would have been but for his next move. He had been simmering in the dock throughout the session, now he lashed out with both arms. One guard was knocked sideways, the other just managed to grab an arm but could only hold on. Maclean was not being restrained, only held.

Then he roared from the dock.

"It's all over isn't it. You've stitched me up. You've made it all up." Then a brief pause before an anguished plea, "WHY! What have I done? I could not hurt David, or anyone else. Why is this happening?"

The judge banged his gavel and looked at Humphries. Humphries stared back helpless.

"Be quiet, Mr Maclean, or I shall send you down again."

This time Maclean dispensed with any remaining respect he had for the institution of the law. He looked at the judge and said, hotly, furiously, "Who gives a fuck! I'm going to be found guilty anyway, send me where you like. I want no more to do with this."

Humphries made a move to calm him again, "Mr Maclean, you are doing your case no good whatsoever..."

"Forget it, judge. I'm done for. Just hurry it up will you."

"Mr Maclean, don't you want a chance to put your case?"

"What chance have I got. I'll wait while they find me guilty."

Humphries knew that the jury process was shortening with every outburst, he would not have to wait much longer.

"But I'll say this to all of you here..." Now the voice was slightly calmer but laced with steel and determination.

"Someone will pay for what's happened here."

The courtroom fell completely silent, including Maclean. No one spoke for several seconds. The judge sighed and banged his gavel again, "Mr Maclean, you leave me no choice, the rest of this trial must be heard in your absence."

There was only Maclean's evidence left to hear anyway thought Humphries, if he refused to play ball the outcome was inevitable.

"I'm not saying any more. I've had enough, I just want to be out of it."

Not if you knew what was waiting for you in prison, thought Humphries.

Hoskins was now on his feet. "M'lud my client's reactions are regrettable but understandable."

"That may be so, but I will not have my court being used as a substitute for the House of Commons. This is a court of law where cases have a right to be heard properly and fairly."

He directed his gaze again to the dock. "Mr Maclean you

have done yourself no good at all with these outbursts."

By now Maclean's fury had withered, as strong emotions do. He did not roar back his return, but delivered it firmly, "I see no point in my speaking, sir, it seems to me that it's all over."

"That is for the jury to decide, Mr Maclean. You still have the right to be heard in the witness box if you so wish."

"No chance, no point."

He sat down, resigned, defeated. Pauline was looking at him imploringly, but he could not bring himself to raise his eyes to look back. Hoskins rose again to make his concluding remarks.

Preston and the mystery young man, Bill, were in the middle of the city's biggest park filling in details. Preston used the voice recorder on his phone, Bill refused to be videoed.

"Let's start with the old man!"

Bill took a breath and began recounting his days at the James Institute.

"Him and his wife were a pair. She didn't care what he got up to."

"Why the odd names, not your real ones?"

"None of us had names in there. We were all given silly ones, it was like they were reinventing us for their own purposes."

Again that sophistication.

"Are you really called Cooper?"

"Yes, I kept my birth certificate well hidden. They never knew I had it. I've always had a strong feeling about who I am, I didn't get sucked in like the rest. I think I was a mistake. If they'd known more about me I wouldn't have gone there. They wouldn't have risked it."

Preston wondered why this lad had such strength when everything pointed to them trying to break it.

"What did they call you?"

"Barker, Billy Barker."

"Any idea why?"

"It was a stupid name, but I think it was because I used to make a howling noise when I was hit. It hurt, they wanted it to."

Preston took some seconds to get past that.

Bill looked at him. "No I didn't like it either."

"Did Jack ever know his real name?"

"Jack never really knew much about anything. He was only average. He used to cry a lot."

"Do you know Jack's real name?"

"I always thought it was something like Bates, but I can't be sure. It was all I could do to hang on to my own name."

"Was Jack singled out for special attention?"

"I think so. I knew him quite well and he used to tell me the stories of what they did to him."

He paused. "But everyone got something from them. I just got beaten about, I was lucky."

Like you're lucky if you lose one leg but keep the other, thought Preston.

"Why did they go for Jack?"

There was an uncomfortable wait before he answered.

"He was a pretty boy and he wasn't very bright, he never fought back or resisted."

"Sometimes he'd go very quiet and not speak to anyone at all. I think he expected to be treated roughly."

"But he still cried."

"We all cried."

Preston, not for the first time in this incident, felt impotent. Why hadn't Jack thought it wrong? Surely he must have felt the endless fear was unnatural.

"How could he accept that as normal?" he asked, exasperatedly.

"Don't forget where we all came from. We had been taken into care. Something was wrong from the very beginning in our lives." He paused again. "But some had it worse than others. I struggled with the beatings but Jack was brought up to take whatever he was given." Bill looked away.

"Where does your defiance come from, Bill?"

The young man grimaced for a moment and tried to hide it. He was silent for a few moments before saying, "I'm an orphan. I lost my parents when I was five and there was no one else to look after me." He stopped for another few seconds while he held Preston's gaze. Then, "Jack was a throwaway – that's what they called themselves."

"You mean discarded by his parents?"

"He never knew who they were, none of them did."

"So they'd never known a family."

"No, and I had. I was loved, Simon..." he looked away again, "Then I wasn't."

They were talking about a different universe; Preston steeled himself and continued.

"We need to find the old man's wife."

"She could tell a lot but she probably won't," a quiver developed in the light voice: "She's an awful woman."

"She never did anything to you herself did she Bill?"

"That's not the point. We were in there because we'd been taken from our parents or lost them. She was supposed to give us support, warmth. She did nothing."

"Bill, we have to find this woman!"

"I know where she is. I always made sure I knew where they were."

Preston's eyes lifted. "You mean you've kept track of them?"

"Always. It wasn't easy, but you only need one break: that came when I saw them in town one day. I had no idea where they had gone to after the James Institute, none of us even knew their proper names. But then I saw them in the market, about three years ago. I followed them wherever they went that morning. They finally caught a bus, and I got on behind them. They lived in a small semi-detached house in one of the new housing estates."

Preston whistled. Breakthrough!

"And you know their names...or should I say hers?"

"I do now. Barnes. Felicity Barnes...and Jeffrey."

"Why have you kept such a close eye on them Bill?"

"I wanted them to pay some day, I wanted them to know they couldn't get away with what they did to us."

"Like Jack did!"

"No, not like Jack. He wasn't clever enough to know any different. And he was treated a lot worse. No, one day, when I was grown and didn't have to be scared, I was going to turn up on their doorstep and tell them who I was, and who they were. Then we'd see who was scared."

"Jack's taken care of all that now."

"No, he killed him, that bastard deserved worse than that. He deserved to be scared to death."

A cold shiver ran through Preston's body. Bill's calculated revenge would be far worse than Jack's.

"So, if Jack wasn't that clever, how did he manage to track this Barnes man down as well... did you tell him?"

"No, I didn't see Jack again after the James Institute. Anyway, he may not have been bright, but he wasn't stupid. Maybe he got lucky and saw them in the street as well. They didn't seem to care about who saw them, it was like they were invulnerable."

Until that point, they probably had been.

Di Sanders heard the security alert and looked at the small video screen. It was Preston with a youngish looking man.

"What?"

"Di, there's something I have to talk to you about. Please let us in!"

She sighed, thought about turning him away, then relented and buzzed him in. When they reached her apartment she was waiting at the door.

"Come in, it had better be good!"

"Di, meet Bill Cooper."

A young voice, articulate but unsure, interrupted before she could say how do you do, or who the hell are you!

"We've met."

It was news to her. She turned to Preston and ignored the other one. "What's this about Simon?"

"We'll tell you everything in a few minutes. Bill, how do you know Di?"

"I never forget a face, she was at the James Institute."

He turned towards her. "You had a uniform then, it was after the Barnes's did a runner. We'd been left there for two days without anything and you came along to look after us, tried to get us to say something."

She was taken aback, "You were at the James Institute?"

It was Preston's turn to butt in, "I promise you we'll give you everything in a minute Di."

Sanders kept looking at Bill. "So, I talked to you then?"

"You did, but I didn't talk to you."

"No one did as I remember."

She pointed to the living room. "Sit down, I'll make some tea."

Bill wandered into the room, seemingly unphased by the encounter, Sanders returned with tea.

"Who were the Barnes?"

"They ran the James Institute. They were the ones Jack was out to get," said Preston.

"And succeeded in getting..."

"Not quite. He died we know, but she's still around."

"Have you told anyone at the nick?"

"Only you so far, and I had trouble convincing Bill I should."

"Why me?"

"Because I don't trust anyone down there, no one at all, especially after what Bill's told me."

"OK, start at the top, and don't leave anything out."

The usher entered the courtroom to announce the return of the jury. They had been out for no more than 30 minutes. There was little doubt of the verdict.

The judge resumed his seat, Maclean sat in the dock unmoving.

"Foreman of the jury have you reached a verdict?"

"Yes My Lord, we have."

"And is it the verdict of you all?"

"It is."

"How do you find the defendant?"

"Guilty My Lord."

Maclean shook his head. His wife yelled "No!" and then slumped into her seat and went silent. The judge prepared to hand down the sentence.

"John Maclean you have been found guilty of a most serious crime. You were put in a position of trust and you abused that trust. You have tarnished the life of the boy entrusted to your care. For that I sentence you to ten years imprisonment."

Maclean winced: ten years!

Prisoners did not like child abusers. They found ways of making them pay for their crime way beyond being put behind bars. Maclean would have to watch his back, his front, his food, everything. And just in case he thought he had it cracked he would have to watch the prison staff as well because accidents will sometimes happen in jail.

The murmur in the court died down as the formalities of costs were sorted out.

"Take him down jailer!"

Preston read Sanders' reluctance.

"You don't want to believe it do you, Di!"

"No, I don't!"

"Neither do I!"

She looked away and then at Bill.

"All right, I'll accept what you say and, Bill, there's stuff you know that none of us have revealed. But it's a big leap from that to the Maclean case. They're separated by seven years. How can you prove it?"

Preston was deflated as the reality struck him. "I can't, I only have a threatening telephone call, and of course I didn't record it because I was lying on a pavement in shock."

Sanders asked herself what she was even doing listening to this.

"Are you sure the accident wasn't playing tricks on you? If you were in shock you might have dreamed it."

"I did not dream that call. It happened!"

"It's just so fantastic if it's true."

Bill looked across at Preston and his downcast eyes held a silent plea.

Preston read the look and tried again, "No one likes the idea of such a big deceit. Maybe when we hear of something as big as this we want to run and hide. It means we can't trust anyone, or anything. Not the law, not the police, nothing."

Bill looked up sharply, "I never had the luxury of trusting anyone."

For the first time Di Sanders considered properly the young man before her. She had been busy absorbing the shock of what she'd been told, but here was a young life which had been a never-ending betrayal from the beginning.

"Why are you trusting us, Bill?" she asked, quietly.

"I'm not. I'm just telling you."

"But what do you expect to gain?"

"Something for Jack, something for all of us."

"You mean justice."

"Yes, I suppose I do."

Preston chipped in, "But you don't trust justice."

"No, I don't." He stopped to consider what he was saying. "Sad isn't it!"

Preston continued, "Admit it to Di, Bill, you've virtually told me: you want revenge."

Bill became animated, his arms moved around in a whirling figure, his face reddened, his voice became harsh, and for a moment, strong.

"Yes, for fuck's sake, I want revenge! You can stuff your justice. If there was any of that in the world I wouldn't be here now, I'd be living in a comfortable house with a nice mum and dad and maybe some brothers and sisters and we'd all play tennis and go swimming in the summer."

He slumped back on Sanders' sofa, the animation gone from him as quickly as it came. There was a silent pause before Sanders spoke. "Simon this tie up with the Macleans is too tenuous, how do we make it stick?"

"Why don't we watch it again Di!"

She looked at him with frustration.

"It's in the nick, I can't get at it."

"It's still on my phone."

"You mean you kept it."

"Only for reference. It was only for the Jack stuff and I promise you I wasn't going to break our agreement. The Maclean interview was an accident. I didn't mean to copy that, but it's there."

She looked and simmered. Preston saw it and found himself intimidated but defiant.

"Di, we have different ways of doing things. I may have broken your rules, but they're not my rules. Anyway, I have not betrayed your trust."

A knowing look came over Bill's face which both adults picked up immediately. His own trust was hardly being restored by this.

Sanders sighed, "All right Simon, show me the bloody video

and to hell with all of it!"

Humphries and Pauline Maclean were led through the court again and downstairs to the jail area. It was slow progress, she could barely put one foot in front of the other and had to stop every few steps. As they inched along the echoing corridor Humphries heard two raised voices.

"Fucking nonce!"

"Bastard!"

That was followed by a thudding sound and a loud gasp of pain. There were two more thudding sounds, similar to a suitcase being hit, and the sound of desperate breathing.

Humphries looked at Pauline who had again faltered in her step. Humphries was not familiar with post-trial court cells but he knew what it meant, it had already started, Maclean faced ten years of this.

They approached the jailer who had remained unmoved outside the door to the cell.

"I'm John Maclean's solicitor, and this is his wife."

"What do you want?"

"We want to see my client," said Humphries firmly.

"I ought not to let you anywhere near here. You deserve to be hung", said the jailer looking at Pauline malevolently.

Hanged, thought Humphries but decided against the correction.

"Just let us see him please!" she replied.

There was another thud from inside the cell, and another gasp. Humphries thought he heard a sob. The jailer couldn't be bothered to argue any more. He jangled his keys officiously and opened the door. They walked in and saw Maclean lying on the ground clutching his groin. Humphries looked up to see who had inflicted this extra punishment and drew his breath sharply. There were no other prisoners in the room, just two uniformed prison officers, neither looked apologetic. One smiled and said, "He must have fallen while we weren't looking." "Slippery floors." said the other, and they both chuckled.

Maclean looked at them with a stare which suggested he would have done anything at that point to break them in half.

They saw it and chuckled again, because they knew he could never do that, not while he was in prison. And by the time he got out he would be broken himself.

"Is that the way you looked at the boys?" sneered one of them.

"It's not so easy when they fight back, is it!" said the other.

Pauline looked at them with horror, then she focused on her husband lying in agony on the cell floor. Humphries was upended by the scene. This was life in the raw, nothing like the world he knew. He dealt with papers, concepts, civilized people. He dealt with middle class England with all its politeness and respectability, and its sanitised procedures. His clients were incidental to it. They came in and out of his life and they were processed through the system and filtered through the law. Until now that processing was a matter of a filing cabinet. Now he saw what it really was, and it was only the beginning.

He looked furiously at the officers and said, "This is outrageous. I shall complain to the court and your superiors."

"What's outrageous sir?"

Humphries was silenced. He was not in a court, nor in his office: he was on their territory. They do what they like, deny what they wanted. He was powerless. All that authority as a solicitor, an officer of the supreme court, and here he was, impotent. But he still tried.

"You have clearly assaulted this man, my client, while he was in your charge."

"I'm sorry sir, you have got it wrong," replied one of them, "We were only restraining him. He had become violent. I'm sure you saw his behaviour in the court earlier."

Humphries had, and he remembered it had never been directed at anyone else.

"Officer, I insist on having time alone with my client. You are well aware of the rules."

The guards started to move. They knew the rules all right.

Humphries, now riding a wave of righteousness, continued, "I am reporting this incident immediately I leave this cell."

"Don't bother, Mr Humphries," came a still gasping voice from the floor, "You never believed me during the trial, why should you do anything now. It's too bloody late."

His wife knelt on the floor with him, trying to console him.

"John, don't say that to Mr Humphries, he did the best he could!"

Humphries swallowed hard. Had he done the best for them? He had done what he was supposed to do. He had pushed the papers, gone through the procedures, but had he done his best for them? His attitudes were being transformed in this dingey cell. He saw the reality for the first time. It was lying on the ground groaning, it was standing up sneering. It was a lightless cell setting the scene for the dark days ahead in her majesty's prison service. Then amid this gloom Humphries was struck by a flash of light. He had only seen and heard the evidence. All his judgments had been based on that, not upon the character. Maclean's character had been a mystery to him. He had recognised his resilience early but had called it obstinacy, stupidity. Now he saw the man lying on the ground before him.

"What are you doing here, Mr Humphries? Your job's done now. You can go home can't you!"

The contempt in his voice was undisguised in spite of the apparent respect.

Humphries deflected the accusing eyes by again addressing the prison staff. "I must insist that you leave." The two looked at each other, sneered again and walked towards the door.

The three were left together, and Humphries now wished the officers were still there. This intensity was unbearable. Maclean spoke again, "Pauline, even if everyone else believes I did this please tell me that you will keep faith in me!"

His voice was breaking up. She held him close. "I know John. I am going to keep fighting until we get the truth out."

Humphries felt wretched. The officers could be heard talking behind the door.

"John, I'm going to see that reporter as soon as I get out of here. He'll listen."

"He wasn't here was he, he didn't see any of the trial. He doesn't care about us Pauline."

"Which reporter are you talking about", asked Humphries.

"Nothing to do with you, Mr Humphries, you've finished now."

"John, stop that. Mr Preston from the Television news."

"Ah, I see. He knows something does he?"

"He only knows what we all know, Mr Humphries."

"Do you think speaking to a reporter will make anything better?"

"Speaking to you didn't help did it, Mr Humphries!" countered Maclean who was now sitting up.

Humphries bit back a reply. One of the officers called from behind the cell door, "That's enough. You must leave now."

Pauline Maclean looked fearful. Maclean had a look of resignation. He knew what would follow.

"Please keep hoping John!" she said, her voice imploring, then she couldn't find any more words as despair took over. They hugged each other tight. One of the uniformed men broke in roughly and separated them.

"Say goodbye sweetheart!"

Humphries railed at the inhumanity of it.

"Goodbye John," her voice tailed off at the end.

"Goodbye Pauline." His face was flat and expressionless. He was already adopting his prison mask.

The officer opened the cell door and the solicitor and the trembling wife were almost pushed out. Humphries took a last look back and saw Maclean staring at the other officer. There was no fear in his face. There was nothing at all.

They walked wordlessly back along the echoing corridor. Pauline was silent.

Humphries felt cold and uncertain.

They watched the interview on Preston's Macbook. He mentioned, unnecessarily, "I've backed it up to three cloud systems."

Sanders looked at him as if he were a boy wanting reward for doing well.

"Very clever, Simon, can we get on please!"

Bill smiled while a chastened Preston pressed the play button on his Mac.

"Hello David, my name is Diane Sanders and I am going to ask you some questions."

Her tone was businesslike but still soft. She had known not to put the boy off, although it might have seemed formulaic.

There was no response.

"I am trying to find out if someone, anyone, has ever hurt you."

More silence.

"It's all right, David, you trust me, I won't hurt you."

Young David stared, then whispered, "I'm not allowed to say anything. It has to be a secret."

Sanders and Preston looked at each other and then at Bill who nodded and then looked away.

There was more silence lasting several seconds.

Sanders pressed gently on the interview, "Was it your daddy?"

Another pause, then a very weak and uncertain "Yes".

It did not ring true. The boy did not seem to be lying, but his answer was hesitant and uncertain. Then Bill looked spoke, "Which father!"

Preston struggled to understand what he meant until it became obvious.

"You mean his natural father?

"Unlikely," said Bill, "more likely one of the so-called guests at the house.

"Huh!", said Sanders.

"There's so much you don't know yet, isn't there?" said Bill, then without stopping to register the effect of that he added, "The chosen ones were told to call the men daddy.

Preston and Sanders looked at each other again. Sanders asked, "How do you know if you weren't a chosen one as you call them?"

Bill regarded them with something which could have been contempt then said, "We lived under the same roof, they told me everything that happened to them."

The two adults looked at him expectantly.

"Jack used to speak of someone at the James Institute who insisted he call him 'Daddy'."

All three stayed silent for several seconds. Finally Preston took a deep breath and spoke, "So this network is still alive and operating."

"Yes," said Bill, I never thought anything else. Nobody ever got caught, everyone went to ground. They only had to wait for us lot to clear away somewhere and they could set up again."

"But not at the James Institute", said Di.

"No, it had to be somewhere else."

"Where!" said Preston frustratedly.

They sat in silence.

Preston broke the mood, "We have got to get to David. Do we know where he is?"

"No, but we can find where he came from," said Preston suddenly blinded with an idea. His records may have been wiped from the computers, but they're around still. Pauline has a copy."

Preston was driving and automatically reached for his mobile as it sounded but Sanders stopped him.

"For Christ's sake, Simon, it's bad enough without you causing an accident!"

There it was in one sentence, the difference between them. "You and your bloody procedures!" he exclaimed and instantly regretted it.

"Shall I answer it?" she asked, quietly.

Preston grunted assent. She picked up the phone and pressed the button. "Hello."

At the other end of the call Louise Brown was flummoxed by the familiar voice which she couldn't pin down. Temporarily off her stride she stuttered, "I'm sorry, I was expecting to speak to Simon Preston. Is he there?"

Sanders bridled at the well-modulated RP tones. She recognised them from somewhere. "Can I tell him who's calling?" she said, stiffly.

Dr Brown briefly toyed with the idea of just ending the call – no complications, no questions, no-one would ever know. But, no, she was supposed to be grown up after all. "My name's Louise Brown. I'm not interrupting anything am I?"

"Oh, it's you Doctor! What could you possibly be interrupting!" Sanders' stiffness turned to ice as she clocked the name. Then, irritatingly, Preston spoke, "Who's calling Di, come on?"

"It's your doctor friend."

"I don't have a doctor friend, who are you talking about?"

Brown smiled at the other end and then said, "Friend is a charitable word, I think we're both agreed we're not that."

"Why are you telling me?" snapped Sanders, "What makes you think I care?"

Quite a lot thought Dr Brown but left it unvoiced.

Preston raised his voice, "Just give me the phone, Di!"

Sanders' police officer mindset overruled his command and she pressed a button to put the phone through the car speaker system. "We can all hear each other now," she said, "You're speaking to Dr Louise Brown. I know you've met."

Dr Brown wearied of the row and had no intention of being its cause when there was no justification for it. She spoke firmly so that everyone in the car heard her, "I'll start again, I am Louise Brown, I can hear Simon, but who else is there?"

Sanders remained quiet, Preston introduced her, "I have Detective Sergeant Di Sanders next to me and …" Sanders grabbed his left arm and shook her head at him. He saw her turn her head to Bill and realised what she meant. "..and … and another person." While this played out Bill sat impassively in the back looking at the couple in front and listening to the conflict.

"Who?" Asked Dr Brown.

"It doesn't matter. What can I do for you?

Preston said with a calm voice, "Doctor Brown, I'm in the middle of something important right now..."

"Right, so is this."

"What?"

"Mr Preston… Simon… much as I hate to do this I think we have something in common and I need to tell you about it."

"Yes?"

"It's to do with those files you saw."

"What files, Simon?" demanded Sanders.

A mental switch flipped, Preston read the connection and moved quickly, "That's enough on this phone, Doctor Brown, stop now! Let's meet. I'll call you later."

He quickly ended the conversation, swerving to avoid an oncoming car at the same time.

"You're going too fast", said Sanders, grumpily.

"You can't do me for speeding, you're suspended."

"Well, thanks for reminding me."

"Suspended?" said Bill.

"Later, Bill. We're changing direction."

"Why?" said Sanders.

"She can help. We're going to meet her at the hospital."

"How do you know she's there?"

"She's always there!"

He indicated to go left and pointed his car towards the hospital.

A couple of miles across the city an expensive ballpoint pen made a note of the time and duration of the call, and the names used. The writer made no attempt to log the call digitally, that was too dangerous.

The office was empty, the case files on King's PC were full. If only Di could get herself sorted out and come back to work. He stopped to lick his lips, he told himself he could still taste her. If she did come back to the department, well, he could always get a transfer, it was about time he had one anyway. He could put in for promotion, that's what he wanted after all.

His phone rang. He sighed and answered. It was ten in the evening. Leave me alone he thought. But he said: "DC King, who's speaking please."

A cheery, warm voice countered his negativity.

"It's Nurse Patel, Tony – Mandeep, how are you?"

The detective flushed with confusion. The image of Di was still etched from when he left her; she lay almost smiling with her ruffled mid-length dark hair on a cream-coloured pillow. He forced out a cheery response, "Mandeep, it's been a few days. Is this a social call, or something else?"

"It's something else." His fast-beating heart calmed by a few beats.

"But I'll make it social as well." Oh! He needed time.

"Good to hear," he said trying neither to put her off, nor encourage her... yet!

"OK, I think it will pay you to come to the ward." The warmth cooled by a few degrees.

"Now?"

"Right now!"
"Why!"
"Your Elsie is talking!"
"But how?"
"She's gabbling, it might be the drugs she's been put on. I should hurry up, I must get back to her bedside, I've got a nurse there. I'm trying to make a note of what she's saying."
"But..."
"Just hurry up, Tony!" The last was spoken with urgency from a voice used to command.
"I'm on my way." He, pocketed his phone and pen, walked briskly to the door picking up his jacket on the move. At last something was coming good.

Louise Brown's office table was strewn with cups, a coffee pot, a milk jug, and a sugar bowl. She had made two brews as she listened. She knew about Jack, but she did not know about Bill; she knew about the Macleans and the missing records, she had never actually mentioned the Carter boy's name to anyone but it was all tying in. Now she knew about the call to Preston after his attack by the car.

When she'd heard Preston's summary and Bill's corroboration she said, "What can I do?"

"Pauline Maclean still has a copy of David's original file."

"How did she manage that?"

"She must have got it before the computer documents were doctored."

"But why hasn't she told anyone?"

Di Sanders shifted uncomfortably. She had been silent until this moment.

"She told me but I wasn't listening. I was more interested in getting David to say something and it didn't seem important at the time. If I needed his file I could get it from the Social Services. At least that's what I thought."

Brown gave her a rueful smile.

"That's how I became suspicious," she said, "I just didn't know what to do about it."

"So you're a detective now as well as a hotshot doctor?"

Preston headed her off. "Di, it's her job to be watchful, just like you. I know you've had a rough deal but don't take it out on the doc, we're getting somewhere!"

"Thank you," said Dr Brown, "I think."

Preston poured yet more coffee and asked, "Did you ever get any further with that other case, the one you wouldn't name?"

The doctor paused, the Carter boy hadn't come into it yet, but he might be connected so what did she do now? Did she voice what she thought was the link or stick to the strict code of patient confidentiality? What the hell, she was already in deeper than she ought to be.

"No further. It was the same as David Maclean... I suppose that's all right now, his name's out in the open, at least with us four." She cast her eyes to Bill, uncertain of what his role should be. He had one to play, but he seemed so young.

"How about letting the other name out now Louise, we might be able to get somewhere with it!"

"It's still confidential, you must understand that."

Bill sat up, angrily. "Doctor, you have a nice place to live, a nice car, you're respected, and you probably had a fabulous childhood?"

She looked at him uncomfortably. Preston stared in surprise, this was a cohesive speech.

"Neither David Maclean, nor this other bloke have had any of that, and maybe they never will. This other one is probably being used right now and he won't thank you much for your bloody principles."

Sanders looked on uncertainly; she had sympathy for this la de da doctor she had not liked at all until now. But this was articulate outrage from the youth sitting on the settee and he was the best qualified person in the room to make any judgements.

Dr Brown made a decision, "His name is Nicholas Carter," then looked away.

"Thank you, doctor."

Preston made a list on a piece of paper. "Here's what we know: a child abuse network exists somewhere; It has links into some parts of the system but we don't know where; it may still be operating in a different place..."

He paused with his pen, Sanders took up the theme. "We

think some members are common to the James Institute seven years ago and to whatever's happening now."

"How?" asked Dr Brown.

"Daddy!" replied Bill from nowhere and not feeling it necessary for further comment.

"Yes, so-called Daddy," said Preston turning to acknowledge Bill, "Plus my so-called accident, and the phone call just after."

"I still find it hard to believe that a monster like this so-called Daddy can exist. He sounds inhuman." The other three looked at the doctor silently.

Then Sanders continued the thread, "We believe an innocent man has been sent to jail; we believe a police statement may be fabricated." She faltered as she said it. She knew now something was wrong at the police station, but she still struggled to acknowledge it.

"What don't we know?" asked Simon.

"We don't know why my original interview with David Maclean wasn't used in court," said Sanders.

"We don't know where David, or Nicholas are now," added the doctor.

Preston attempted some familiarity with Brown, "We'll make an investigator of you yet, Lou...Doctor Brown. How do we find out that information?" Brown dismissed his clumsy compliment with a look away. Sanders caught it and smiled before saying, "That's where we came in. Let's check Pauline's file copy. We might at least get a clue. David had to come from somewhere, Nicholas may have come from the same place."

Preston asked Brown if he could use her office telephone extension. Just as she was about to agree the door opened and Paul Bowes entered.

"Hello," he said querulously, "I wonder who you all are?"

"Paul, sorry, I needed to use your office, this is an important conference," said Brown.

"Should I know about it?" asked the consultant.

"Probably, but I won't bother you with it now, we have to get going."

"Fine and thanks, I've got enough to clutter my life at the moment."

"I know, Paul."

Preston had stopped on his way to pick up the phone. He did not resume the action. Bill looked apprehensive and Sanders thought it necessary to say something. "We've met before Doctor Bowes."

Bowes looked at her more closely and then said, "Sergeant Sanders, of course. I was sorry to hear about your little difficulty."

"You and me both. News travels fast," she added looking accusingly at Brown who stared ahead.

"We have to go" said Preston, and the four left the office. Bowes closed the door behind them.

"...Father said you must never tell anyone. Why Father? Did I do something wrong? Yes you did, Helen, you were a very bad girl, you made Father do what he did to you and now God will punish you forever. But Father I'm sorry, please don't let him hurt me...You must be quiet Helen..."

Tony King came in on the end of the stream of words, there was Elsie, or should it be Helen, in apparent delirium. Mandeep Patel was listening.

The old woman – Elsie, or Helen – went silent, a distraught look fell over her face.

Patel turned to King. "She's been like this for a couple of hours."

"Was it all like that?"

"Mostly! There was some stuff which could have been from her early childhood. But most of the time she's been repeating pretty much what you heard about her father."

"What does the doctor say?"

A tired voice just behind him butted in, "The doctor hasn't got a clue, who are you?"

King turned to see a youngish man, probably early thirties with the obligatory stethoscope hanging around his neck. He looked fatigued.

King showed his warrant card. "I'm acting detective sergeant Tony King. I'm trying to find out who she is."

"And that gives you the right to barge in here, does it?"

"I invited him, Doctor," said Nurse Patel with authority, "We need to know who she is and where she came from. She hasn't exactly helped us very much."

The doctor retreated from his antagonism. It was Nurse Patel's ward and what she said went. "Very well, whatever you want. At least she's saying something now." The doctor withdrew. King inwardly seethed at the young doctor's arrogance but tried to hide it. He asked, curtly, too curtly, "Is Helen likely to be her name?"

"It's likely," said Patel, withdrawing.

Then Elsie-Helen's eyes opened and looked straight at Tony King. He felt the intensity, but she was not seeing him, she was somewhere else. "I'll never tell, honestly Father. Please don't do it again, no please...," and her face creased into a mask of fear. She seemed to be bracing herself: she was shaking and her whole body was rigid. Patel and King looked at each other. They were getting an idea of why she had kept her secrets, they were too awful for her to know herself.

Then her body relaxed, the face turned tranquil, the eyes became normal.

"So, we think she's called Helen, but we don't know where she comes from, who her family are, or how old she is."

Patel adjusted the bedclothes slightly. "That's about it, we probably won't get much more from her now."

King, half-jokingly, said, "You couldn't just give her another shot of what she was having right now could you?" Patel's face went neutral, her tone formal, "No, I could not!" King cursed his misjudgement and said, "Sorry, bad joke!" It took some moments for Patel to unfreeze her look.

They started to move away when Helen's lips moved again. They stopped and looked back. The voice was strong and clear, "I can see you, I know what you're doing!" Her eyes continued to stare, they were still wide open and looking straight at him. But they did not see him, she was somewhere else again.

"I know what you're doing. You're messing with that old man's drip!"

King looked around the ward quickly, there was no man there.

He whispered to Patel, "What man?"

"None here, it's an all-female ward."

Helen continued, the voice as firm as before, "Hey, what are you putting in that man's drip?" Peculiar. Where had she been before this ward?

"Before you ask," said the sister, "she was in the ICU before she came here. She was in a really bad way."

"ICU? You mean Intensive care!" Patel nodded.

Helen continued, "He's dead now isn't he. Why did you do that? I saw you!"

"She could be talking about anything," said Patel, "We don't know how many hospitals she's been in during her life.".

Then Helen went silent, her eyes closed, her head rested back on the pillow, she breathed evenly.

King found himself saying without stopping to think, "How can I thank you? A meal perhaps?" and regretted it immediately. He tried to take it back but she beat him to it saying, "Italian, at my place, two days time."

Bloody hell, sometimes being bold worked. His triumph faded quickly as he turned to go and remembered his night with Sanders.

The only thing for it was to turn up directly at Pauline's door. Trying to find a working phonebooth or cubicle in 21st century Britain was impossible. Pauline looked amazed to see such a disparate group and was wary at first, but Preston convinced her of their intentions.

"You're the only who's listened to us, Mr Preston, so come in," she said, finally. She made hot drinks then got out her files and digital back-ups. They were looking for the missing links between David's birth, and his arrival at their foster home when Louise Brown said, "This is it!" as she held up an A4 paper from Pauline's printoffs.

All five gathered around the file: Louise Brown, Simon Preston, Di Sanders, Bill Cooper, and now Pauline Maclean looked at it expectantly.

"You're absolutely sure none of this was on the social services file you had?" asked Sanders.

"None of it," said Brown!

"What does it say?" asked Preston insistently. Doctor Brown

picked up another sheet of paper from the plastic file-pocket and put it in front of him. It had a social services logo, and a social worker's name. And it had the name of a care home to which David had been sent after being taken from his young mother. Lacey House. He spent three years there.

They looked on silently then Preston said, "Maybe we can get to that social worker? We can track her down through County Hall."

"Who can? You and me!" said Sanders, "Unlikely, neither of us has any clout at the moment, and they never let anything out."

"Including complete files," added Brown, "It was the doctored files which made me suspicious in the first place. They had to have been changed at the Social Services Department, and by a member of that department."

"And I can't think", said Sanders, "that I've ever met this woman in my two years doing this job." She looked across at Brown, "What about you, Doctor?"

"Me neither and that's in three years... please call me Louise! The doctor only matters in treatment or consultation."

Sanders said, reluctantly, thought, Preston, "Very well, Louise it is. And I am Di."

It should have been warm but while the words were the intent seemed less so.

"Why do we need this social worker woman?" Bill spoke for the first time in several minutes. He had watched and listened closely but kept his thoughts to himself; even now he was asking rather than answering a question.

"Who else would have access to the computer and the hard files!" explained Sanders.

"No idea, I haven't known who to trust for a long time so can you be sure that she'll be straight even if you do find her?"

"Or if she even exists at all," added Preston.

He got up from his chair and walked across the room to the window, stopped, turned around to face them and said, "Notice any similarity between this Lacey House and the James Institute? Cocky bastards aren't they! S*ure,* she's going to be reliable?"" The last sentence was laced with deep sarcasm.

Pauline looked shocked. She was used to dealing with problem children, that came with being a foster parent. Bill had seemed so *confident*, she assumed he was a normal child. She was a shy woman, she had a view of where she stood in the pecking order of life and that was not very high, so she'd kept quiet as the clever people talked among themselves. But she wanted to know what was going on.

"Is this official? she asked, "because if it's not I don't want to put John into any more trouble than he already is."

Pauline had remembered Di Sanders from the original interview, and she knew Preston because of his earlier visit. Those she could handle; but now there was a doctor from who knew where and strangest of all this boy-man, Bill, who looked wise and beaten beyond his years.

"This is all getting beyond me," she said to no one in particular, "Please explain before we go any further! I don't know if I'm helping or hurting John, here – or David!"

Preston looked at the other three in turn and knew he had to take the lead, he revealed all that they knew so far and the conclusions they were coming to. As the story unfurled story Pauline's eyes grew wider with each new development. Finally they stopped widening and narrowed into fury.

"And you are certain that the same people who were responsible for this young man..." she looked at Bill, "And the other one who died…"

"Jack," said Preston.

"Yes, Jack! Are you sure they abused David?"

They nodded.

She raised her voice, "So John has been sent to jail by these people? Why don't you go straight on television tomorrow and say so, Mr Preston?"

She turned furiously to Sanders, "And why don't you arrest them?"

Preston tried to explain but this kind of anger repelled reason. "It's not that simple, if it was we would have done it."

She was not as clever as them and she knew it, but Pauline Maclean was also not stupid, she knew how people worked, especially damaged people. Her voice maintained its volume, her face creased in a reddened glare, "Why not! If you know it, you can prove it!"

But what *did* they know? They had built their entire case by extrapolating on a phone threat. The only tangible piece of evidence they had was the hard copy they had just spotted in Pauline's file.

Louise Brown saw Pauline's state and the healer in her came out, "Mrs Maclean this is a breakthrough for us. Until fifteen minutes ago we were only guessing. This tells us something."

Pauline remained quiet, but not silent. She did not need words at that moment to speak volumes. Brown looked at the two investigators, police and reporter, and noted, "I have been working here for two years as a paediatrician, and I cannot remember anything about a Lacey House. I don't know where it is or who runs it."

"Does it say anything on the piece of paper?" asked Bill.

"Nothing at the top... nothing in the middle...Ah, a charitable organisation."

"So it wouldn't have been under the permanent gaze of the social services department", noted Sanders, "Or if it was, the invigilator was in on it!"

"Shit!" said Brown, "It doesn't bear thinking about."

There should have been a new energy in the room after the discovery but they were leaden, weighed down by the enormity of it.

"Pauline, do you know where it is?" asked Preston.

"I never knew, and I never went there. They always brought them to us."

"How many of their children have you had here Pauline?"

"It must be five including David."

"Was Nicholas Carter another?" asked Brown.

"How did you know that?"

"Lucky guess," said Bill coldly.

"So you have his file here as well?"

"We kept all of them; David's was the most important because we adopted him. I've got it here somewhere."

She went off to search for it leaving the visitors in her front room.

"So, there's a chance both of them were taken back to this Lacey House," said Preston.

"How come not one of us has heard of it, and with all that Louise and I know about these places?" said Di Sanders.

"Once they were sent there you didn't need to know." said Bill.

"No, But I should have heard something," said Doctor Brown, "Three years is a long time not to have come across a child from a place like that."

"But you have come across one, you just didn't know it until today, that's all," said Sanders, "You may have come across a lot more than that. How were you to know, you're a hospital doctor, you treat then when they come in to you, the social services have the details."

"That's fine as far as it goes, but someone had to be giving them medical attention at the Lacey Institute. It wasn't me, nor any of my colleagues I assume. So which GP practice was it? for instance who sent Nicholas Carter to hospital in the first place?"

"Did you see his referral notes, Louise?" asked Preston, perhaps more forcibly than he intended and managing to leave an unspoken accusation hanging in the air. She looked at him sharply. Of course she had looked at his notes, what there were of them! They weren't her problem. At that time of night she only needed to know what medication he was on and what the diagnosis was. Her later inquiries had drawn a blank as everyone present was aware. "Yes, I did! All I can say is that he was looked at by one of my colleagues in the Paediatric Department, there was nothing else."

"Is there a chance the kids have been looked after privately?" asked Sanders, "These people seem to have money, they can afford the set-up, perhaps they can keep the health care quiet by avoiding the NHS."

Brown looked at the detective. It was a reasonable point. "Possible but not likely. You see it's just so unusual for neither me nor my colleagues to have come across it. Even if they did treat on site, and even if they hived off serious treatment to a private surgery they would have to come by us at some stage. We would have to hear of it purely through professional osmosis."

"How does that work?" asked Preston.

"We would meet them somewhere along the line, at a conference or a social event. If they are on the medical register it's almost impossible for them not to be known."

"True, but you wouldn't know what they were doing, especially if they didn't want to tell you."

"There is one thing to think about." Everyone turned to Bill. He had been quiet for a several minutes while he listened to the conversation. "When we were at the James Institute we were given medicines by the old hag!"

"...Mrs Barnes," corrected Preston.

"I don't ever remember being seen by a doctor, or if I was I didn't know that's what they were. Anyway, I never got really sick so I didn't need much looking after..." Sanders and Brown looked at each other but said nothing, "But I know some were. They had to be, there were more than twenty kids in the place."

"That's true", agreed Brown. "The idea of twenty kids staying permanently healthy without even a cracked fingerbone is impossible to think of. Every kid needs a doctor's attention somewhere."

"But what's all this driving at, Bill?" asked Sanders.

"I'm saying maybe doctors are part of the Network!" He said it calmly, but it fell like a bomb. They stopped and looked at him for several seconds. Finally Brown broke the silence, "Impossible! It just does not happen like that."

"Upsetting your precious standards again are we, doctor. Oh you're all wonderful people really, I know. I bow to you, really I do. Silly of me to even think such a thought. I mean for God's sake you people sit at the right hand of God don't you. There's nothing you can be blamed for..."

Sanders stopped him. "That's enough Bill. Getting angry isn't going to get us there any quicker!" Bill said no more and shrunk back into a corner muttering. Doctor Brown was temporarily silent in her thoughts.

Sanders spoke more calmy, "It has the makings of a theory. If they treated them on site no one would ever know."

"But they still have to be sent out to hospital sometime." said Brown, quietly, "I or my colleagues would have come across them. That's how we know about Nicholas Carter."

"Not if they weren't local." said Preston, "If they came from other authority areas and never made contact with the local health service, you would never know."

"It still doesn't make sense. They have to become known when they refer kids to hospital."

"Not if they arrange for the records to be doctored," said Preston, "You saw what happened with Nicholas Carter. You had no idea who had referred him or where he came from."

"It would mean they would have to be a real emergency. That way the paperwork would be delayed." The paediatrician was slowly and reluctantly coming around to the possibility, but she had to be dragged. It was hateful that people from her own profession could be capable of the bestiality she had been hearing about.

"That makes sense," continued Sanders, "They'd want to keep it away from the hospital unless it was a dire emergency. They'd refer everything to either a private clinic or deal with it there and then. Nicholas Carter must have been a one-off." She turned to Brown, "What happened to him in the end?"

"He disappeared before I could find out any more. I did think it was a premature discharge."

"They probably wanted to rush him out before he could be connected with this Lacey Place."

"So it might just be possible then, Mrs High Priestess Doctor," sneered Bill. Brown stared at him with some hostility and some fear.

Sanders jumped in again, "Bill, she's helping here, you're not!"

Pauline Maclean re-entered and broke the tension. She carried a small folder and a USB stick. "I've found it, Nicholas Carter's file. He wasn't with us very long, just a couple of months, then the social services took him back."

"Back to where?" said Sanders.

"Lacey House, and they have an address here for it. We backed up the files to a hard drive as well. She held up the USB stick, so this will be the original."

"Now that was careless of them", said Bill with energy, the hostility gone.

Pauline tried to share their excitement but there were only

two things on her mind: where was David, and "Does this mean we can get John out of jail?"

"I hope so", replied Preston, "But we still have a way to go."

"We are going to get him out, though, aren't we!"

Preston put an arm around her shoulder and tried to calm her. Sanders and Louise looked on without saying a word. There was little they could say. They had stumbled upon something so apparently fantastic it was unreal, even when they had talked it through, rationalised it, and concluded they were probably right, they still thought they were more wrong.

Bill had turned his head away a long time before. This was no part of his world.

Sanders stood up abruptly and shot an order at Preston, "Give me a lift home, there are things I have to do!"

"Like what?"

"It's better that you don't know right now." She had seen enough, her blood was boiling. Her career was being sacrificed for this blasted network, all because of that tape and the interview with Jack. She was off the case and suspended, and someone else was on it. It was time for a showdown, or at the very least some risk taking.

"Don't cut out on us now Di, we need you more than ever!" pleaded the reporter.

"You've got enough to be going on with. Louise will be doing some checking among her medical friends I presume." She looked at Brown who nodded assent. "And you will be taking a look at the Lacey Institute I have no doubt, Simon?" He nodded as well.

"I have other things to do, which I cannot do with you, I'm afraid."

"No secrets, Di, please! We have to stay together," replied Preston.

Pauline started to twitch again: "Please don't fall out among yourselves. John will never get out if you fall apart."

They looked guiltily at each other. Pauline had a way of reducing things to basics and getting it right.

"I promise you I'm not falling out with them, Pauline. This is something I must do."

"We haven't got any idea of what the police should be doing

in this Di, we need you," said Preston. No response. "Who can we TRUST there Di!" said Preston loudly.

Sanders eyes narrowed and her fists clenched as she responded through gritted teeth, "That's what I need to find out."

Louise Brown lacked the professional cynicism of either of them. She said, "There must be someone safe to talk to, they can't all be in it."

"There probably is, there are probably several, but I don't know who they are. I begin to suspect I know the ones who aren't safe."

"Are you going to put yourself at risk?" asked Brown. She considered it for a moment.

"Yes, I probably am."

She paused to think. Tony King would not thank her for it but she was sure enough of him. He was a good man.

"All right, speak to Tony King if anything goes wrong."

"Your sidekick?" questioned Preston. She was surprised to hear him being talked of like that but it was true. Their relationship had changed rather since then.

"How can you be sure of him?"

"I just am. Trust me, he's all right." and she looked at Brown, knowingly. The doctor returned the look.

Preston saw it and felt a pang of something but he didn't recognize what it was. He moved to the door saying, "Let's go, then!"

She was going to break into the police station and was shaking at the thought of it. Her plan was to go in through the back entrance at a time when she knew everything would be quiet. It was midweek and the cars would be parking up out in the city, the control room would be down to a bare minimum, and the shift would be taking a rest as it went quiet. She just prayed that the security code was accurate for the back entrance lock. It changed every week. If she got it wrong she would alert someone inside. Tony King had relinquished it without much of a struggle, just, "What are you planning Di?"

"I can't tell you, Tony, it's better that you don't know."

"Just be careful, I'm worried about you."

Yes, she supposed he was. He was that sort of man. Not a lifetime partner, not for her anyway, but a good, honest man. She was clinging to him like an island in a sea of sulphur. The previous few hours had left her desperate about the male of the species. Was there a single one of them not burning with bestial desire? She knew that wasn't true but right now it didn't seem like it.

She planned carefully, it was a damp night, the rain glistened in the security lights of the Police Station's back yard. She wore soft shoes to avoid any echo in the car park and she put her phone in silent mode. She dressed in a black sweatshirt and jeans and gingerly danced around the security-camera blindspots. When she got to the rear door she pressed the 6-figure code number into the device and waited anxiously for what were only microseconds, but seemed like days. The door opened and she ducked in quickly. In her hurry she did not see the dull glow of a cigarette end at the far end of the yard. The eyes behind it noticed her, though.

So far, so good, she thought, but she had to get out of the corridor area, it was the busiest part of the station and anyone could come out of a door on their way to somewhere else. She wore a rain hat to disguise her if the corridor camera picked her up, but if anyone saw her she hoped they would just assume she was on duty – not everyone knew of her suspension. Fortunately for her she knew the reality of the night security video: no one looked at it until after something had happened, it was never monitored.

She made her way rapidly to CID, trying to avoid the soles of her trainers squeaking on the linoleum tiles. No one was around, she made the twenty metres without incident. It was a different office to her own but she knew the layout well, she had been there often enough. The door was open so she could walk straight in without a noise. She had been lucky so far, no one had come out into the corridor. She did not know what she would do if they did, she had no cover, she would be exposed no matter who stumbled upon her: friend or foe. Even if they were entirely innocent it would take a very short time for the guilty ones to find out. And then what!

She knew what she was looking for, Sam Spencer's diary. He

had a role in this she was certain, he had to be involved if the Maclean cover up was to work. She had found it just as hard to imagine her colleagues were part of the Network as Louise Brown had for her own profession. But when everything was taken together it added up. For such a conspiracy to work there had to be high level agreement among the very agencies put in place to prevent that sort of thing. The facts were beginning to take on a life of their own, and they weren't so much speaking as yelling for themselves. It should have been less of a surprise to her because she was used to dealing with the ugliness of humanity. She knew better than most what uncontrolled men can do to defenceless children. She knew there were people not held by the constraints of morality, or law. Insinuating themselves into positions of authority and innocence, and most of all access, was easy.

Her heart thumped at 100 beats a minute, tension stiffened her whole body. Still no one was around although she could hear noises from different parts of the station echoing through the corridor. Mostly it came from the custody area where the usual crop of drunks and assaults would have been processed prior to their appearance before the magistrates later in the morning.

Jack Spencer's diary would be in the office next door to the main area. It would not be locked. Spencer's reluctant modern cop reputation was well-known: he believed women had a place in a police station, serving tea in the canteen. He had a good record for arrests and he had been mostly courteous to her, but always patronising as well. He did not think much of her outfit, the family unit, he thought it was a waste of time and all the effort would be better directed to picking up real villains. Leave the rest to the social services! She had never even felt a frisson of sexual interest in the man, and he had never shown any towards her. He was not a man's man either, not exactly a loner, but a man who only ever stayed for one drink.

She knew where he kept his diary; it was in a drawer in his desk and she headed straight for it. That was the reward from the gamble of this foray into his affairs, he was a caveman when it came to IT and struggled with computer apps, so he was even more old school with his records than he was with his coppering. She wanted to know when Spencer spoke to David Maclean.

Still the station only echoed to distant sounds as she pulled open the desk drawer, her heart rate didn't lower and as she reached in for the diary it threatened to overwhelm her, but she breathed in deeply and pulled it out.

She scanned the entries for the last two months, from the date of her first and only interview with David, until now.

There was no sign. Everything else was there in brief but proper detail: interviews with suspects, appointments with superiors, evenings with the department, but absolutely nothing about an interview with David Maclean, or a social worker.

She'd wondered why her interview hadn't been brought up in court and now she knew why: Jack Spencer was one of them! There had to be more, he could not have done it on his own, there had to be help from someone more senior, otherwise it would have been given to Tony King to continue the investigation. It was his job after all, despite his workload. Instead, Jack Spencer had been taken from his area of expertise and put into one of which he knew nothing, at least nothing in the police sense.

There was a noise in the corridor, she froze. Steps could be heard approaching the CID office although she was now hidden in the DI's room she was still vulnerable. If they came in and turned on the light she would be seen. She noiselessly sank below the level of the desk and tried to hold her breath, her heart, already pounding, had almost jumped into her mouth.

There was no need, the steps receded down the corridor, probably on their way to the canteen. She breathed again and pulled out her phone to start tapping an SMS to Tony King. It read: "Tony, Jack Spencer did NOT interview David Maclean, it's not in his diary. I and others believe he gave false testimony at the trial." She wrote brief details of what and the others had deduced. Each message was no more than 30 words and then sent. She accounted for the police access to the boys, the social services were obvious, in fact probably the key to everything, she just did not understand how the medics could be an active part of it.

She finished saying, "Ring me at home when you have read this." She hesitated before finishing with "Love Di." As she pressed the final send button she regretted the last part of the message already. Love?

Her heart started to settle, her work was done. The corridor had been quiet for some time and she felt relaxed enough to sit back for a few moments, before making her way out. Then she froze again. More steps were coming down the corridor. Possibly two sets of feet. She was still in the dark and did not think she could be seen. They slowed as they reached the CID office, then stopped. Her heart started thumping again, so hard she feared it could be heard and would alert whoever it was.

Then the nightmare came true, the light snapped on and no amount of dark clothing could hide her presence. She looked at who was standing in the doorway and her eyes widened with horror. Her hands were still concealed from their view and she managed to hide her phone in a fold of Spencer's surprisingly luxurious chair.

Too much was swirling in King's head. He got out of bed to make a drink. Di Sanders's earlier call was only partly responsible, he was concerned about her of course because he knew she was asking for trouble sneaking into the police station. That alone might have kept him awake, but it was compounded by a nagging inquiry which had been growing ever since he had left the hospital ward. The euphoria of having got somewhere in his quest for who he now knew as Helen's identity had not lasted long and when he came down to Earth Helen's last words repeated to him.

"I can see you, I know what you're doing."

See who? Why that childlike telltale voice?

"You're messing with that man's drip aren't you?"

She obviously knew what a drip was.

"...What are you putting in that man's drip?"

Had she seen it being done, had she actually said those words at the time? The memory of her previous utterances came back, but that was a different kind of voice. It had genuine fear and terror. He had no doubt the conversation with her "father" had taken place, it sounded real enough. But the second voice was more secure, as if she were enacting it the way she wanted to. She was in control of the situation. Or was it just another bit of whackiness from her? She had led them all a dance so far, why not speed up the tempo!

The maelstrom of his thoughts meant one would quickly push out another before he had time to think about it. He switched to Di Sanders: what was she up to in there?

Then Helen reasserted herself. When was she admitted? How long was she on intensive care? Who else was in there? What old man?

He poured a cup of decaffeinated coffee, and as is always the way, when the mind stops thinking about something, it makes the link. Half way up the cup the thought jumped into his head: the old man in the shooting! The old man who is now dead! The old man who they now knew ran that crooked care home seven years ago which Preston had televised.

That old man!

Was Helen telling them he had been killed by a hospital insider? What was being put into the drip? The inquest said he died of natural causes, hadn't it!

Now he was completely alert. There was no chance of sleep. He thought of calling Mandeep Patel to tell her, and to listen out for anything else. But it was unlikely Helen/Elsie would say any more as the drugs wore off, and was it reasonable to call her in the middle of the night? Helen had probably revealed more in that half hour than in her entire lifetime. Poor sad Helen!

He paced his kitchen thinking it through. He would have to tell someone of course, in the morning. Probably his superintendent, not Jack Spencer. He would have to work it through from the beginning and speak to Helen again when the drugs had worn off.

Maybe someone else had seen the drip as well, he could talk to whoever disposed of it: the nurse on that ward, care assistant, cleaner? When did it happen? Night or day!

He was as alert as if it had been midday, then out of nowhere he yawned and his eyes drooped. He left the remains of his coffee and went back to bed. He did not see the string of texts from Sanders on his phone, he'd been in his kitchen and the boiling kettle had masked the alert-noises. He would return to it in the morning. Daylight had a way of rationalising things. If there was anything left after all the dark corners had been lit up then he would continue.

Her eyes accustomed to the light, her phone-torch shone uselessly in her hand, illuminating a small patch of a desk. There was no mistaking who was there: Jack Spencer, and the one person she least wanted to see at that moment, the person who had suspended her and banned her from the police station.

"Well Sergeant Sanders, what exactly are you doing in the CID area?" asked Hawkins.

She stalled, should she tell him about the diary? No, not yet! Should she ask about the David Maclean interview? Yes, good idea! Should she tell him of her suspicions? They were still unproved but the evidence was gathering its own momentum. She did not want to betray her fellow investigators, but after all she was a police officer, albeit suspended. It was the job of the police to root this thing out even if they were in some way involved themselves. Yes, she would tell him!

"Well Sergeant Sanders!"

The superintendent was not in uniform, there was no reason for him to be at that time of night. He might have been staying over in the station, it often happened that the area commander stayed in special quarters. He had probably been having a drink with Sam Spencer. He remained silent by his superior's side. He was looking at her as if he knew she had found something.

She summoned her courage and started, "Sir I believe there has been a serious miscarriage of justice."

"Really?"

"Yes Sir, I believe the John Maclean trial was a fit up from the beginning to cover up a much bigger syndicate." Spencer shifted uncomfortably. The superintendent raised his eyebrow in surprise. "Upon what do you base that Di?"

She expected resistance, it wasn't there.

"Trial evidence sir. My own interview with the boy was not used, and I believe Detective Inspector Spencer's interview was fabricated!"

Spencer jumped in, "What do you mean?"

Hawkins raised a hand and said, "This is a serious allegation Sergeant Sanders, coming as it does from a police officer on suspension."

"Sir why wasn't my initial interview offered as evidence?"

Spencer replied, "It was inconclusive, there was not enough detail. We needed him to nail his father. My interview did that where yours did not Di."

She looked at him accusingly. "You never spoke to him did you Jack!"

"It's Guv, and how dare you, of course I spoke to him, and I have a witness to prove it, not that I need to. The trial's over, Maclean's in jail where he should be."

"What do you mean by a larger syndicate, Di?" asked the superintendent.

She launched into an explanation without pausing to think, "There's a paedophile ring which has been operating for possibly ten years in the area, and Jack Spencer is party to it." Spencer remained unmoved.

"How do you know that?" continued the superintendent, evenly..

She explained all that she knew about the James Institute and Lacey House.

Spencer said nothing, his face now an impassive mask. The superintendent took in a deep breath, "You realise if this is true it will scandalise the entire area!"

"Of course it will sir, but we have to do something about it!"

"Who else knows?"

She felt a sickening feeling at the bottom of her stomach. Why did he need to ask that?

"I can't say at the moment!"

"Oh I think you can," said Spencer, menacingly.

"Steady on Jack, it may not be all it seems."

She looked at both of them. "Why are you trying to protect

him, sir!"

"We look after each other in the police force, Di, you know that." Suddenly he was friendly.

"You haven't exactly been looking after me."

The two men looked at each other then the superintendent nodded and turned to her again. "No I suppose not, but then why should I? You're only a woman." As she was listening with mounting worry she did not see Spencer move to her side. She did not see him reach into his pocket and pull out a tiny phial. She did not see him until it was too late. The last thing she remembered was seeing a sinister look on the face of the man she used to call sir.

A phone sounded, a hand reached out and picked it up. It would not be good news, not at this hour.

"Yes."

"They know!"

"Who knows?"

"Impossible to say how many. But it's out, and they've made the connection with the other place."

"Well surprise surprise", came the exasperated response. "I'm amazed it took them so long, we gave them enough bloody pointers."

"That's a matter for later discipline. We have to act fast. We have already taken out one problem, but we don't know where the others are."

"OK it looks like windup time again. Strip the place out, get there fast, make sure nothing is left!"

"What are you going to do?"

"Stay by the phone, make sure it's all happening, there are other things to be done you know."

"Of course! You stay where the guns are loudest, by the phone. We'll do the easy work, like sorting it all out. Meanwhile we have to get someone out of the bloody police station without being seen."

"All right, cut the sarcasm, just get on with it!" He ended the call.

There was no going back, no trying to keep down the body count. He started planning his own escape route before working on the rest of the clear out. The Middle East or South America? He would have just upped and gone and left everyone else to their fate but he had to cover his tracks and he needed them.

He picked up his phone again and started making calls. Needs must when the Devil drives.

Hawkins turned to Spencer and said, "No help there, but no surprise either. Any ideas?"

"Fucking CCTV everywhere, how do we get round that?"

"OK, I've got that. I'll call the custody sergeant to create an emergency, he can bring help down from upstairs and leave the screens unattended. We'll get him to make it last as long as we can."

"What emergency?"

"He can give one of the thugs a kicking, that'll stir it up."

"Smart. And you?"

"I'll get into the video room and wipe the files. We'll disconnect the cameras long enough for you to get her out without being seen, everyone will be in the Custody Suite anyway."

"Get her out, how?"

"For fuck's sake, Spencer, how did you get to be a DI? Over there!" He pointed at a documents trolley left in a corner close to Sanders' unconscious form. "Load her on that and get her into the boot of my car."

Hawkins handed Spencer his keys and then picked up the internal phone and called the Custody Suite. The same sergeant who had spotted Sanders in the car park answered. A short time later the dark hours of the morning were pierced by the tannoy calling for urgent assistance.

King had a fitful night's sleep and now stood under his high pressure shower distractedly doing his ablutions while thinking about his next moves: check the hospital records for the time Helen, and let's assume that's her name, was in intensive care. Just to be sure, but it was bound to be the same time as the old man was in there, he could remember it well enough. Then check the old man's medication with the Intensive care consultant; check the pathology report on the cause of death; speak to the people who get rid of the hospital waste material; and of course, speak to Helen again.

And call Di Sanders.

Why not just walk away from it? It was not his problem. Just forget about it, go back to work and leave it all behind for someone else to find! But didn't he owe them something? Or was it all story-chasing bravado, ego-stroking glory? No he did not owe them something, how could he, he didn't do any of this and nor did he have anything in his life which could lead to it. They got a shit deal, yes, but he was being threatened and so were his people. It would be easy to throw in the towel, then he looked across to the door to his spare room where Bill was staying. He felt he owed Bill something. He did not know why, but he had formed a bond with him in the last couple of days.

Those boys had been put into a secret Hell. It would last a lifetime, they would never be happy, never know true peace of mind. And with that his resolve returned.

Preston's movements had stirred Bill and he emerged into the living room.

"We're going there today, Bill," he stated.

"What good will that do?" was the weary reply.

"We might find something, you might even recognise someone."

"Some hope!"

"Come on Bill, we've come a long way, don't give up now. Think about Jack, think about all the others. Think about yourself! Let's get them."

Bill looked up as he drank a mug of tea, "In the end I don't care so much about them. I know I say a lot, and I like to think I would help them if I could, that's why I came to you." He looked down to add milk, "But it's bigger than even I thought. It's too big?" he looked at Preston.

"We can't just walk away, Bill, not now. We're in too deep."

"But all I really want is to stuff that cow, the rest is less important."

"You'll get your chance, Bill. And if you like we'll make it very public. But there were others who did worse damage than she did."

"In your eyes, Simon, not in mine." He took another sip of tea. "All right we'll go today, but don't forget what I've said!"

Louise Brown had been troubled all night; who could these doctors be that they could drift in and out of the hospital without being suspected? Maybe her colleagues had suspicions? It would mean rebreaking the ice with Martin Tench but she had to start somewhere and Paul Bowes was in too fragile a state. Somehow that did not seem such a galling idea now, maybe because she was wrapped up in the inquiry, or maybe because the plight of these children made her issues look small by comparison.

She resolved to get to it first thing in the morning.

King made a cup of instant coffee and contemplated preparing a breakfast before abandoning the idea in favour of a fry-up in the police canteen. He carried his coffee back into his bedroom to check his phone. The dark screen fired up to his touch and he saw immediately a stream of texts, all from Di Sanders. He took a sip of coffee and accessed the messages with his left thumb. Then he yelled with pain as coffee spilled on to his bare arms and legs.

"Jesus, what the fuck!" he yelled. He touched the call icon on the first message but there was no response after ringing four times, instead it went to her message service.

"Di, what the hell… Call me as soon as! What have you been doing?"

Buried deep in the folds of an office chair in the DI's room Sanders' phone lit up with calls and texts, but no one knew, it was still on silent from the previous night.

It was uncomfortable crouching behind the bushes, but Preston and Bill put up with it. They had their eyes trained on Lacey House. It had taken some finding even with the help of a detailed Ordnance Survey map. In the end Bill had typed it into the app's search facility and it threw up a map reference. Preston wondered how navigators survived on just the stars and a dangling magnetic stone before the IT revolution. The building was Victorian, large, and at the end of a long drive. They had left the car on the roadside half a mile from the entrance and walked the distance. It was still uncomfortable for Preston's hip, but he had been told to exercise so he grinned and bore it.

There had been no movement since they arrived. Nothing in the spacious and well-kept gardens, nor inside that they could see. There was a solitary Black Range Rover parked in the front driveway.

"It's strange that nothing has moved Bill."

"Perhaps they've been tipped off again... like at The James Institute?"

Then the front door opened and a middle-aged man walked out. He looked each way as if he were crossing the road. The two spies held their breath, although why they did they didn't know, they were at least 200 metres from the man. They could make out his grey hair and casual dress. There was something about the way he carried himself that suggested middle class. It was the way there was only slight movement of the body, the shoulders stayed in the same place, the head erect, the arms moving gently by his sides. He had carrier bags at the end of each of them. If not middle class then military?

What's more he looked familiar to Preston. He was sure he had seen this person somewhere before, not for long, and a while ago, but he knew him.

Preston pushed the record button on his phone video camera and kept the man in shot. Even with sophisticated cameras getting close on him would be hard, but the camera did a decent enough job.

"Bill", he whispered, "Your eyes are younger than mine, Do you know him?"

The young one stared intently for a few seconds, they watched the figure walk towards the car parked about twenty metres away. He got in and there was a pause while they waited for the engine to start. Finally it did and the man drove closer to them on his way out. They retreated further into the bushes to avoid being seen.

"The face is familiar but it was a long time ago. Let me think about it!"

They trained their eyes back on the front of the building. It was now completely silent outside, there were no more cars, not even a bicycle.

It was time to make a move.

"Bill we're going to knock on the door," he announced as he rose from his hiding position and emerged into view.

Louise Brown was in the middle of a consultation, an asthmatic eight year-old who had been waiting for an appointment for two months. She tried to give the girl her full attention but it was difficult. She kept telling herself to be professional, but the events of the previous evening were gnawing at her and she looked at the clock repeatedly waiting for coffee time to come around. She made an effort to concentrate on the patient; in fact so hard she developed a deep furrow on her brow which alarmed both the girl and her mother.

"Is something wrong doctor? Is it very serious?"

She looked up, drew a strand of her dark brown hair from her eyes, and forced herself to smile.

"Nothing that we can't handle."

She continued with the examination; the girl had a breathing problem, probably not helped by an overprotective mother. She prescribed a course of drugs and an inhaler. The GP could probably have done it just as easily, but better to be safe than sorry. As the hands on the clock came closer to ten thirty she became impatient to get away. She did her best to deal with the mother's insistent concerns and in the end managed to usher her out into the outpatients' corridor. They went in one direction, she turned on her heel and went the other to avoid any more conversation.

As she walked into the Doctors' Mess she took a deep breath. There sitting at a familiar table were Paul Bowes and Martin Tench. They looked serious.

It was the first time she had been there for two weeks. She had been avoiding Tench; she knew it was adolescent, but some aspects of youth stay with you forever.

She sat down beside them.

"Louise!" It was Paul Bowes with a cheerful look on his face for the first time in ages. "How unexpected. You haven't been here for a while."

"What's kept you away," asked Tench, politely.

As if he didn't know... but maybe he did not know.

"I've had a few things to sort out, you know how it is." She looked at Tench who returned the gaze with a smile. Blast, just when she thought it safe to start talking again!

"What have you been up to?"

Maybe she was unbalanced by finding Tench there, because she didn't stop to think about her response – and she knew later that she should have done. "I've been playing at detectives," she said, and then possibly even more indiscreetly, "Have either of you come across anyone who has ever worked at a place called Lacey House?" The two men looked at each other quizzically. Then Tench asked: "It's not around here is it? I haven't been here very long."

"Where is it...what is it, some sort of scientific research place?" continued Bowes.

"It's a charitable home for kids in care. It's a few miles northwest of the city and it's a den of perversion," said Brown. They looked at her askance.

"What are you talking about! How come we've never heard of it?" said Bowes.

"You'd think we'd have heard of it with our combined time here."

"Why the interest?" said Bowes.

Brown took a deep breath and plunged in, "We've never come across them here, never met anyone who's treated them, and never heard of the place. Yet I know it exists, I've seen proof of it."

The two men again looked at each other. Then Tench said, "Tell us what you know and let's see if we can get to the bottom of this."

"Yes, but ..." Bowes was cut off as she got up to get a coffee from a dispensing jug and took it back to the table. Then she let them have what she knew starting with the missing file information and finishing with the night with Pauline Maclean.

The two men listened attentively giving sympathetic nods.
At last she was getting somewhere.

The file before Tony King's confirmed what he had suspected: the old man had been in the Intensive Care Unit at the same time as Helen. She was removed from there a day after he was found dead. She could easily have been awake and aware when he pegged out so she might have seen something.

The next stop was the hospital maintenance office, that's where the workers got rid of all drips, dirty bandages, used plastic protection gowns, masks and hats and everything else.

He met with a disappointing response when he got there. The friendly admin clerk probably didn't mean to be downbeat but it set King back. "You won't stand much chance of finding anything there, have you any idea how many of those we get rid of in a week?" He could imagine but he had to try. The maintenance block was a brick building 20 metres square with a large chimney which used to be the outlet for a furnace. It was not a triumph of architecture but what hospital building is? There were plastic sacks piled up close to a set of double doors and some caged trolleys linked in a train running away from them. He made his way to the entrance and called out. There was no reply. The incinerator had been decommissioned 25 years before but he could still feel a warmth contrasting with the ambient temperature. So much so he took off his jacket, taking out his warrant card as he did so.

"Can we help you!" He could not see where the voice came from because the gloom inside was fooling his eyes. "I hope so." He identified himself showing his card blindly to whoever was looking. Gradually his eyes got used to the dim light and he saw two men sitting in canvas chairs drinking tea.

"I'm Danny Smith, this is Pete Thompson, we run this place."

"Doesn't it ever get boring?" asked the detective looking around at the spare space and the empty brick walls.

"Sometimes", said Danny. "But if you can't stand the heat..."

"Do you get rid of everything the minute it comes in?"

"We never keep anything. If it's come here it has nowhere left to go, except an onward journey to landfill oblivion," said

Danny.

"What if something gets held up, like a used drip?"

"They don't. They're useless once they've been pierced. They come down here immediately."

"Even if there's a lot of it left!"

"Every time," answered Danny.

"Unless the coroner has a need to keep it back for analysis." added Pete.

"You both know a lot about procedures," observed King

"You can't help but pick it up working here. In the end you get to meet everybody and they tell you how it works. You can't deal with the amount of stuff we do and not want to know where it's come from or what it does," explained Danny. The unexpected eloquence took King by surprise. Never jump to conclusions, Tony, you should know that by now.

"Then I suppose there's no point in asking if you kept any back from a few weeks ago," asked King.

"What are you looking for exactly, Mr detective?"

"It's a longshot. I'm looking for any peculiar drips which may have come your way. It's a daft question, but you don't get anywhere unless you ask them sometimes. The sensible ones don't seem to work."

"In what way peculiar?" asked Pete.

"I don't know myself. Perhaps it had been tampered with in some way." The two men looked at him.

"What's going on then. Something dodgy in the hospital is there?" asked Danny, not unreasonably. King had already given away enough to set a rumour flying through the hospital and that was the last thing he wanted. He was on to something all right. But the more he asked them to keep quiet the more they were likely to think there was something up and spread it around.

He laughed it off, "Nothing that I know of. I'm just curious, can you think of anything?" They looked at each other then Danny said, "There's not much to remember about a drip you know. They all look the same and we don't take much notice – we just empty them out and throw them."

Danny couldn't care less, but Pete remained quiet for a few seconds. Then he spoke, "There was something a while ago.

I'd never seen it before."

King became more alert

"I can remember picking up one three quarters full and as I squeezed it I spotted a funny leak in it. It spurted from the top, straight into my face. I didn't think anything about it at the time, I just thought it was a duff one."

"What has made you remember now?" asked Tony clinically.

"Precisely the opposite of what Danny said. Drips are all the same, they're pretty ordinary, but you do notice when one is slightly out of line."

"Did you report it?"

"I didn't see the need. Someone else further back up the line should have spotted it."

True, thought King.

"I suppose it would be too much to ask if you remember the date?"

Pete shrugged his shoulders, "Sorry." King was about to thank them and walk away when Pete suddenly offered, "I can tell you it happened the day after the Manchester United versus Arsenal match."

"How do you know that?"

"It's silly really, but you know how your mind wanders when you have nothing much to do."

"I was reading about a winger having a spurt of speed that teabreak, just after I'd emptied that drip. It struck me as funny." he looked at Danny, "I think I said something about it to you! You know something about the Arsenal winger being a drip."

"Oh yeah," said Danny. "It was quite funny. That winger was a drip but he had a good spurt on him. Clever, Pete."

King tried not to be distracted by the sports chatter. "

"It might be the key to everything," said King. "By the way, was it League or cup?"

"No idea, but two weeks ago won't be so hard to narrow down will it. Why don't you check the fixtures?"

He would.

It was a nervous walk to the front door of Lacey House; as they stepped up to the doorbell, Preston did his best to be purposeful, to put his mental effort into the physical things he was doing. Bill hung back and approached the door reluctantly, but he came. Preston took a breath and pushed it hard. A distant ringing could be heard. They waited for twenty seconds and then pressed it again. Still no response.

"Let's take a look around!" he said. They set off at a slow pace, peering through the windows as they went. Every now and again they thought they saw a movement, but it might just have been the light playing tricks.

When they got to the back there was another entrance. Preston tried again, nothing!

Bill half whispered, half spoke, "I don't think there's a soul here."

"There has to be, it's a children's home."

"I think they've cleared it out, just like they did at the James Institute."

"They still left you there, remember! They left the kids."

"Maybe they've learned not to do that again.

They went to the front again, but before they reached the door Bill looked up.

"There's a window open, next to the drainpipe."

"What are you suggesting Bill!"

"That I climb up and get in."

"Can you do that?"

"I've had lots of practice."

How little he really knew Bill.

"We've got nothing to lose I suppose. I'll watch to make sure you get in all right."

Bill shimmied up the pipe as if he were a circus performer. He reached the second-floor window in fifteen seconds and went straight into the opening without pause.

Preston held his breath as he kept one eye out. No one came.

He went back to the door and waited. After five minutes he became worried. What had happened to Bill! After ten minutes he started ringing the bell furiously.

Then the door opened and Preston stepped back uncertainly. Standing before him was a smiling Bill.

"Look what I've found!"

Preston looked down. There at waist height was a boy of

about six who looked the spitting image of the pictures in Pauline Maclean's photo album.

"Hello David!"

There was no movement at all in Di Sanders' apartment. The bed was untouched although the furniture was in a state of disarray, as was her wardrobe and chest of drawers. The place had been turned over thoroughly. The security phone was hanging off the hook but had long since stopped its pendulum swing. The only activity was the occasional whirring of her answering machine, an antique service she refused to give up because she enjoyed listening to the messages that way.

"Hello boss, it's Tony here. I haven't heard from you, give me a ring as soon as you can, I'm just leaving for the nick now."

"Good morning, Di, this is Simon calling at nine thirty. Just wondered if everything was all right. We have things to do today. Phone me soon, let me know what you've been up to."

"Hi, it's Tony again, I've got lots to tell you. I've left loads of messages on your mobile as well. Call me at the nick!."

"Hello, Louise Brown here. I've started some inquiries. Perhaps you can call me. I might have something but I don't understand it. It's not my field after all."

"Di, it's Simon again. You won't believe this. It's too incredible even though I've seen it. I'm calling from a phone booth, and for goodness sake don't call me back on my mobile. You know why. But I have to see you, and the others, as soon as possible. I'll call round."

But they went unanswered. Di Sanders could not hear them, she was lying on the floor with a gaping wound in her head, as if it had been inflicted by a meat cleaver. She was no longer bleeding, she was no longer breathing; Detective Sergeant Diane Sanders would never, ever hear those messages.

Preston was in a place he'd managed to avoid all his life until this moment: he'd never married and if a relationship got near to bringing children into the equation he had found a reason to end it. His own memory of a cold mother and a harsh father killed off the idea of affection or love, he wanted nothing to do with them. But he could not run from this, there were eighteen confused and probably damaged young boys before him and he could not simply leave them. He needed to get these boys somewhere safe and the very people society relied upon to do that had conspired to put them here in the first place. He was crippled by not being able to use his mobile phone. He had already used a landline at the home to call Sanders and leave the message. Where was she, anyway?

They would go to Pauline's place and talk to David there. Pauline would calm him, Bill would be able to help. He would call Louise Brown from there, and if he still could not contact Sanders, he would have to speak to Tony King.

He took a reluctant David by the hand. "It's all right David, I promise I won't hurt you."

"There's a good chance he's heard that before," said Bill, "I had."

The reporter half closed his eyes and reopened them. Until now it had only been words and he could deal with them no matter how distasteful. But here he was in the reality of it; here, standing in the deserted spaces of Lacey House he was sickened. It was Bill's turn to show some tenderness. Uncharacteristically he put his hand on the reporter's shoulder and said gently, "Come on, let's get on with it!"

Bill took David by the hand and between them they escorted him through the grounds to Preston's car.

As they left they did not see another car draw up to the entrance and a man get out, the same man who'd left only 30 minutes earlier. He made his way to the door and saw it was unlocked. He went inside and saw the children. He did a headcount just to be sure, as far as he knew it would be the last time he did it. Seventeen! One of them was missing? Who? He counted again.

They've got David Maclean. He pulled out his phone, urgently.

King walked into his office and called the coroner's officer first through the police exchange. "Denis it's Tony King."
"Yes, DC ... sorry, Acting Detective Sergeant King?"

"Have you got the report handy on the old man who died after the city centre shooting?"

"Somewhere in the pile. There wasn't much to that though. He died of a heart attack after being shot. The Coroner wasn't even sure if he could call it unlawful killing."

"I need to go through the detail. Do you know if the pathologist took a blood sample?"

"Of course!"

"And!"

"It was normal. He had a high cholesterol count, hence the heart attack, but nothing else."

"Not even traces of drugs from his hospital treatment."

"I'll take a look."

There was a lengthy pause. King could hear the sound of a keyboard being worked..

"Here it is! No, none at all."

"Doesn't that surprise you!"

"Well, it did surprise me but it didn't surprise the pathologist so it didn't surprise the coroner. Where the medic goes the coroner always follows."

"Is the Coroner a lawyer or a doctor, I can't remember?"

"Lawyer!"

"Thanks Denis, by the way are you a football fan?"

"Sometimes."

"What was the big match the night before the old fellow died?"

"United against Arsenal, I was watching it."

"How can you remember that?"

"It was a big death, you tend to remember what happens around it."

"I get you."

He put down the phone and thought for a few seconds. If it was the old man's drip that had been tampered with then surely there would have been at the very least a trace showing up in the blood. As for there being no sign of any treatment drugs, that had to be daft. What was the point of having a test if it did not show that!

A voice came from behind the door, "All right Tony, how are you dealing with it?"

It was Sam Spencer. King steeled himself, he didn't have a clue what Sanders' texts meant but she'd made it clear Spencer was at the heart of it and it was bad. He'd barely had time to absorb what she'd written and he needed to cause a diversion.

"Fine, guv, making progress now, could do with DS Sanders, though, how long's she going to be out?"

Spencer was quiet for three seconds, long enough to heighten King's concerns.

"We're looking at that now."

Preston wasted no time once he'd reached Pauline Maclean's home. He used her landline to call Louise Brown. She picked up immediately.

"Louise, this is Simon, I'm calling from Pauline's place."

"Mr Preston... Simon, what's up?"

"Can you come around here immediately? It's serious!"

"Of course, but why!"

"I've just come from Lacey House I have David Maclean with me and I need you here to help me with the details of what happened to him."

"What about Sergeant Sanders?"

"I can't get hold of her, she's disappeared."

"I'll come right away." She put down the phone and turned to Paul Bowes who was in an office with her,

"Paul can you take my clinic this afternoon, I have an emergency?"

"What sort of emergency?" She knew she was supposed to keep everything quiet but he deserved an explanation, "I'm going to talk to John Maclean's son. We need to find out from him what really happened."

"Good grief, John Maclean's son, why would you want to speak to him? He's in care isn't he?" She looked down at the floor, Bowes continued, "What's going on Louise? Do you know what you're doing?"

"I don't know Paul, but sometimes you have to bend the rules."

"What does that mean?"

She fought with herself for several seconds before finally

deciding that she could not keep what she knew to herself any more. She unloaded everything on Paul Bowes and then slumped into a chair.

"This is madness, are you sure about it? "

"Yes, I'm afraid I am, Paul. It's hideous and dangerous but I can't walk away from it."

"No, I suppose you can't. Neither can I now. Shouldn't you at least call the social services first?"

"I don't think so, and please don't you do it, Paul!"

He sighed, "All right but you're taking a risk."

"I'm doing this for the right reasons, not the wrong ones."

"Is there any way I can help?"

She thought for a second, "Maybe you can. I'll call you later." She put on her jacket and left the room. When the door closed Bowes thought for a few seconds and then picked up his phone.

Preston had not anticipated the wave of emotion which would greet young David when Pauline Maclean opened her front door. When she saw him she screamed, "David, why are you here! Never mind, you are," and she threw her arms around him. David said tentatively, "Mum?" but although he returned the greeting in part, his inbuilt reticence stopped him doing much more than smiling a little. Bill stood back unable to share in the joy.

"Let's get inside!" said Preston hurriedly. They went in where Pauline was unable to control her delight. She had wanted someone to simply hug for a long time, that was one of the reasons they had adopted David, so that he could share her love. Then she looked at Preston. "How…?"

"We found him at Lacey House. It's deserted just like the James place was. Just a bunch of kids left. I brought David away because he can help us get to the truth of what happened with John. And we don't want him being swallowed up by the same people again."

"What about the others?" Asked Pauline.

"I had to leave them there. I didn't dare call the police and I could not contact Di Sanders. We know the social services are a problem, so I did the best I could. I brought him here."

It was Bill's turn, "If we're going to talk to him, let's do it with the right people. If we can't get a police officer, get the doctor." Sensible, rational, clinical, cold, that was Bill.

Preston made the call. Then, as he watched David and Pauline appearing to enjoy each others' company he called Sanders number again. Same response. So he took the step he had not wanted to and called Tony King's number at the police station.

As he pressed the numbers David asked, "Where's Dad?" The boy was a lot different in the flesh to the sad uncertain image he had got to know from the video.

"He's not here right now, David, but we hope to get him home soon," said Pauline turning her head away to hide her grimace.

"Is he coming home soon, I want to play with him?" What was peculiar about the boy's speech? There was something important there and he just could not pick it up.

Then Tony King answered, "Acting Detective Sergeant King." Preston picked up an edge in King's voice and was even less confident about bringing him in, but he had no choice. "Tony, this is Simon Preston. I have to talk to you. Have you heard from Di Sanders?"

King paused, why would he want to speak to a TV reporter, especially a former boyfriend of Di Sanders?

"No, I haven't," he said, giving nothing away.

"Look I don't want to talk on the phone but Di says you're all right. I must speak to you."

"What is this, Mr Preston? I don't just come at your bidding you know!"

"Of course not, but it's crucial that I talk to you and I'm not messing about, really!"

King pondered this imploring and dare he even say deferent version of Simon Preston. He kept his reservations but said, "Meet outside Di's apartment in thirty minutes!"

They finished the conversation. Preston looked around Pauline's house and decided David was safe enough. "Bill, stay here with them please, I have to go for a while. I'm meeting someone at Di's place."

"What good will that do if she's not there?"

"Just look after them please Bill; and David and Pauline, stay here, don't let yourself be seen. I doubt that they would come here first of all, especially as the police haven't been told yet…"

"We don't know that, they could easily have been. Remember who's in this!" said Bill.

That was worryingly true.

Robin Humphries had not been able to sleep since he left Pauline Maclean the previous evening. He knew nothing of the developments elsewhere, he only felt that he had somehow misjudged his client. Perhaps it was a mistake to make any judgement at all on clients, just supply them with legal advice. But human nature is what it is and he had got it wrong. He did not know why he had got it wrong because nothing had changed since the beginning of the case. The evidence remained the same, the conclusions drawn by the jury were inevitable. But Maclean's angry demeanour throughout had foxed him until finally he saw in that awful Crown Court custody cell that somewhere there had been a terrible miscarriage of justice. He saw in Maclean a father who cared; he knew what one looked like because he was also a father who cared. If only he could pinpoint where the failure had been: himself perhaps, had he not given the case enough thought?

No, he may not have trusted his client but he gave him everything he could. So, what could it have been? The police, don't be silly; the social services, equally daft; the teacher, totally honest and why would she want to anyway! The medics: nothing in it for them either. But there was something very wrong.

"Want some coffee," his secretary asked as he sat bleary eyed at his office desk. "No. I'm going out. I need some air and some time." The secretary looked on mildly alarmed, he rarely displayed behaviour like this. He put on a coat and walked out into the street.

When he added it up they could all be part of it, and yet to think there was a conspiracy was ridiculous. He had rotary dinners with some of these people. But something was amiss and if he couldn't see it, perhaps someone else could.

He looked at the clock in the city centre then made up his mind and strode quickly back to his office. "Hold my calls for fifteen minutes please, Lucy." He scrolled up his phone contacts and got the number for his old friend Superintendent Hawkins at the police station.

"Hawkins, who is this?" demanded a suspicious voice.

"Phil it's Robin Humphries... from the rotary club. I'm sorry to bother you like this but I've been plagued with doubt about the whole Maclean case."

"I'm sorry, Robin, which case?"

"Of course, I suppose it was too small for you to be in contact with. Your CID put a fellow called John Maclean away for ten years for abusing his adopted son."

"Oh yes, I remember, it was yesterday wasn't it?"

"The fact is I thought he was as guilty as everyone else!"

"Did you say you were representing him?"

"Yes, and I still thought he was a bad one."

"Didn't say much for his chances did it?"

"That's what worries me. Phil, I know all the evidence was against him, but I never queried any of it. And now I have an awful feeling he's been set up."

"Set up! By whom?"

"I can't begin to know. I just feel he didn't do it and something has conspired for him to take the blame."

"Are you sure you're all right Robin. You're calling me saying there's been a cover up and the wrong man has been deliberately sent to jail!"

Humphries sighed. He knew how absurd it sounded, he was even tempted to throw it in and simply say the jury had found him guilty. It was out of his hands. But a voice nagged him from within. He was determined to listen to it this time because not to do so would betray both his client and himself.

"I know it sounds daft Phil, I have no evidence, just a feeling. Are you sure everything was straight at your end?"

"What possible reason could there be for it to be any other way. Why would my officers want to invent something?"

"I don't know, Phil, I'm sorry."

"I think you'd better go home and sleep on it. You won't do

yourself any good spreading around crazy rumours like that."

He ended the call without another word. Superintendent Phil Hawkins had another urgent call to make on what would become a sleepless night for him too.

"You're telling me they have that little brat! After all that work! Fuck: how did it happen, you were supposed to shift him out?" The voice was shouting into a telephone and the recipient could be heard to feel uncomfortable.

"I wasn't gone for long, I was moving some files. They must have got in while I was out."

"This is a mess. It'll be as bad as the James affair. I wanted those kids moved fast, spread out to different locations."

"We can still do it!"

"Anyone can close a gate after the horse has bolted. This particular pony is away and gone, and I presume you have no idea where."

"Sorry!"

The phone crashed against a wall, his face a mask of rage. His temper had been masking a mounting fear and now it overwhelmed him. He was going to be found out. Found out for the sake of the Devil; uncovered. He was shaking, his limbs went weak. The anger which had kept him standing while he shouted, had given way to all the anguish he had battened down in his life and he fell on to a hard chair.

It had become too big for him. Him, Mr Big himself, and it was too much for him!

He sat hopelessly in his chair trying to regain his balance. He fought and kicked for it to return. He drew on all the strength he had built up in the decades of monstrosity which had brought him to this moment.

Then slowly the shaking stopped. He regained control of his limbs and his mind returned to a state of equilibrium, although not equanimity. It would never be that. Thank the gods that no-one else had seen him like that. He would have been a sitting target for them. He had done it enough to others in the past, he knew how much they would have enjoyed it.

King and Preston stood outside Sanders' town centre

apartment block.

"Sorry we've never had the chance to talk much, Tony," said Preston.

It was wasted on King. "Why would you? I'm only a Detective Constable after all."

It was true, ground level contact was rare these days, there was no time for it.

"You can't know everyone…"

"No, you can't. So it's best to concentrate on the big ones, I suppose."

King couldn't make any clearer his opinion of Preston if he shouted it in a megaphone."

"Let's sort that out later, we need to talk to Di and I haven't heard from her since yesterday."

King kept his counsel, the messages on his phone remained there and in his mind, no one else's. He did not like the reporter, possibly because of Di, possibly because Preston was famous, or possibly because he did not like journalists.

"Come on, let's ring the bell!" said King urgently. He pressed it. They waited for a few seconds. Both knew the distance from the furthest part of the apartment to the security phone. Sanders had enough to time to get there, and she had not.

"Right, I'm worried, Tony. She's been missing since I dropped her here last night, and she was going somewhere she wasn't able to tell me about." King nodded, he knew where she had been. He was even more worried.

"Let's go in!" said Preston .

"How?", replied King as he went to push another button on the door. The reporter's hand stopped him.

"No need to disturb a neighbour," and he flashed a key in front of the detective.

"Where did you get that?" asked King irritably.

"That should be obvious," replied Preston as he turned the key in the lock and pushed open the door.

They quickly mounted the stairs and knocked on the door. Still no response. Preston produced another key for the door, this time King said nothing. They pushed it open and walked in a couple of steps. Then they drew back at the mess in the flat; the place had been turned over, it looked as if it had been searched and wrecked in the process. But how could burglars get in here thought King.

Preston walked further in, to the bedroom. The bed was made, there was no sign of Sanders. He glanced at the answering machine which was still switched on and registering calls. King said as he advanced into the flat, "Who uses an answering machine, these days?"

"Some people still like them. I know Di thought it made life easier for her."

King raised his voice irritably when he saw Preston picking up a piece of paper, "Don't touch anything, the place has been burgled."

The remark brought Preston's gaze from the floor to behind the sofa and he gasped in horror.

"What have you seen?" asked King as he made his way quickly to the sofa. Preston was unable to speak and as the detective looked down he could see why. There on the floor was the lifeless body of Di Sanders. There was no doubt that she was dead, her skin was coloured blue and purple and when he bent to touch her, as he inevitably did, she was ice cold, and stiff. Neither of them could see any peace in her face, the way you're supposed to when you encounter a corpse. She had died badly.

He had never regretted it, never believed he would have to pay any sort of price because he was the banker as well as the spender. But just at that moment he realised he was not immortal, just human, with human frailties. It was unnerving. The fact was that they were closer to discovery than they had ever been and this time the bodies were adding up, the more they did the worse it could be for them.

He grabbed his phone and punched out a number he hoped he would not have to use. It was the prison where John Maclean was being held before being put out into the dispersal system. Curiously this was no governor or prison officer he was calling, just a lowly clerk in the administration section. He needed contacts everywhere and for some reason the prison service had run dry on him in recent years. So he had to take what he could get.

The number rang twice: "Hello."
"Fix Maclean!"
"How?"
"Transfer him to a normal wing, make it look like a bureaucratic cock-up!" He ended the call.

The clerk was still hanging onto the receiver wondering what it was all about. That word "Fix" was important, the Network wanted Maclean dead, not just beaten up. How could he do that, then he started flicking through the files in the administration area, looking for someone with a bad psychological profile, someone who had been abused himself and needed to take it out on anyone he came into contact with.

Fifteen minutes later the clerk's eyes lit up: there he was, on C wing, serving life for murder, attempted murder, grievous bodily harm, and drugs. That was just a sample. He pulled his psychological profile. It boiled down to one thing, dangerous!

Now all he had to do was find a way of moving Maclean into C Wing, today, and casually letting it be known to the screws just why he was there. He started working with the prison computer.

They retreated a few metres from the body, both were dazed.
"All right Preston, what do you know?"

The reporter had gathered himself and tried to think rationally, but his mind kept going back to the cold body on the floor. The body which had been so warm when he had known it. They had their problems, but they had become friends again.

"I just know she wouldn't tell me, or anyone else, what she was doing last night."

"Why should she want to?" King knew the answer well enough he thought, but he was still keeping it to himself.

"It's a very long story, it's why I wanted to see you in the first place. Now it's more important than ever."

"Get on with it then!" The detective was making no secret of his impatience. He had other things to worry about than politeness.

"Look, I know you don't like me but can we forget that for a while? Di's body is lying over there, I was only speaking to her last night."

"Screw you! Who do you think you are! I knew her, she was my friend, my very good friend," He shouted the last.

Preston raised his voice as well. "What makes you so special, she was my friend too!" They heard the sound of their rage trying to banish what they could not. No matter how much they shouted Di Sanders would still be lying there.

They stopped.

"We'll have to tell someone, the Police." Preston's voice returned to normal.

"I AM the bloody Police..," said King, despairingly, "And there's no one I can think of to tell right now."

They looked at each other in silence for a few moments, always conscious of the body a few feet away.

"All right, here's what I know", said Preston, and he gave the detective everything, including David Maclean's location.

"OK, you're in as deep as I am," said King, "And you're right, I don't like you but we need each other right now so I'll work with you."

They simultaneously looked across the room to the sofa behind which lay Sanders' corpse. "Fuck it, we can't stay here and we can't tell anyone yet. Let's leave… but make sure we're not seen. We'll use the back exit. And if you've touched anything either bring it with you or wipe it down."

"Why?"

"Motive, we've both been her lovers…"

"Oh," said Preston, non-commitally.

King was almost shouting and Preston shrunk into himself.

"It's as bad as you think, that's why I can't think of anyone to call."

"No-one!"

"That's what I said," and he went on to explain why in only a slightly reduced voice.

Louise Brown was uncertain about calling on Pauline unannounced but she didn't have a choice. She wanted to be sure of what she was doing and she was not, it seemed too far-fetched. The more she thought about it the less likely it was: none of her colleagues had heard of Lacey House, did it really exist or was it a figment of someone's imagination? Had Simon Preston been more seriously affected by his recent injuries than he realised? Had he been blown off course? Any sane person would question what she was faced with. On the other hand it was her, Doctor Louise Brown, who had started it in the first place; it was her suspicion which had prompted the series of discoveries, but the evidence seemed so impossible.

And the idea that David Maclean would be back at his adoptive mother's home: kidnapped effectively! That was hard to take in. Even harder was the thought that she could not go to the police or the social services.

It was unreal.

"The whole police force can't be rotten, there has to be someone you can talk to," said Preston, incredulously.

King was expecting it, "I have to go through my line manager, and that's Sam Spencer at this moment, the very one she named in her texts."

"Well, we can't just sit here with her body just a few feet away and tell no one. It's wrong Tony!"

"I don't need you to tell me what's wrong. I have a good enough idea without lectures from you." King's wounds were open. The fact that Preston had a key to this apartment and that he had been a lover of Di Sanders made him a perfect target. It was hard remembering he was an ally. Even when King told himself he had no romantic future, even when he didn't want one, he couldn't quite give up that little possession he had when they were joined, however briefly. The act was over, the tenderness consigned to memory, but still something told him she was his even when he knew she wasn't.

"Stop shouting, Tony!" said Preston, "We have to make some sense of this." He looked around again to the sofa which hid her cold form. He shivered, it was one of the ugliest moments of his life. He had seen bodies before, plenty, scores, but he had never known any of them, not intimately.

"You've got to hold on to it. You're the only one we know who can do anything."

"I'm just a lowly acting sergeant. I haven't got any power. I can't take on a DI and higher."

"You're all we've got. Now Think! Who can we go to?"

King scowled but calmed down. "No one in this division. I can't go to Spencer for obvious reasons. The superintendent sounds as if he's suspect after keeping Di suspended for so long. It was him who reorganised the Maclean inquiry."

"You can't rule out everyone, there'll be no one left!"

"It looks like it. I can't trust anyone there, they could all be in for all I know."

"Bollocks, DC King, you're not in it, there will be others like you, plenty!" Then Preston went cold as he looked again into the detective's face, "Are you?"

King had wanted to hit something hard for the last ten minutes, he grabbed hold of Preston by the throat and raised a fist ready to bring it crashing down onto the reporter's jaw. It was going to be the first of many blows to vent his rage

"Of course I'm fucking not!" he roared.

Preston, versed in the streets of Cairo, Belfast and Mumbai, had learned how to take care of himself. Through the pain and hysteria of being attacked he saw the detective had left himself vulnerable in the groin and he brought up his knee quickly, King fell away winded. He slumped to the ground and the rage converted to sobbing.

"Jesus I'm sorry. What was that all about!", he stammered.

"I preferred you when you were angry," said Preston, "It's about something neither of us understands, Tony. But Di's gone, we have to do something about it."

The detective remained on the ground recovering his breath, the worst of the rage had gone.

"Concentrate, is there someone in another division we can go to. Who do you trust?"

They sat for several seconds while King thought through the force's divisions.

"Of course, Juliet Neilson!"

Preston looked at him quizzically.

"She's a chief superintendent at headquarters. I knew her five years ago when she was an inspector here. She's going to be a chief constable somewhere, eventually."

"Can you approach her?"

"She may be the answer."

"Let's get out of here and call, I can't stay here another second. This is foul!"

John Maclean found himself being led along a landing. Nobody had bothered to tell him but he was on the upper level of C Wing. He was flanked by two prison officers neither of whom said a word, they just scowled at him. They stopped and one of them turned a key in a cell door.

"Right Maclean this is your home, get in!" Maclean walked in slowly to see another man, not very big but with staring, unreachable eyes, sitting on the top bunk.

The door closed with a bang, the sound of jangling keys and chains briefly filled the smelly cell. Then there was nothing except the staring silence of his cellmate.

Maclean had enough to think about without trying to be sociable with his neighbour.

Nevertheless, he introduced himself slowly. "I'm John Maclean!"

There was no response. Maclean shrugged his shoulders, what did he care. He moved to sit on the bottom bunk and accidentally brushed his companion's legs. The man's face creased into a formidable mask of hate. He ground out the next words in a low voice.

"Don't touch me you fucking nonce!" and he lashed out with his foot catching the new prisoner square on the cheek. Maclean was surprised but accepted it. He knew it was not going to be easy. Then his mind was changed.

"I'm going to fucking kill you, you fucking child molester. I'm going to pull your balls out. Do you hear!"

All concerns for his position, all resentment about the injustice dealt to him were thrust to another part of his mind. Naked fear took over.

He beat loudly on the cell door and shouted: "Someone, for god's sake, get me out of here. I'm in with a madman."

He beat the door and repeated the message five times. It started a clamour in all the other cells on the landing. He could make out the words "Shut Up" and "Fuckin' nonce" in the general confusion. Then the footsteps of prison officers could be heard on the landing.

"Shut up the lot of you!" came a gruff voice which Maclean could not identify. His cellmate was staring at him unforgivingly as the clamour slowly died down. Whoever had spoken had some clout. Then the spyhole to their cell opened and a mean eye appeared.

"What are you shouting about Maclean?" came the unsympathetic question.

"This man has threatened to mutilate me. He says I'm a nonce. I'm supposed to be on Rule 43, why aren't I in a separate cell?"

"Well MR Maclean, we didn't want you to get lonely did we! You're in here because they say you're in here. Too bad if you don't like Charlie here, he's not very good with nonces. Still I'm sure you won't come to too much harm." Then the spyhole snapped shut and two sets of footsteps could be heard echoing along the landing as they receded. Maclean thought he heard a chuckle. He looked to see Charlie, he was not smiling, just baring his teeth through the face that had not changed since he had made his last threat.

Louise Brown pulled up outside Pauline Maclean's house and quickly locked the car. Pauline let her in and she was greeted by Bill, and a still very shy David.

"Hello David, my name's Louise." She bent down to shake his hand. He was not certain.

"Come on David!" cajoled Pauline, reassuringly, "Shake Dr Brown's hand!" He seemed even more uncertain but he held out his hand limply.

"Why don't we sit down and have a talk, David!" She led him by the hand to the sofa and sat down beside him. Bill looked on from the side. "First of all, are you feeling all right?" He nodded. "That's good. Are you pleased to see your mummy again?" He smiled, "Yeah!" a pause, "it's nice being home again." He looked around to see where Pauline was. She looked on dotingly from the other side of the settee. "It's nice seeing mum again." Then he looked at her directly, "When's dad coming back mum?" Pauline tried to hide her distress. "He's away for a few days David. I did tell you. You'll see him soon, we'll all see him soon," and she shot a meaningful look at Brown. The doctor returned it trying to look positive. But she had to get something definite from David.

"Will you be pleased to see your Daddy, David?" He looked at her, quizzically.

"Don't you mean Dad?"

"Why do you say that?"

"We've never called Him Daddy have we Mum!"

"No son, he's always been Dad."

Brown did not see it, but Bill sat bolt upright, like a man electrified. "Sorry to interfere Doctor. David, who DO you call daddy." The smile disappeared to be replaced by a worried frown which looked wrong in such a young child.

"Who, David!" Bill was not shouting but his voice carried more weight than any of them had heard before.

"What are you driving at, Bill, I don't get it?" said Brown, worriedly. She was trying to gain the boy's confidence and this kind of pressure might make him clam up.

"OK, I'll back off but you'll have to ask him the difference between Daddy and Dad. I don't think he'll tell me."

"Why! What's so special about it?"

"With a bit of luck he'll make it clear himself." She turned back to David who remained hunched up. The openness of before gone.

"Is Daddy not the same as Dad?" He shook his head unwillingly.

"Who is Daddy, David?" she asked softly, as if she was stroking her own child.

He looked back as if wanting to trust her. But something held him back. "It's a secret", he muttered.

Bill broke in, "David, did Daddy ever hurt you?" The doctor went to shut him up but held back as she saw David reacting. His already furrowed brow had intensified and he now looked tortured.

"Did he hurt you, David?" repeated Bill, more softly.

The doctor watched on not knowing what to do. It was important but David was being made to suffer and she could not allow that. It was her job to relieve suffering in children.

She could see the anguish tearing him up. Her heart went out to him and perhaps through the ramparts that he had been forced to build he managed to get a sight of it.

"It's all right David, you're safe now. You're with us. You're with your Mum and me. You don't have to have any secrets."

The anguish lessened in his eyes, but only a little.

"I thought I was safe before when I came here. When I was here with Mum and Dad."

"What changed it?"

"They took me away again. They took me back to it all."

Bill crashed in again, "Back to what?"

David froze again. "I can't tell you."

Brown interjected quickly, "Bill back off, will you, you're doing more harm than good!"

She turned again to David: "What did they take you back to David?"

He looked at her and finally burst out, "Back to Daddy, back to all of them." Then he burst into tears: "They hurt me. They were always hurting me." Brown hated to see a child cry, she hated to see this one in such distress and for all her skill as a paediatrician she had no medicine for this pain. But she had got what she needed: David had confirmed everything they suspected. She cuddled him and beckoned Pauline over at the same time. David's adoptive mother took the sobbing child into her arms and stroked him.

Brown slipped quietly off the sofa and up to Bill who had moved away from the tender scene. He struggled to look her in the eye and murmured with his face almost at right angles to her, "It's obvious: Daddy is someone completely different from his Dad. Daddy was one of the bastards at the James Institute. He used to give Jack a bad time. I never knew who he was."

"So that's the one mentioned in the interview. We'd better tell Simon."

Pauline looked up, "We'd better tell Mr Humphries, our solicitor."

Then the doorbell rang and the room froze.

"It must be Simon," said Louise. They all breathed a sigh of relief and Pauline went to the door. As she got closer she could see through the frosted glass that it was not Preston. The shape was unfamiliar. She opened the door gingerly and recognised with horror the figure standing there.

"Good afternoon Pauline, we meet again. I understand you have a young lad by the name of David Maclean here. He's supposed to be in care isn't he? I've come to take him back," said Detective Inspector Jack Spencer with practiced ease. Louise Brown heard part of the conversation, Bill heard all of it. They both watched David's reactions as he cowered in a ball as soon as he heard the policeman's voice at the door.

King and Preston came in one car, the detective was driving, neither had said a word since they left Di Sanders' flat, carefully closing the door behind them. Preston fiddled with his phone filling time and realised he had a video of someone at Lacey House. He rigged the phone through King's screen consul and played it. "Who's he, Tony; do you know him?" King glanced down trying to concentrate on both the road and the screen but as soon as he saw the image he said, "Deputy director of social services, why?"

"He was at Lacey House taking away documents or something."

"Shit, you mean the social services are deep in this as well?"

"They had to be. How else could the rest have got away with it!"

They both fell silent until they reached Pauline Maclean's street. As they drove into it they saw two cars parked outside. One was Louise Brown's, Preston recognised it, the other looked familiar to King, he had seen it in the police car park but it was not a police car.

Then he saw Jack Spencer standing at the door appearing to talk to Pauline.

"Christ it's him, Jack Spencer!"

Preston shouted hoarsely, "Back up quick!" King did not need to be told twice. He thrust the gearstick into reverse doing his best not to crash the cogs, then reversed beyond Spencer's line of sight. The detective inspector had been concentrating on what he was doing on the doorstep and had not turned to see them.

"That means they've tracked him already! Jesus, how did they do that?"

"There are no others there, just Spencer. No uniforms, no social workers. What's he trying?"

"He's trying to get David before anyone knows he's gone," said Preston, 'I think that will be it for David if we don't do something now."

"There's a way round the back. We'll have to park the car out of sight and hoof it over a couple of fences."

"How do you know?" asked Preston.

"I'm a copper. I've had to work nearly every part of the city in one way or another. Stop wasting time."

The noise of the car reversing and driving off could be heard in the house but no one was listening. They only heard the sound of Pauline slamming the door in Spencer's face.

"That'll make him mad," observed Bill.

"What do we do?" asked Brown.

Her question was punctuated by a loud battering of the door.

"Come on, open up, Pauline, or I'll break it down."

Bill looked worried then in desperation he said, "Tell him you'll call the Police."

She looked at him askance then did it anyway.

"Go away or I'll call the police!"

"Don't be silly Pauline, I am the police," but the battering stopped temporarily.

Pauline tried to gather herself. David was as tense as a board, he had heard the voice on the other side of the door and Bill had watched him.

"Is that Daddy, David?" he whispered. The lad shook his head.

"It's someone else."

"From Lacey House?" He nodded.

Pauline was panicking. "There is no way out the back, it's someone else's garden."

Doctor Brown was nonplussed, this was a far cry from her treatment rooms. She had no control over this, but she could see that unless she took command nothing would happen and they would lose David again.

"Let's get out there anyway. Come on!" She shooed them all into the small garden. She was the last of the four to come out, she was looking directly at David trying to make sure he was all right. She did not look straight in front of her and could do nothing to prevent a pair of arms encircling her and a hand going over her mouth. Her eyes widened with terror until she heard a soothing "Shush" it's me, Simon Preston. I didn't want you yelling out."

She continued to struggle and said, loudly, "Let me go! Who do you think you are!" Preston's sotto voce was insistent, "Shut Up! DI Spencer is one of the baddies." She fought on for two more seconds but only because she had programmed herself to, the words got through and she went quiet. Just for half a second she surrendered to it and then regained her wits.

"How did you know?"

" No time for talking now, this is Acting Detective Sergeant Tony King." He pointed out the detective. "David, climb on my shoulders, we've got some cross country to do. The car's over this way."

As they mounted the first hedge and cleared it they could hear the renewed sound of a door being battered, followed by the tinkle of breaking glass.

"He's gone? How the Hell did he get away? You... ! Do you realise what this means? You have been *seen*, they know who you are. For Christ's sake why didn't you just beat her out of the way and get to the kid!" Another time Sam Spencer would have thrown it right back but he knew he'd failed and right now he was more terrified himself. He was meant to get David Maclean. He got no one.

"She slammed the door on me before I could do anything. I thought she would swallow the line, but she seemed to know. They got out through the back, then they just disappeared. I don't know where they went. I heard a car drive off but didn't see which one." His gasping responses were accompanied by a thumping heart.

"All the other cars are still there. They must come back for them sometime!"

"That will be too late! And why haven't you checked them through the DVLC? You could still have choked this off, but you keep screwing it up." There was a long cold pause.

"You're on your own now, you had better make your own arrangements." The finality in the voice sent a shiver down Spencer's back and into his hands, he had trouble holding his phone.

"You mean you're winding up the Network?"

"There is no Network now, you're on your own. Goodbye!"

The conversation ended. Spencer held the phone in his shaking hand not knowing what to do. He was breathing harder than at any time, perspiration seeped through his upper body, he felt a twinge in his left arm. His heart seemed to be beating its way out of his chest.

Then he felt a sharp stabbing pain which was like bad indigestion, except that it was worse than that. It spread to his left shoulder, very quickly, so quickly he did not have time to yell out for help.

Spencer knew he was having a heart attack but the knowledge did him no good. By the time it had entered his mind he was gripped by a pounding dreadful rhythmic pain in his left lung and he verged on unconsciousness as his heart failed to pump enough blood to his organs. He slumped slowly to the floor of the pub from which he made the call and stayed there motionless. He had found a secluded area so no one saw him collapse. He did not have time even to return the address book to his breast pocket, the book with so many important numbers. Because Sam Spencer was old school and didn't keep the numbers in his phone or on his sim, he hardly knew how. A few seconds later Spencer was dead and would not be discovered until the barmaid came round to collect glasses. That would not be for another 15 minutes when the body and the book would be found.

"Can we get your chief superintendent in on this now, Tony?" said Preston as he manoeuvred his people carrier through the city, thankful for once that it wasn't the Porsche he'd been so keen on when buying a new car the year before. King was in the front seat, Pauline and David were at the rear and Louise

Brown and Bill were in the middle.

"Just as soon as we find somewhere to offload this lot!"

Pauline was doing her best to stay calm for David but she was in a world where nothing made sense. At least she wasn't alone in that.

"How about my place?" offered the doctor, "They won't think to look there will they?"

"Sounds reasonable," replied King.

"We can't be certain of that," warned Preston, "Somehow they knew David was at Pauline's place. If they tracked him to there they must have something on us somewhere. What is it?"

"You haven't used your phone have you, Simon?" he asked.

"Not at all, not at any stage since the accident."

"That doesn't mean they don't know where you are – or at least your phone. It's the police, don't forget, we have this kit now, we can trace a phone if it's switched on – sometimes even if it's not."

"Isn't that illegal?"

"Nothing is illegal to the security service, you should know that. Sometimes we ask for their help. Anyway, It's not that. It seems strange that we kept him there for all that time until fifteen minutes after Dr Brown got here. Then we get the knock at the door." Bill looked at Louise suspiciously.

"Did you do anything Doctor!" he asked as the car progressed through the uneven traffic,

"I told my consultant I was going to meet David... I felt I had to."

"You did WHAT!" yelled Preston.

Brown was temporarily destabilised by Preston's exclamation, but she would not let this showpony dominate her. "I didn't say where. I had to explain why I needed to go, I can't just leave my patients. And anyway, I needed to tell someone I could trust – I mean I don't know any of you, I do know Paul Bowes."

"Maybe not as well as you think," said Preston, quietly this time.

"So, Inspector Plod turns up," said King, bringing them back to their current dilemma, "Everyone turn off your phones and take out the sim, let's at least give ourselves a chance. I don't think we can go to your place Dr Brown. They're clocking you as well." Her heart jumped. "Why me, what can they know?"

"Maybe it's because you know me," answered Preston, "Or maybe it's because you were on the case at the start. He's in your Risk file after all. Whatever it is we can't go to your place, and neither can you," then, suddenly his face fell, his eyes widened and he said desperately, "Where do we go?"

For the first time in Louise Brown's admittedly intermittent relationship with him he looked lost and was unable to stop his vulnerability from showing. She saw it and knew it for what it was.

Then King broke in, "Dr Brown do you know Mandeep Patel?"
"Vaguely, she's a senior nurse on the geriatric wards isn't she?"

"That's her. Do you trust her?"

"As far as I know her. Why?"

"We can take David to her."

"Who?" said Preston.

"Just be quiet, will you! I know what I'm doing." With that he directed Preston to the address on the piece of paper Mandeep Patel had given him recently. She would not enjoy being woken so early before her nightshift but this was crucial. It would be a safe phone and he could bring in Juliet Neilson. Not before time either, he was in so deep he doubted he would ever climb out. What a stinking pit. The image of Di Sanders' body with the wound to her head skipped into his mind and he winced.

Mandeep Patel was in a dressing gown and yawning when she answered the door. "Tony, I thought we said tomorrow night?" Then she glanced over King's shoulder to see the carload.

"What's going on."

"Please Mandeep, don't ask now! I can't tell you everything, it's better that you don't know." He turned and indicated the car with his open hand, "We need somewhere to stay for a few hours." She looked at him with her mouth slightly open and an unformed question struggling to get out. King stopped it before it could make any progress, "Mandeep, I wouldn't ask you this but we have nowhere to go."

"But you're a policeman. You can get help anytime you need it." She looked at him suspiciously and said, "Have you done something wrong?"

"The exact reverse. I can't tell you right now. Please just let us in!" She looked at the desperation in his face and altered hers to a smile.

"Come on then, bring them in!"

She watched the car empty and the look of surprise returned when she saw Louise Brown get out with David and Pauline.

As she made room in the doorway she greeted her colleague: "Hello, Dr Brown, this is a surprise."

"Hello Nurse Patel, if you only knew the half of it."

"Just a quarter would be a start!"

"Nothing yet, Mandeep," repeated Tony King, "As far as you are concerned we are not here and you know none of us. I promise I'll make it up to you, now where's your telephone." She pointed the way.

"Right, Preston, Dr Brown, with me please!"

"Just call me Louise please, that goes for you as well, Mandeep!"

The nurse smiled and closed the door on them as they went to make the crucial call.

"Let's get this Dad and Daddy stuff straight, you're the only credible witness. David says he was abused by someone called Daddy, but not John Maclean who he calls Dad."

"That's it exactly."

He said no more but dialled a number he seemed to know from memory.

"Here goes, let's just pray."

Brown looked despondent. "Hasn't done us much good so far has it!" Preston took her hand and squeezed it gently. She made a move to take it away but the unexpected tenderness was welcome and she let it happen.

"Where has this bitch gone now."

"She's not at home, her mobile hasn't been used for more than two hours."

"And Preston."

"He seems hors de combat. We haven't seen or heard from him for most of the day."

"Find them, then find the boy. Now!"

Chief Superintendent Juliet Neilson answered after three rings.

"Juliet Neilson."

"Guv… Juliet, it's Tony King."

"Tony! You're using my workphone so I assume this isn't social?"

"No, it's the wrong protocol and I should go through my line manager in my division but I can't do that."

"Why not?"

"You're not going to like this." He told her everything that had happened.

"Have you been taking something, Tony? Have you broken into the confiscated Drugs store?"

"No, Ma'am."

"Forget the Ma'am and the Guv, we go too far back."

"Right, Juliet, we're hung out to dry here. We have Sam Spencer and Phil Hawkins in on it and I'm just a DC…. Acting DS."

"You were never just a DC, Tony, you'll be a DI soon enough. But what can I do? I'm a chief super, yes, but I can't just crash into someone else's division and start throwing my weight around."

King realised the truth of it.

"No, I suppose you can't. But you can bring in high command, they can do what they like."

"You realise what you're asking me to do? Risk my career – no, trash my career – on a wild series of accusations from a DS in the Family unit?"

"All right, Juliet, you know me better than that!"

There was a pause before she said, "Yes, I suppose I do. All right, I'll go straight to the chief with it. And I'll get a couple of uniforms from another division to go to Sanders' place… and where was it… Lacey House?"

Her brisk professionalism pulled King back into active police work instead of being on the run.

"That's it... Guv!"

"And send me those texts from Sanders straight away – whoever is listening out for calls won't be able to pick up the messaging! And make sure you text me her address!"

"Straight away."

"And you get back to DS Sanders' place now!"

"Er..."

"Don't hesitate, Tony, get on with it! I'll meet you there."

No wonder she was flying so high, so young.

He ended the call, fired up his phone and told the rest as he forwarded the texts. He closed down his phone again immediately.

While he did Preston picked up the landline receiver and dialled the newsdesk.

"Who are you calling," said King.

"Work, in all of this it's easy to forget what I do for a living."

"Can't you leave it until we get ourselves sorted out?"

"I've been out of contact for too long..." He stopped speaking as Geoff Donald answered.

"Newsdesk."

"It's Simon."

"Where the fuck have you been?"

"Long story, here's the short version..." He told Donald everything so far.

After a short pause the news editor exclaimed, "Fuck my old bones. What do you need?"

"Back up! Get Jonesy on it."

"Got it. Now, this time stay in touch!"

"I'll try, got to go." He replaced the handset without waiting for Donald's response.

"Happy now?" said King.

"No!" replied Preston, looking him straight in the eye.

Donald wasted no time, he called Mike Jones at home, explained the story and said, "So I need you to get to this DS Sanders' place with Steve Topping, ASAP!"

There was a brief pause while Jones took in the information, then he said with a rueful, "He's a jammy sod, isn't he. He only has to tread on a turd and it turns into a story. I don't know how he does it."

"He's good at his job, Mike, so are you. Now if you want to be part of this can you get a move on. We're about to bust a paedophile ring and it's huge."

"Isn't it just. Right, I'm on it."

"Good. Don't let jealousy get in your way, your turn will come again, it always does."

"No, I don't begrudge a mate a bit of success. I'll call when I've linked up with Steve."

He ended the call.

Neilson was already waiting for them with two female PCs by the apartment block door when they arrived. She was dressed casually in a sweater, jeans and trainers.

"Who is this, DC … Acting Detective Sergeant King?" she asked.

"Simon Preston, I was with Tony when we found Di."

"Mr Preston? The TV reporter?" She looked at King, "Tony?"

"Without him we wouldn't be here now, Guv, we need him – and I don't like it any more than you do."

Neilson paused for a moment then said,

"All right, I'm putting a lot of trust in you Mr Preston, don't abuse it!"

He made no mention of Steve Topping whom he'd spotted on his way in but who was keeping a discreet distance. He looked for Jones but felt the pressure to add to his exchange with Neilson.

"This is too big to score journalistic points, Chief Superintendent, you have my word."

"I hope that means something. Hurry it up Tony… DC King, let's get in and have a look!"

Preston opened both doors with his keys and stepped back. He did not want to go in. It had only been a few hours since they were last there but already a smell was developing. It was April, the days were becoming warmer even though there had been no heating in the apartment.

"OK there's obviously something. Let's see!" said the chief superintendent as she marched in.

"If you don't mind, Guv, I've already seen as much as I want to," said King, hanging back at the door with Preston. "Look behind the sofa," he said and they both waited. It was only a few seconds.

Neilson stopped and said nothing for 20 seconds, then, "You poor girl Di. What have they done to you?" She remained composed. "That's it!" She pulled out a mobile phone and made a call. "They're right, she's here and very dead, I'm afraid, Ma'am."

A short time later they heard the sounds of feet coming up the stairs and everyone looked to see who was approaching. The reporter recognised her first but King was soon after him. She was not dressed the way they would normally see her, in a uniform with shiny silverware on her cap and epaulettes and blue collar tabs. She was in a sweatshirt and jeans and very few would have known her to be the chief constable.

Tony breathed to Preston: "If she's on our side then we're through. If not then we can kiss everything goodbye.

"Good evening DS King." King stiffened to attention, "and I believe it's Mr Preston, is it not? How different you look away from the television screen." They nodded at him.

"Where's DS Sanders?"

"Here Ma'am," replied Neilson pointing behind the sofa. The chief constable's face had worn a political smile until that point. But when her eyes went down to the body it changed. "Oh no!" she moaned quietly. She stood over the body not saying a word. King knew it was the sense of family loss which hits all police, no matter the rank. And it hits the boss hardest of all. Only Preston saw the very slight change of stance in Juliet Neilson. She had almost imperceptibly moved to the chief's side and he thought he heard her say "Petra!" but in a very low voice. The Chief snapped back upright and her face now bore a scowl of command. "All right DS King, tell me everything you know and let's start to understand this!"

John Maclean recoiled in pain and dropped his food tray on the floor of the communal dining room. It was called free association at meal times but it did not feel free to him. He had just been jabbed hard in the thigh with a sharp object while standing in the queue. As soon as the crash of the tray sounded the place went quiet. No one said a word.

He looked around to see who had done it as he clutched his thigh. It could have been any of them, they looked as if they could happily have done more.

"Dropped your food have you Maclean! Shame, you'll have to wait until breakfast now won't you!" The voice came from an officious looking man wearing a white shirt, black tie and bearing two pips on his epaulettes. By now he had learned that meant he was a Principal Officer, one of the most senior in the establishment, the very one who should be protecting him from this intimidation.

He was too close to home. He had gone to a dispersal prison ten miles outside the city while it was decided where he should go next. News had travelled there faster than he had. "Why aren't I on Rule 43?" he demanded of the uniform, his voice echoing off the yellow painted brick walls.

"Shut your fucking mouth you nonce!" came the reply.

"You're here because that's what the piece of paper says. And if it's in black and white on a piece of paper, it's true."

"What are you trying to do to me?"

"What did you do to your boy?" snarled the man in the uniform.

The pain eased slightly although blood was beginning to seep through his prison issue trousers. It must have been a knife. Maclean looked at the mess on the floor and started to walk away.

"Where are you going Maclean!"

"Back to my cell."

"Clear up that mess, you'll go to your cell when I say so!"

He could not fight the officer and he had no friends among the inmates.

"Where's the brush", he asked wearily.

"No brushes Maclean, you dropped it, you clean it up with your bare hands." Maclean sighed and started to scoop the food from the linoleum floor. As he bent down a foot lashed out from a nearby formica topped table. Maclean's arm went into the pile of mashed potatoes and he hurt his injured thigh trying to recover himself.

And that was just the start of the humiliation.

They were drinking coffee, David had an orange juice. He remained quiet. Bill had probed a couple of times but got nowhere. "Who was the copper David? Where did you meet him before?" Nothing! David had clammed up tight again. Mandeep Patel was doing her best to be calm but she didn't really understand what was going on and she said so to Louise Brown.

"You're not the only one. It's a frightful mess. Murder, intimidation, abuse...and we just happened to stumble upon it."

"Are you on the run in some way?"

"Yes, in a way!"

"Not from the police surely?"

"In a manner of speaking."

"But what about Tony, he hasn't broken the law has he? Have you?"

"No, we're trying to uphold it."

Patel looked none the wiser. Brown tried to elucidate.

"It goes back to the shooting a few weeks ago. Simon Preston has stumbled upon a paedophile network, and Tony King now thinks an old man who died in the hospital was murdered." She hoped that would do but she'd reckoned without Patel's intelligence. The nurse went quiet for a few moments as she digested the information. Then she said, "So that was what poor Helen was going on about." Then she looked again at David cuddled up in an armchair.

"What's his role?"

"He's the son – adopted son – of the man sent to jail for abuse yesterday."

"Poor lad!"

"Yes, but not because of his dad. It was this network again. They blamed it on the father and got away with it with some doctored police evidence." As she said it she realised that it seemed like a scattered 1,000-piece jigsaw puzzle.

Patel must have felt the same way, she fell silent, her eyes wide open.

"And there's more to it than that."

Brown had been wrestling with a dilemma as she related this to Patel. She knew she'd been told to take out her sim, but she couldn't afford to be out of contact with the department. They were overloaded as it was. She took the decision to restore the sim and hope that King and Preston had already smothered any threat elsewhere.

Immediately the room filled with the trilling sound of messages crowding into her Inbox.

As she started to retrieve them the phone rang. She did not recognize the number and was tempted to close down the call and take out the sim again. But it might be from the ward and she didn't want to risk it.

"Hello, Dr Brown speaking!"

"Ah Louise, got you at last. We've been trying to find you for hours." She did not automatically recognise the voice but it was familiar.

"Who is it?"

"Martin Tench."

Only a few days before she had been mithering about Tench and now she didn't recognize his voice! That made a nonsense of her self-obsession, she thought.

"Paul's been trying to get hold of you at home but there's been no reply. We tried bleeping you but you didn't respond..." She looked down the electronic pager in her bag. It was switched off at the same time as her phone. She had forgotten about it in the scramble of the last few hours.

"And we desperately need you back here."

" What's the problem?"

"We've got a minibus crash in and there's a backlog of overnight cases. We can't deal with all of it. You have been away quite a long time Louise, where are you now?"

"I'll come in as soon as I can."

"How soon is that?"

"In the next few minutes."

"All right, but please get your skates on!"

"See you in a few minutes, Martin," and she ended the conversation.

Elsewhere in the city a man picked up a telephone.

"Right! Juliet get a team up, make it people you know, and get that boys' home surrounded!" The chief was in the car that had brought her and Juliet Neilson to the scene. King and Preston were with them.

"King, get back and make sure you stay with the boy. I'll get a family unit woman officer to meet up with you. I'm calling Assistant Chief Constable Norris, I want him to go into the city police station and find out who else needs to be turned over." She looked at both his officers then barked an order, "Move, please!"

King left the car and returned to his own.

"Mr Preston you may care to help us locate Mr Maclean's solicitor. I shall need a judge's approval to have him released on license pending a pardon. One thing is certain, he should not be allowed to spend one more night in jail."

"Thank you, chief constable, I have his number in my phone."

He accessed the number and bluetoothed it to Neilson, then he left the car and located Topping.

"What have you got, Steve?"

"Lots of police activity going in and out but no bodies coming through."

Preston winced at the response. Any other time it would have been fine but this was personal and it was Di's body. He fleetingly thought of Mike Jones and how he would have understood, but the urgency of the moment moved him on.

"OK, Steve, I'm going to the prison, you follow and bring Jonesy along when you eventually meet him."

Topping nodded assent and they parted.

Robin Humphries had sat down to a quiet evening at home. The telephone rang and his eyes widened as he listened to the chief constable reveal what he knew. "I'm calling the judge straight away," he said. "Perhaps you would like to join Mr Preston at the prison. One of my officers will deliver the paperwork and I will call the governor."

Humphries was too surprised to say anything more than "Certainly, straight away, and thank you!" Then as an afterthought he asked, "Is Mrs Maclean aware of what is happening?"

Back in his car the chief constable looked at Preston and replied: "She will be very shortly. I advise you to go Mr Humphries." Humphries replaced the receiver quickly.

He put his suit back on and called to his wife that he could be out for some time.

Elsewhere in the city they had never thought to bug the chief constable's mobile phone and the eavesdropper remained oblivious.

"I have to go back to the hospital Mandeep," said Louise Brown, "I've been away too long, they need me."

"I'm on my last nightshift, I have to go as well," said Patel.

"I can't leave them here without you."

"What would Tony want?" asked the nurse because the more you tell me the less I understand."

The doctor shrugged helplessly and said, "You and me, both. I'm in way over my head here." She looked at Pauline, Bill and David and she knew she couldn't just leave them. Pauline was obviously a wonderful mother but she was a simple woman and the last few hours had knocked her sideways. Brown made a decision, an unwilling, reluctant one, she would have to take them to the hospital. They would be safe enough there, at least for the time being.

Pauline's house phone rang. It was Preston in a callbox.

Mandeep Patel answered, "Hello!"

"Mandeep, this is Simon Preston, please let me speak to Pauline!" She handed her the telephone and Pauline let out an involuntary gasp as she listened to the developments.

"He's going to be freed!"

"Yes Pauline, we're on our way now. Mr Humphries is coming as well." Pauline nearly jumped down the telephone line, "I want to be there as well."

"All right, we'll pick you up. Do you want David to come as well?"

Pauline's up until now mild and confused manner was replaced by a vehemence which took everyone aback. She shouted into her receiver, "No, I don't want him anywhere near a prison. I want him to make a clean start and I don't want him to see his father walking out of a prison gate."

Preston deferred, coming out of prison was nothing to be proud of even if you'd been falsely sent. It was a relief, not a triumph.

"OK, let me speak to Louise!"

Pauline handed the phone to Louise who had heard every part of her end of the conversation.

"Hello, Simon, is it all right?"

"It's getting better. Is everything all right there?"

"No I've been summoned back to the hospital, they've got a logjam, they need me to help clear it. I'll take David. I can leave Bill here now." There was a pause.

"Are you sure he'll be all right?"

"Of course what can happen to him there!"

"There are two corpses you could address that question to," he answered, firmly and without humour.

"All right, I take your point."

"I'll see you there." The phones went dead.

Tony King arrived at Patel's house just as she was leaving.

"They've gone, and thanks for mixing me up in this mess," she said, scaldingly.

"Gone where?"

"Dr Brown had to go to the hospital, she was called on her mobile. She's taken David with her."

"I told her not to use her phone, damn it! Where are you going?"

"To work Tony, where do you think, have you forgotten?"

King was annoyed with himself despite the urgency. It had only been forty five minutes since he had left the scene of Sanders's death but he knew he owed a lot to Mandeep Patel.

"And Bill?"

"He's inside. I have to go." She attempted to brush past him and he sensed that if he did nothing now their relationship would be dead before it started. He tried to put aside the memory of Sanders' corpse, and the importance of getting back to David. "What about tomorrow night?"

"That's up to you. I'm quite angry now... I may not be tomorrow." She rushed out to her car and got in.

King had no more time to, he ran into the house and yelled

for Bill to follow him. Together they bounded to his car and headed off in the same direction as the senior nurse but much faster.

The time was approaching mid-evening in the jail as Maclean, still bloodstained and covered in food, lay on the bottom bunk. The wound was superficial but a declaration of intent. They were banged up, and now Maclean was truly alone with the man with the staring eyes.

"Jesus you fucking smell, nonce!" said his companion, "You smell of food and you smell like a nonce." Then suddenly he was staring the man in the face. He had swung his torso over the top bunk and was leaning into his space. He spat at him full in the face. Maclean was not used to dealing with this.

"Why did you do that?" he said.

The man laughed. "Because you're a nonce!"

"What's a nonce?"

"*You're* a nonce you wanker. Someone who fiddles with women and kids, that's what a fucking nonce is, that's what you are!" The shock of what had happened to him had suppressed Maclean's tendency to anger, but that was enough to make it surface again.

"No I'm not", roared Maclean, his breaking point finally reached, "I never touched any kid in my life and I never will!"

"Yeah! that's what they all say. You gutless bastard, too scared to admit it aren't you. Well I'll get you to admit it." and he jumped down from the top bunk and aimed a kick at Maclean's face. It hit him a glancing blow on the forehead. Maclean was now furious, the rage which had erupted in court came out in full again, only this time he did not have to worry about guards at his side. He reared up from his bunk and slammed his head into his cellmate's jaw, the man was temporarily stunned. Maclean brought down a fist onto his neck and followed it with a left-handed swipe to the stomach. The element of surprise had given him the edge. His attacker backed away winded and dazed. But then he felt a sharp pain in his thigh where the knife had gone in earlier and it made him stop. It was enough for Charlie, only this time he was rushing at Maclean with a knife in his hand. Where did that come from? There was no time to think about the answer, Maclean had his work cut out dodging the blade in the tiny space of the cell. There was no running on to the landing, the door was locked. He avoided the first thrust but banged into the cell wall at the same time. It restricted his movement and aggravated the thigh injury.

He lashed out a foot to put him off while he cried out for help.

Then his attacker came at him again this time scoring a direct stab to the shoulder. Maclean did not have time to attend to the wound because he was coming again.

"Fucking nonce, fucking nonce," he chanted as if in an altered state.

He parried the next but it cut a slash through the shirt and into the left forearm. Maclean was virtually immobilised, his cries for help had become weaker, blood was spreading across his prison issue clothes and he was feeling faint. The man came in again, "Fucking nonce," he shouted as he plunged the knife into the area of Maclean's groin.

He was too weak to know what happened next. Neither of them had heard the key turning in the lock, nor seen the collection of people on the landing. The duty governor, an officer and a man in a suit.

Robin Humphries had heard the cries from down the landing as he rushed with the entourage to give his client the happy news that he was a free man. Something possessed him when he saw the prison officer open the door and instead of letting him take care of the security work he pushed him out of the way and dived between Maclean and the knife. He took the thrust on his wrist suffering a deep slash. It started to bleed immediately but it stopped the blade getting to Maclean. The officer followed in behind and disarmed the attacker who was still chanting his enraged mantra.

Maclean lost consciousness. His first act as a vindicated man.

He came round a few minutes later. The prison doctor was staunching the blood and had injected some adrenaline to keep it circulating. He was on a trolley being taken to the prison hospital. As it charged down the landing Charlie could still be heard chanting "Fucking Nonce," despite being held down by three prison officers.

Others on the landing took up the chant again, they had no idea what had happened or of Maclean's innocence, they probably did not want to know. He was something on which to vent their rage. Maclean looked at Humphries, then at Preston, "Well well, such dedication Mr Humphries, and it's not even visiting time." He looked contemptuous and Humphries felt it burning into his face, smothering the pain from his wrist. Preston butted in as he kept up with the trolley, "John, Mr Humphries has just saved your life!"

"You want me to say thank you?" said the soon-to-be ex-inmate as he rolled down the jail corridors. He was speaking slowly but every word was meant to hurt.

"Mr Humphries, I don't know many long words but I go to church." Humphries looked on uncertainly, the blood from his wrist still seeping through his makeshift bandage.

"You've got your absolution now, you can go!"

Humphries turned away and slowed down. He let the stretcher trolley get ahead, he was not going to follow it any more. The governor said, "They're taking you to the prison hospital, and from there to the main hospital. You're a free man, Mr Maclean, you're innocent."

Maclean, now beginning to feel the effects of the sedation, and already weak, replied, "You mean that's it?"

The governor looked down. "Yes, that's it. Your wife is waiting for you."

"My Pauline, thank god for that," and what little energy he had left was converted into gentle sobbing which lasted all the way to the hospital wing.

He did not hear the animated conversation between the governor and the principal officer, but others did.

"That he was an innocent man sent here is not our fault but you deliberately ignored Rule 43. You're suspended."

The uniformed officer knew he had no defence and did not try to mount one. He fell back.

Louise Brown raced into the hospital with David following and went straight to her office. There was no sign of Bowes or

Tench and she assumed they would be dealing with the minibus crash. She should be doing the same. She could not take David on the wards with her, she would have to leave him in the office.

"David, I have to go for a few minutes. I'll be back very quickly. You must stay here. Don't leave the office!" David looked unhappy but nodded. The boy was as quiet as he had been since she first saw him. The only times she knew he was panicking were when he fidgeted more, or seemed to breathe more heavily. Right now his breathing was heavier and his hand movements were jerky. But compared to the earlier drama he was under control. She smiled, patted him on the head, and closed the door behind her. Halfway down the corridor going towards the wards she met Tench going crossways.

"I'm sorry", she said as she went at right angles and fell in with him, "Where's the emergency?" His eyes lit up when he saw her, just as if the two of them had rejoined after the awful break.

"Don't worry, it was a hoax call to the ED, turn the fire engines round," and he laughed. His voice was as soft as it had been that night. She felt a familiar feeling tugging at her. She found her eyes reluctantly but inevitably moving to look at his face.

"Everything's all right I hope?" he said as they slowed to a stroll along the corridor.

Then she drew herself up sharply. She had been through a hell of a day, and David was still in their office.

"Everything's fine," she lied.

The police radio crackled into life in King's car, "Message for DS king. Are you receiving?"

"Receiving", he replied automatically.

"You are instructed to find a telephone landline and call Chief superintendent Neilson immediately."

"Understood!" He scanned the street for a phone box as he drove.

"There's one", cried Bill, and he braked hard to bring the car right alongside the box. It had not been vandalised.

He was put straight through.

"Spencer's dead, Tony. Might be a heart attack we're not sure."

"Where was he, Guv!"

"In a pub close to Pauline Maclean's place."

"Thanks, Guv."

"That's not all, Tony. We're matching up forensic at Di Sanders place with anything we might find on him." That was good he thought.

"But there's something else. He had an address book on him which we're going through. It doesn't have real names, just strange ones, but they all have numbers. We're checking them with the phone companies now."

"An address book? Who does that these days? Right Guv. I have to go. The boy's at the hospital with the doctor, I'm trying to catch up with them."

"Get on with it, Tony!"

"Yes, Ma'am."

Steve Topping had his camera switched on but slung down by his side. It was ready to go straight on to his shoulder the second the small door in the prison gate started to open. He had waited 45 minutes after watching Pauline and Robin Humphries go inside. He had watched and listened as the keys jangled before and after the entry.

He had seen an ambulance go in five minutes later and wondered about it but did not make any connection. He filmed it anyway, why not!

A flurry of jangling keys behind the gate broke the quiet of the mid-evening. Topping's camera was on his shoulder instantly and trained on the small door.

But he was surprised to see instead of that opening, the big gates slowly parting with a prison officer on each one.

Then he saw the ambulance in the prison's security chamber and Simon Preston was right alongside, making towards him.

Standing by its side was Robin Humphries and Preston started shouting as he loped forward. Something had gone wrong.

"Start running Steve, he's in that ambulance!"

"Are you sure?"

"Please just shoot!" The cameraman pressed the record button on his Sony and pulled out to a wider view at the same time. Preston ran to the side to get out of the shot.

The ambulance drove out and past them. Humphries walked up and said resignedly, "Someone must have put it about that he was in for child abuse."

"Bastards!" breathed Preston. He had not seen Topping swing the camera around to Humphries.

He looked at the solicitor's bandaged forearm. "How is it?"

"Absolution!" answered the lawyer, dejectedly, as if that was enough, and then slowly walked back to his car. Preston had no more time. "Back to the car Steve, let's get to the hospital!" and they ran quickly, passing the solicitor who did not give them a second glance.

Preston said breathlessly to Topping, "Where's Jonesy?"

"No idea, should I?"

"He's supposed to be with you here, now."

"I know, that's what Geoff told me, I haven't seen him at all tonight."

"What!"

"No idea, mate, nothing to do with me. I got in my car and came here straight away. I expected to meet him but no sign."

What are you playing at, Jonesy, thought Preston.

She felt some weight lifting from her shoulders. She had given an outline of what had happened, enough to make the picture clear. Tench looked into her eyes and stroked the back of her hand. The doctors' mess was empty except for them. The kitchen staff had long since gone, only snack and hot drink dispensing machines remained.

"So what happens now?" said Tench.

"Simon Preston's with the detective talking to the police."

"So it's being taken care of?"

"Yes, at last... sort of. The kids will be looked after but whoever's behind this will still be out there. Oh, Martin it's been horrible. I still can't believe that so many people could be doing that sort of thing. I mean what makes them do it?"

"Your guess is as good as mine. All we know is that we have

to pick up the pieces when they bring them in here."

"And I'm not sure we do that so very well!"

"Maybe not, we can only do our best. Come on Louise, it's not your problem anymore."

It had been a full twenty minutes since she had left David and it was only then that she remembered.

"Yes, it is, I still have the boy with me."

"Good heavens, where?"

"In our office."

"You mean you left him there alone!"

"I didn't have any choice Anyway what harm can come to him here?"

"Maybe none but it's best not to tempt fate. Let's get back there. I'll just get hold of Paul."

"Fine, tell him I'm here. I hope he's not too cross." Tench smiled reassuringly and squeezed her hand again.

The ambulance arrived at the Emergency Department and John Maclean was transferred to the treatment area.

Preston and Steve Topping were just behind. Topping leaped from the car as it was still moving and raced around to the back of the ambulance to film Maclean on his short journey through the doors.

He tried to follow them inside but was met by a security guard who asked, "What the fuck do you think you're doing!" He abandoned the idea and re-joined Preston who had parked haphazardly close by.

"I'll go in and see what's happening," he said to the cameraman. He walked through the doors unimpeded and saw Pauline waiting anxiously outside a cubicle.

"He's in there, Mr Preston."

"How serious is it?"

"They're just sorting it out now. I pray he's going to be all right. To have gone through all that only to end up like this...." Preston touched her arm gently. "It sounds like they wanted him out of the way as well. They have a lot to answer for when we finally get them."

A doctor emerged from a curtained cubicle.

"Mrs Maclean?" She nodded. "He's not in any danger, he's

lost some blood but he's going to be fine. Do you want to see him now?" She nodded again as relief flooded her face. The doctor walked away to another cubicle. Preston followed Pauline.

She leaned over the bed stroking her husband's brow. Then they both noticed the reporter.

"John we have a lot to thank Mr Preston for."

"I don't have anyone to thank. I've always been innocent, why should I thank someone for my freedom?" Preston thought that this was ingratitude, but he kept quiet.

After all, the man was right.

David looked up worriedly as Louise Brown came through the door to the office. Only twenty-five minutes had elapsed since she had left him there but leaving him for any length of time would have been enough to reinforce his sense of abandonment. Brown had enough child psychology to be certain of that. He had been abandoned throughout his life, and just when he had been reunited with his new mother he had been whisked away again.

"It's all right David, it's only me. We'll soon have you back."

"So this is the young man is it? Hello again David, my name's Martin." David looked up suspiciously at Martin Tench, shrank back and said nothing.

"It takes a long time for him to say anything at all," said Brown. "He's been through a lot and we think he's still scared by the secrecy business. Just smile at him and be reassuring, he'll come round."

Tench looked again at David and winked at him. David curled himself up into a ball.

Brown went to hold him, but he would not unfreeze, even for her.

"The sooner we get him back to his mother the better. With a bit of luck he'll see his father again," she sighed as she gazed at the tense figure trying to hide himself in the unfamiliar surroundings of their office. "There's a lot of rebuilding to be done, he'll probably never get over it fully."

"Sad isn't it," said Tench, "And we, or people like us, will be picking up the pieces for years to come."

Yes, they would, but the here and now was more important than anything.

"I need to find out what's happening with the others, Martin. Can you keep David amused while I make some calls?"

"Sure, who are you calling?"

"I'm going to try to reach Simon Preston, he needs to know what's happening."

"Good idea. All right, young David let's see if we can bring a smile to your face shall we," and he winked again. David remained as stiff as before.

Brown took out her phone and pressed Preston's number. It sounded four times and she wondered if he had replaced his sim yet.

Preston *had* replaced his sim, he couldn't see how he or the others could operate without it and the tumult of the moment outweighed the risk of being overheard. The familiar call-tone sounded in his breast pocket. He pulled out his phone and eyed it suspiciously, then saw it was Brown. He was now on a general ward where John Maclean had been taken. Patients and nurses were looking at him expectantly as he toyed with the idea of answering it.

He pressed the button fearing the worst. They were closing in on the Network and they could be trying anything at the moment. Calling him on his mobile was already a tried and tested method for them. He answered, "Simon Preston, hello."

"It's Louise Brown."

"What's up?"

"Everything's fine but I've had to bring David into the hospital with me. He's in my office with Martin Tench."

"Who!"

"Dr Martin Tench, one of my colleagues on the paediatric ward."

" Why did you do that?"

"They needed me here. They called me in – I had to put my sim back in. There was nowhere else to leave David so I brought him here. Where are you now?"

"I'm probably about a hundred yards away."

"In the hospital? But…"

"Never mind that, let's get David to Pauline and John!"

"Of course, I'll bring him to you – where?"

He told her the ward name, just one floor below her, and they finished the conversation. Preston turned to Steve Topping who had now been let in and said, "They're bringing David here and I want to get the pictures."

Topping understood immediately. He nodded and smiled.

Brown put down her phone and looked across at David and Tench. David was no longer curled up into an impenetrable ball but he was still tense. Tench was obviously getting through to him. "Come on David," she said, "You're going to see your dad." She went to take him by the hand when the door to the office opened.

"Hello everybody," said Paul Bowes, "Glad you could make it in, Louise! He smiled good naturedly at her. Then he looked down at David who had curled back into a ball. "Is this the young man I've heard so much about?"

"That's him. Dr Bowes, meet David Maclean," said Brown, smiling.

"Hello, young David", said the third doctor, cheerily, "How are you!"

David remained tight-lipped.

"We're just about to take him to see his father," said Tench

"Good. He's all right then?"

"As well as can be expected," replied Louise, then querulously, "Why do you ask?

"You know how it is, word gets around quickly."

"Word?"

"Nothing stays a secret in this place for long, Louise, you should know that."

"But how could you know? Why would you want to know, Paul?"

"Never mind that now, you be a good boy and don't say anything to upset your daddy now will you," said Bowes to David in mock admonishment. David looked up at him submissively. Brown was on edge, not just from the activity of the last few hours, but from what was happening in the office at that moment. Why say that, and how did he know Maclean might not have been all right? He'd been in prison, not a place Paul Bowes needed to know about. Then her curiosity was satisfied and her discomfort worsened.

"No Daddy!" David's voice was weak and fearful. Brown took half a second to realise what he had said. Then she looked at Bowes. "You're Daddy!" The shock of the realisation made her go weak and she slumped into a chair.

"What are you talking about, Louise?" asked Martin Tench.

She had to be wrong. It was impossible. But one look at David was enough to tell her she was right. He was cowed, scared, and avoiding everyone's gaze.

"Paul is one of them," she said finally, her shock converting to icy fury

"What are you talking about Louise," repeated Tench.

"He's one of the men behind the ring, the so-called Network."

"How can you possibly say that?" said Bowes.

"So you know of the ring then, Paul?" she said nervously, "Or do I mean *Daddy!* Martin please watch over David, I'm going to call for help."

She walked two paces to the desk to get the telephone again, but a hand came down strongly on hers before she could reach the receiver.

"I don't think so Louise," said Bowes, "You already know more than is good for you."

"What are you doing Paul! It's over. The whole scheme has been found out. We know everything."

"Not quite I suspect, but enough. I'm sorry Louise. I always quite liked you," he glanced across at David's cowering form, "But I'm afraid I have a weakness which I just can't seem to completely satisfy."

"Martin, quick, do something," she called. He was by the door, his face appearing shocked.

"I'm not sure what. What should I do?" he called, uncertainly.

"I should close the door. Martin," said Bowes, "That would be a start."

"Good idea", he replied. And he did exactly that. Brown looked at him questioningly then she understood what was happening.

"You as well!" she gasped. She looked down at David who

was now shivering in a corner. "Do you know him as well David? Is that why you wouldn't say anything to him?"

David said nothing.

"Good boy. Yes he does Louise," said Tench, "He won't say anything because he's been told not to, but he knows us both."

She summoned up the courage and made a run for the door but Tench beat her to it. He grabbed her roughly and threw her away. She was sent spinning across the compact office and crashing into a desk. It hurt but her mind was elsewhere.

She looked up at Tench. "How could you be like this? I loved you, you were special."

"Just an act, Louise. I needed to divert your attention. I don't like women that much."

She felt dirty. She had fallen for a monster and he had been *inside* her.

"Why you, Paul, you of all people? You have a wife and family. You were supposed to look after these children." She looked down again at David.

"Good cover don't you think. Easy access to the kids and no-one believes for a minute that you can be anything but a caring human being."

"Works for me," added Tench. She looked at him in disbelief. She must be in the middle of a nightmare.

"Martin this just can't be true. What about what you just told me?"

He stared back, the ice glinted in his eyes. "Don't be stupid. Even if I did want a woman it wouldn't be you." She gasped with shock.

"Take a look in the mirror sometime Louise, you're past it old girl." He was spouting pure spite now. She was helpless, let down by everyone she had respected in her profession, disgusted by what they had done. And now trapped. The very people she would normally turn to for help were here with her.

Tench spoke again, this time to Bowes, "This is all very well but what do we do with them?"

"Shut up and let me think!" said the senior doctor, "We have to assume the police know where we are and our friends there won't help."

"Why not?"

"Because if they could they would have done so by now and the place wouldn't be infested with them. We had Hawkins and Spencer and still we're in a corner."

He pulled two syringes from his jacket pocket and took the plastic caps off.

"What the hell are you doing?" shouted Brown.

"Be QUIET!" said Bowes, "You know what this is, it's Isoflurane, you know what that does?"

"General anaesthetic, you're going to knock me out?"

"Hold on, Paul, said Tench, the body count's mounting and they might already be on to us."

"Body count!" said Brown, weakly.

"But they might not and one more body won't increase a life sentence," said Bowes, "If we leave them here alive they can testify, if we take them out we can get away and they'll only have the bodies."

"You're going to OD me on Isoflurane?" said Brown, weakly.

One floor down on the general ward Preston and Topping were getting impatient. How long does it take to walk down a flight of stairs?

"So you were behind the James Institute, and the Lacey Foundation?" she said mechanically.

"I was there for the former, yes. Martin only joined us recently, so he knows little of those times," replied her consultant in a matter of fact voice.

She gazed around her. She could not outrun them, nor could she leave David in their care if she did make a break for it.

"What happens now?"

"I'm afraid that's it for you Louise, and young David here. You both know far too much, and neither of us relishes the idea of going to prison, they tend not to like people like us in there."

"What do you mean?"

"I mean you will have to be disappeared as some people say rather uncouthly."

"You wouldn't dare. That would be murder."

Tench leaped in, almost wilfully, he was enjoying the

atmosphere of fear around him.

"You wouldn't be the first Louise. We tried to keep the body count down but you people kept getting too close." She sunk deeper into her chair. "Who else have you killed?"

"You knew one of them I think, not very well mind. Sergeant Sanders. Nice woman I'm told."

"You did that!" she gasped.

"Not us personally, it was taken care of by other members of our fraternity."

She was temporarily relieved. "So you haven't killed anyone yourselves yet?"

"Of course we have. Perhaps you've forgotten the sad death of the old man in the intensive care unit. So many people die there I suppose it's hard to remember just one."

"So that was you. Why, what had he done?"

"Nothing really. But he was old and on drugs and we were worried he might be indiscreet while waiting to die naturally," said Tench, "I just helped him on his way."

"And I suppose the other was Jack."

"Absolutely right, Louise. Well spotted", said Bowes, "That was Martin of course. Once your reporter friend had seen me there I had to make a quick exit. Martin turned up a little later."

She let the information sink in through her terror. The awfulness of what had happened opened up and she was nearly sick. "That was the night you went out with me, Martin," she struggled to say.

"The night I fucked you, that's right Louise. I did a pretty good job although I do say so myself. Good enough to leave you sated and sleeping."

She became aware of David listening to it all. "And now us!"

"And now you," said Bowes as he reached for one of the two anaesthetic syringes.

As he picked up one the other fell to the floor, close to David. The boy looked at it and then Brown. She nodded to him and David picked it up and handed it to her. Brown had hoped he would do that but couldn't expect it, she thought he might have just as easily given it to Bowes or Tench, but he didn't.

Quickly she flicked off the plastic cap and plunged it into Tench's leg. He had been focusing on Bowes and did not see any of it coming. His adrenaline was already high and his heart rate at 100 so the drug found its way very quickly to his brain and three seconds later he slumped to the floor. As she pressed she saw how much there was of it and stopped just before the halfway point. The drug was meant to be drip-fed through a regulator, not injected directly, the full syringe would kill him.

"For God's sake, Tench, what are you doing?" yelled Bowes who now had the other doctor blocking his way to Brown.

"Only one syringe left now, Paul," said Brown.

"Shut up you bitch, or I'll…"

The door burst open and King, Preston and Will bundled in as Mandeep Patel and Topping looked on from the entrance.

"You'll what?" said King loudly.

Tench, in his hurry, had not locked the door and Bowes found himself staring at the three of them. He clocked Bill last but his eyes narrowed as he did. "I know you," he said.

Bill looked on with sudden fire in his eyes.

"I'm Detective Sergeant King," said Tony, loudly, "What's happening here?"

"Don't believe anything he says!" said Brown, "he's one of the Network".

"What network don't be foolish, Louise, the game is up. Officer, she was trying to kidnap this young boy and I was attempting to stop her."

"How?"

"With a general anaesthetic by the looks of it," said Patel from the doorway. Bowes looked down at the syringe in his hand and said, "I'd already taken this from her but it was too late to stop her from injecting my colleague here, Doctor Tench."

They looked at him wordlessly.

"She's childless, it's upended her… I'm sorry Louise but you know it's true!"

Brown fired back a look of pure hatred.

"Perhaps you'd like to put the syringe down Doctor Bowes," said Preston, "You won't be needing it now." Bowes hesitated for a second and then slowly lowered his hand to the nearby surface and released hold of the syringe.

"Move away from there now Doctor Bowes, we don't want any accidents do we!" said King.

Bowes again hesitated but then moved away. "Right Officer, well you have things under control here and I must get back to my patients," said Bowes as he tried to barge through the crowd of people in his office.

"No Doctor, you stay where you are. There's more we want to talk to you about – and your sleepy colleague here," he added pointing to Tench's limp frame.

Two uniformed officers had appeared at the doorway as Bowes tried again to force his way through. "Stay there or we will restrain you," said King.

While this confrontation continued no one saw Bill move stealthily to the desk and pick up the syringe. He flicked off its cap and rushed towards Bowes.

"Yes, you knew me, *Daddy!* You knew all of us, didn't you!"

"What nonsense is this?" asked Bowes but then stopped dead as Will pushed the needle stingingly into his left Carotid artery.

"For God's sake be careful with that, there's enough in there to fell a horse."

"Really?" said Will, "Good!" He pushed the hyperdermic straight into Bowes' neck. Bowes yelled in pain. "Now then, I've got you by the balls and everything else, you shit! But I'm going to talk to you before I press the plunger here, because I want you to understand what you've done."

Preston stepped up, "Will, no! Think of what it will mean for you!"

Brown said, "He's a late middle-aged man with a heart condition, it will kill him."

"That would be Murder, Will," said Preston. "You'd go down. Think about his life from now on! He'll be on Rule 43 for the rest of his life and even then someone will get to him because they don't like paedophiles in prison, they really don't."

Bowes eyes clouded in terror, "Paedophile, don't be ridiculous, I've only ever wanted to look after children. What is all this nonsense?"

King felt his phone buzz and looked down to see a lengthy text referring to Jack Spencer's address book. He read it and then said to Bill, "We've got him, Bill, he can't get out of it, his number is in a book we've found, together with the others we know about and a whole lot we didn't. We've got him, he's going down and it will be a living hell for him. Wouldn't you prefer that?"

Preston added, "Revenge is a dish best served cold, Bill, ever heard of that? Kill him now and he's gone and won't suffer any more. You want him to suffer don't you?"

Bill looked around the group then said, "All right, he gets to go to court." But he didn't withdraw the syringe immediately, instead he pushed it in deeper and smiled as Bowes squealed in agony as it pierced a neck vertebra; then he pulled it out without depressing the plunger. He put the syringe back on the desk and Louise Brown quickly took it and put it in a sharps box. Then she fell back in a chair and wanted to cry, but didn't, instead she told King everything that had happened since she'd last seen him.

King took it in and then addressed Bowes, "Doctor Paul Bowes, I'm arresting you on suspicion of murder, attempted murder and kidnap." He continued with the formalities of his rights and when he'd finished he said, "And I'll be doing the same for your friend on the floor here when he comes round." He indicated to the uniformed officers who had now entered the office to handcuff Bowes and take him to the police station. Bowes started to protest but King looked him hard in the face and said, "We've got Spencer's book, his phone and the testimony of all these people. Keep denying it, maybe you have to, but we've *got* you, *Daddy!*"

With that, Bowes was led away. Two porters arrived to load Tench on to a trolley to take him to the recovery room. King turned to Louise Brown and said, "He'll be in handcuffs when he comes round."

Then he turned to Mandeep Patel who was still standing at the doorway looking spellbound. "Hell of a first date, Mandeep! I wouldn't blame you if you didn't want a second." She looked at him as if he was mad then, slowly, her features broke into a smile and she said, "You're dangerous to be around, Tony King. Promise me we don't have to do this again and I'll reschedule."

King smiled and said, "It won't. That's me done for a long time."

Neither of them saw Topping's camera silently filming them until Preston approached and said, "Give them some space, Steve, They've done enough!" Topping put down the camera.

"Well, Tony," said Preston, "we seem to have broken up a paedophile ring, well done!"

"Truce for now, Preston… Simon, without you this would never have happened. Maybe I like you a little more than before but that's not saying much. No offence."

"None taken," said Preston. "Shake hands on it?"

King offered his hand instantly.

"When you've finished your bromance, could you make way for someone who still has to work here! I no longer have a consultant, nor a senior registrar so right now I am the paediatrics department and there's a ward of sick children out there."

Despite everything going on around him and the undoubted antipathy the two had developed Preston was impressed.

"Sorry, Louise," he said, "But how can you go back to work right now, someone's just tried to kill you."

"Duty!" she said, "Something you wouldn't understand."

Preston tried but the events of the last 24 hours caught up with him and he didn't have the strength to mask his disappointment.

"I should rethink that, Louise," said King, "Duty is what brought him to all of this in the first place and saw him through it." He turned to Preston and added, "I'll give you that: respect… Simon!"

Preston smiled and nodded. Brown looked guilty. Bill looked on disconsolately.

As they made their way to the door Preston's phone sounded. He didn't recognize the number and feared the worst but answered, "Simon Preston."

"Simon, it's Janet."

He was taken aback, Janet Jones? She'd never called him before, not on this line.

"Hi Janet, I'm in the middle of something quite big at the moment."

"I won't take long but I wondered if you knew where Mike was?"

"No, I've been wondering the same thing."

"It's just that he took a call from the newsdesk earlier and started to pack a bag and collect up his passport and so on. He said he was being sent to the Middle East about someone who's been in prison out there."

Preston heard the information but struggled to believe it. "Janet, he's supposed to be here at the hospital helping me and Steve Topping."

"What's going on, Simon?"

"I wish I knew. I'll try to find out."

He ended the call and resumed his walk to the door of the medics' office. As he reached it the awful truth presented itself to him and he stopped instantly. He put his arm out to steady himself against the doorframe. His oldest friend in the business had been a fifth columnist all the time. Bastard!

He forced himself to walk on and caught up with King.

"Another one to add to the list, Tony."

EPILOGUE

It was an upmarket eatery in the city centre, the TV company was paying and the guests made sure they took full advantage – especially Louise Brown who had managed to negotiate a week's leave from her current post as acting consultant. Taxis were coming, no work the following day and the wine flowed, she made sure she got her share.

Preston acted as host to the others who had played a part: Tony King and Juliet Neilson from the police and her guest for the night, no less than the chief constable; Bill, Mandeep Patel, there in her own right but attached to King and a seat left empty with a place setting and a picture of Di Sanders. The evening started sombrely with the chief giving a tribute to Sanders followed by everyone else there who'd known her. There had already been a police ceremony and a formal funeral, tonight they would drink to her and remember her.

In a quieter moment Neilson took King aside and said, "You got your inspector's when you got your sergeant's, didn't you? I should know, I coached you through it"

"I did, I wanted to get it done while in study mode."

"Smart, the chief's going to bend a rule or two and jump you up to DI – you're filling Spencer's vacancy."

"Bloody hell, Guv, it was only a few days ago that I was tracking down the ID of old ladies."

"It was only a few days ago that you broke up a paedophile ring. We need you, Tony!"

"Thanks, Guv!"

"You take over his desk on Monday."

"What's happening to Hawkins?"

"We'll find him, he can't run forever, no one can."

"Thanks, Juliet… I mean Chief Superintendent."

"Just for now, Tony, from Monday it's Assistant Chief Constable."

"No surprise but well done, Ma'am."

"It's still Juliet, tonight. Now go on and join that lovely lady of yours! Bit of a purple patch for you, I'd say."

He smiled and joined Patel at her side.

Preston had Bill with him. "Yeah, it's great and all that. We broke up a ring and got some of the big ones but not the one I wanted," said Bill.

"Who's that?" replied Preston.

"I told you at the start, the Barnes woman, the one who didn't lift a finger and laughed at us. That's who. How did she get away, I told them where she was."

"Ah. Yes, we sent a camera and reporter there just as the police knocked on the door. She was long gone and hadn't been seen for weeks."

"Fuck it!" said Bill.

"Well, yes, I suppose, but on the other hand think of her now: old woman, no means, on the run. Rubbish life I reckon. I don't think you'll help yourself by dwelling on it, Bill. You need to move on with your life."

"But I'm not good at anything."

"If that was true then I'd accept it, but you have no idea because you have never tried and you were bullied by those bastards. Go to college, Bill, get some qualifications, don't let them define your life forever!"

"Easier said than done."

"I know, but please try! I'll be here to back you up. You have everyone here on your side. I bet you've never had anyone on your side before, have you?"

"I suppose not."

Louise Brown watched the exchange from a metre away and began to see more to Preston than the version she'd so readily dismissed. Maybe he wasn't so bad! Maybe he could be good company – not for a lifetime, of course. Good looking, that had never been in doubt, but now he had a conscience – maybe he always had.

What the hell, she thought, let's see what you've got, Preston; she moved directly in front of him, looked him hard and long in the eye and said, "*Drink*, Simon?"

They did not acknowledge each other although they were sitting within arm's reach. They were not supposed to be on the same planes but there were so many trying to get out that it couldn't be avoided. Jones and the social services second in command, the one who'd been tasked with emptying Lacey House, who had both gone absent inexplicably, had already changed phones, identities and now waited in the economy lounge at Gatwick for a flight to Thailand. Others had gone before, more would follow. Individually they saw another of their number join the waiting passengers. Ex-Superintendent Phillip Hawkins saw them as well but made no acknowledgement. He sat down and all three avoided each other's gaze while waiting nervously, desperate for the departures board to flip to boarding.

Just as it did and the passengers rose to join the queue a dutiful PC spotted someone he thought he remembered from his training days. Wasn't that Sergeant Hawkins as was? He'd moved forces long since but he looked just like him. The same Superintendent Hawkins now on a watchlist at all ports…

Printed in Great Britain
by Amazon